THE NIGHT HUNTING

RITE WORLD: NIGHT WOLVES
BOOK 3

JULIANA HAYGERT

COPYRIGHT

AUTHOR'S NOTE

I hope you enjoy reading *The Night Hunting*!

This book is set in a bigger "universe", called Rite World, where many of my series take place. This "universe" is still our modern world, but with a large, hidden supernatural society. Because there are many series in this same universe, there will be many cameos in my books, but don't worry. Book 1 of any new series is designed to be a good entry point into this universe. Hopefully, you'll like it a lot and will pick up the other books too! <3

Don't forget to sign up for my Newsletter to find out about new releases, cover reveals, giveaways, and more!

If you want to see exclusive teasers, help me decide on covers, read excerpts, talk about books, etc, join my reader group on Facebook: Juliana's Club!

RITE WORLD

Welcome to the RITE WORLD!

Free Novellas:
The Vampire Hunt
The Light Witch

Novellas:
The Hunter Path
The Light Calling
The Light Witch
The Wicked Alliance
The Shadow Fae

Rite World:
The Vampire Heir (Book 1)
The Witch Queen (Book 2)
The Immortal Vow (Book 3)

The Warlock Lord (Book 4)
The Wolf Consort (Book 5)
The Crystal Rose (Book 6)
The Wolf Forsaken (Book 7)
The Fae Bound (Book 8)
The Blood Pact (Book 9)

Rite World: Blackthorn Hunters Academy
The Demons Kiss (Book 1)
The Hunter Secret (Book 2)
The Soul Bond (Book 3)
The Shadow Trials (Book 4)
The Immortal Vow (Book 5)

Rite World: Vampire Wars
The Darkest Vampire (Book 1)
The Darkest Witch (Book 2)
The Darkest Magic (Book 3)

Rite World: Night Wolves
The Night Calling (Book 1)
The Night Burning (Book 2)
The Night Hunting (Book 3)
The Night Rising (Book 4)

Rite World: Lightgrove Witches
The Midnight Test (Book 1)
The Midnight Spell (Book 2)
The Midnight Flame (Book 3)

And more to come!

THE VAMPIRE HUNT

I have an exclusive novella set in the Rite World that is just for my newsletter subscribers!

Click here to sign-up and receive your book!

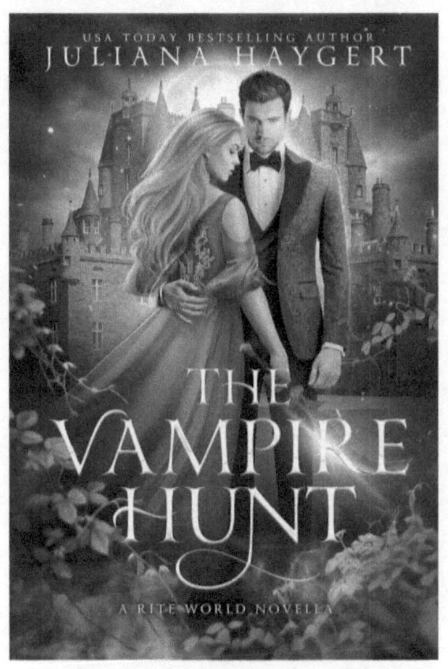

THE VAMPIRE HUNT
A Rite World Novella

Norah is a demon hunter, one of the best graduated from the Blackthorn Hunters Academy. When she's sent to investigate a case concerning demons in a small town, she runs into a very arrogant vampire. Her first instinct is to kill him, after all, he's a supernatural and demon hunters are taught to end all evil.

Cain is a vampire prince. Because of his status, he's in charge of making sure humans don't find out about his kind. During a routine investigation, he bumps into a very sexy demon hunter and he wonders what she's doing on his way.

However, the case grows much bigger for Norah and Cain to handle alone. To find the truth and win this battle, the vampire and the demon hunter will have to hunt together—without killing each other.

How well could this end?

1

RAIKA

I HATED THIS FEELING, THAT I WAS WALKING DOWN A FOGGY street and couldn't see the way to go. That was me every second of every day since I woke up five days ago, my memory gone.

I stared at the large painting above the fireplace—a two feet tall slit in the wall that extended ten feet. The painting, a modern-style watercolor, depicted beautiful black wings, the feathers floating to the ground.

I should remember this place, this painting.

"There you are."

I spun, looking at the young woman walking in the living room. "Hey," I said, turning back to the painting.

Ivy stopped by my side, staring at the painting with me. I gave her a quick side glance. Ivy was pretty. She had long, light brown hair, brilliant blue eyes, fair skin, some freckles on her nose. She was lean and supple, like a ballerina, and an inch or so shorter than me.

She was always dressed up—everyone in this house was —and tonight was no different. She wore a beautiful dark-blue dress that came down to her heels, a slit revealing her left leg. The bodice hugged her tiny waist and large breasts. Elegant, yet sexy.

"Pretty, isn't it?"

I nodded. There were many paintings around this house, most of them colorful abstracts, but this one had bothered me in a way I couldn't explain since I first woke up.

"Why this painting?" I asked, surprised at my words.

Ivy shrugged. "I don't have an answer. I think that when I saw this painting, it reminded me of the battle between the underworld and heaven. Not all demons are bad, not all angels are good. We're not defined by our species or our environment. We can be more. And this painting, of the wings of a fallen angel, seemed like it belonged in a demon's home, don't you think?"

I glanced at her. "Were you always this philosophical?"

Once upon a time, that would have been a rhetorical question, but as it was, I really didn't know.

I had woken up five days before in a strange bed, in a strange bedroom, with two strange people watching over me. Then two more strange people rushed in the room, and everyone rejoiced I had recovered from the attack.

Until they realized I didn't remember anything.

Well, I remembered a few things. My name, my age, my birthday, that my eyes were blue, that I was half-demon and half-wolf shifter. I remembered that a supernatural world existed, and it was hidden from the human world. I remembered how to walk, how to brush my teeth, how to use silverware, how to write, but I had no recollection of this house, of this woman standing beside me, of my past. Memory seemed to be funny like that.

Ivy smiled at me. "Sometimes I have a bout of inspiration." She pouted her lips and flipped her hair over her shoulder.

I smiled back at her.

This young woman, who was a year older than I was, was said to be my best friend.

And my sister.

My *half* sister.

Even though I liked her company and she made me laugh more often than not, I had no lingering feelings for her. Nothing that told me how close we were, how much I loved her. There was a huge hole in my chest that would be challenging to fill until I recovered my memories.

If that ever happened.

She offered me her arm. "Come on. We've been away from the party for too long."

I hooked my arm on hers. "It's not a party."

"Potato, potato."

I chuckled as Ivy steered us away from the living room. We crossed the large hallway that cut through the center of the mansion and walked to the far back, where a sunroom opened to a large porch and outside pool.

I inhaled as we crossed the threshold to the porch, enjoying the fresh air and the day's warmth. It was nighttime, but the weather in Vancouver—just outside the city—seemed pretty good for July.

I tensed when I saw the five men standing at the edge of the porch, wearing suits and holding champagne flutes in their hands.

Higher demons, and one of them was Prince Paimon of the underworld.

My father.

Each time I was near him, I expected a kernel of recognition, a memory to flash behind my eyelids. A feeling to come back to me.

Nothing. I had nothing.

But he saw Ivy and me returning and he smiled at us. Because he was a higher demon, he looked young for his age —midforties—when in truth, he was thousands of years old.

Since I first laid eyes on him, I had been tense around him. The man was tall and well posed, exuding power and confidence from every pore.

I felt small and silly next to him.

But he had been nothing but patient and caring since I woke up.

I gave him a little wave, and Ivy nodded her head at him, before taking us to the side where a full bar was. This mansion was incredible. A modern structure with lots of white and glass, and some wood and metal details. It had a formal living room, a family room, a formal dining room, a breakfast room, a fully equipped kitchen where ten people could cook without bumping into each other, three sets of stairs, a library, two offices, a dozen suites, and in the basement, a gym and training room. Not to mention the extensive gardens, the pool house on the other side, the six-car garage, and the maids and cooks and employees the mansion required.

Ivy had told me she bought it three years ago. About two years ago, our father moved in, and a year ago, I did.

"Here." Ivy handed me a flute with champagne. She grabbed another one and touched mine with hers. "Cheers."

She drank half of the champagne in one go.

Having a feeling I had not been a heavy drinker before, I sipped my drink.

Two maids in black uniforms came out with trays filled

with hors d'oeuvres and passed it around. I almost rolled my eyes. There were only seven people here, and two more inside the house somewhere. This was supposed to be a business dinner, but Ivy was right. It did look like a party.

A maid stopped by our side, offered us food, then at Ivy's request, left the tray on the bar's counter beside us. She picked up a flaky crust topped with a reddish cream and popped it in her mouth.

"Yum," she said, her mouth full.

I shook my head, and was about to reach for one too, when a harsh whisper came from the group at the edge of the porch, and the two of us turned to the demons.

My father had a hand up and he spoke in austere tones, but even with my half-wolf hearing, I couldn't hear each word of what he was saying.

I had asked so many questions when I woke up. Besides the where am I, who am I, I also asked about my mother, where was she, or had I always lived with my father and with Ivy?

They told me everything—it had been a lot in a short amount of time, but I think I got the gist of it.

My father used to be a prince of the underworld. After a long time in power, the king had grown bored and a little greedy, and my father and his brothers—brothers by title, not blood—had been talking about measures they could take to prevent the king from breaking the natural balance of the world, but before they could do anything, King Brikan's ruthless children attacked. They killed him without giving him a chance to explain or to repent, and with him gone, the former princes grew weak. They had to flee the underworld, or they risked being killed too.

In fact, all demons taking refuge in the underworld fled,

afraid of the new king and his sisters. They seemed to have a low tolerance for any kind of demon, even the ones with a good heart.

Weak and alone, my father found Ivy and she took him in.

A year later, when I needed a place to hide, she took me in too.

Seeing the group of higher demons wouldn't turn on each other, I finally reached for the pastry I wanted to try.

My hand almost smacked someone's chest. I pulled my hand back. "I'm so sor—" My words died at my lips when I looked at who had walked up to us. I hadn't even seen him. "Roman, hi."

He smiled at me and my cheeks warmed. "Enjoying the party?"

"It's not a party," I said again.

Roman tilted his head. "We could put on some music and turn it into one."

"Oh, I like that idea." Ivy went around the bar, where the sound system controls were. She pressed a button, then fussed with her phone, and a low rock ballad started playing from the speakers along the ceiling. Since Ivy liked music so much, each room in this mansion had a hidden sound system.

Roman stared at me. I thought he was going to ask me to dance with him, so I looked out at the pool and took another sip of my champagne, as if I wasn't interested in him or anything else.

Roman was a full wolf shifter from my pack.

And my mate.

Long ago, my father had a love affair with my mother, Kali. After they broke up, he found out she was pregnant, but by then, she had holed up inside her pack, and he couldn't get to me.

I had been raised by my mother in our wolf shifter pack, and despite her trying to isolate me from others, I had gotten close to Roman, and we found out we were mates.

Then one day, a year ago, an older man assaulted me. He called me names and slapped me in front of half the pack. I lost control and used my darkfire on him. Everyone found out my mother had been lying, and I was half-demon.

They turned on us.

My pack attacked us. They killed my mother and were about to kill me, when Roman stepped in and helped me escape. He didn't care what I was. He just wanted me safe. He said he had apologized many, many times for not being able to save my mother too, and he apologized again when he told me the story.

I didn't remember any of it, so I told him it was okay.

Thankfully, he had patience and didn't push it. He didn't even try holding my hand or touching me. He stood close by, always within my reach, for when and if I needed him.

"You need time, and that's what I'll give you," he had said.

I appreciated that. I appreciated him.

I drank another sip of my champagne and peeked at him. Roman was handsome. He was tall and wide, and his body was hard and full of muscles—I had seen him training without a shirt yesterday. He had light brown hair and dark green eyes, which contrasted nicely with his tanned skin.

Right now, he wore a dark blue suit that seemed to have been cut for him.

It was easy to see myself falling for him, though with the mating bond, that would happen regardless of whether I wanted it or not, wouldn't it? I always thought that with the mating bond, I would lust after him the moment I set my eyes on him, but it hadn't happened. It could only be my memories. The damage to them was so deep, it was affecting the bond.

"Any news from the office?" Ivy asked Roman.

"Nothing unusual," Roman said. Our father had a fake office front in Vancouver, where he did a lot of business with other demons and gathered allies. Roman went there a few times a week with Rotgar, one of the demons standing with my father right now. The higher demon was the general to my father's army, his left arm, while Ivy was his right. Roman said he went to the office to help out; with what, I had no idea. Apparently, I used to help too, but since I woke up, they kept me away from the office, saying I should rest until my memories returned before I rejoined the family business.

"I need to stop by there tomorrow." Ivy groaned.

"All right, stop," I said. "If this is a damn party, then no work talk."

Ivy pointed to the five demons a few feet from us. "And what do you think they are doing?"

I shrugged. "I don't care about them. This is about us."

Roman nodded. "I like the no-work-talk-during-parties rule."

Of course he would agree with me. He always did. Maybe that was a mate thing?

Loud laughter came from beyond the pool.

A woman wearing a beautiful dark-green gown walked out from the pool house. She was gorgeous with smooth dark skin, dark eyes, and long black curls.

She walked over the pool without getting her shoes or dress wet.

Dot, a Nightmist witch. Probably the last one from what

they had told me. She was powerful and a little nuts, but so far she seemed like a crazy aunt who loved to get in trouble with her nephews and nieces.

"There you are." My father beckoned her to join him. She glanced at us, winked, then joined the demons and their conversation.

"I feel like we're the naughty kids and we're being punished by not being able to join the important meeting," Ivy said. She drained her flute and reached around the counter to get the champagne bottle from the ice bucket.

I frowned. I felt like that too.

After all, hadn't I been told the four of us were now plotting how to take the underworld back and restore balance? Not just plotting, we had been taking action. That was why these four demons were here, to talk business.

And we were not in that conversation.

"Aren't we helping them?" I asked. Honestly, I had been lost in this whole plan since I couldn't remember anything, but my father always said that Ivy and I were playing a big part. "We should join them."

Ivy nodded. "We should."

Roman groaned. "You know, I will do anything for you, but I don't want to headbutt with your father. What if he decides he's had enough of me and throws me out?"

I stared at him. Roman had been crucial to my survival. If it weren't for him, I would have died with my mother, and he had given up everything to be here with me.

"If he throws you out, I'll go with you."

Ivy scoffed. "As if he would let you leave."

"My point exactly."

She narrowed her eyes at me. "Smart." She took my hand in hers. "Let's go."

We turned toward the group as a maid appeared at the doorway. "Dinner is served."

MY FATHER SEEMED like quite a laid-back man. He hadn't raised Ivy or me, or any of our other siblings—I had been told there were many—and he wasn't the most fatherly type. But he had tried. He had been around while Ivy was growing up, visiting her here and there, and he had reached out to me many times, but my mother wouldn't allow him to see or talk to me.

Still, now that Ivy's house had become his house too, he had a handful of rules, and one of them was no business talk during mealtimes, which left us with small talk.

"It was boring," I said as I descended the stairs to the basement the next morning.

Ivy chuckled. "Yeah, it was."

Dinner had been boring, and after, my father had closed himself in his office with the other four higher demons, leaving me, Ivy, Roman, and Dot out of whatever they were planning.

I stopped at the end of the stairs and turned to Ivy. "Is he doing this because of me? Because I still don't have my memories back and he's afraid of overwhelming me?"

She cocked an eyebrow. "How would I know?"

I shrugged. "You're his favorite."

Ivy snorted. "What? I'm not."

I resumed walking into the basement turned state-of-the-art gym and training facility—in a corner were a dozen of big weightlifting equipment and several weight racks, on the back were equipment like treadmills and stationary bikes, and to the other side was a large open area for training.

I frowned as I stepped onto the mat ... thoughts like this always made me stop and wonder. How did I know about weightlifting equipment and such when I didn't remember being in a gym before?

This memory thing was way complicated.

Dot, who was sort of my doctor, had told me that the innate things we do as we grow and learn are deeply ingrained and those wouldn't be easily gone. As for my memories, she was confident they would come back. Every couple of days, she meditated with me, using her magic to prod inside my head to unlock whatever vault my memories had buried themselves into.

"You sure are," I said, and for the first time ever, a little jealousy made itself known. At first, I didn't like it, but then I held on to it. If I was feeling something, then it meant there was a memory attached to that, right? "You're like his general, and I'm ... I'm just a private."

She bumped her shoulder on mine. "That's because of your memories. You are a general too, but right now, you're a little lost. Don't worry. Once your memories are back, you'll see you're his favorite."

I shook my head. "If my memories come back."

Ivy frowned at me. "Don't say that. Be positive. Your memories will come back."

"If you say so," I muttered.

My sister turned and took several steps back. "Ready?"

I glanced at her. My sister and I had traded the formal outfits for workout appropriate clothes—yoga leggings, tank tops, and sneakers. She had tied her hair into two braids, while I preferred a ponytail.

I sighed. "What do you think?"

She chuckled. "Just ... relax. You'll get it."

That was what she had been saying for the last four days. When I woke up five days ago without any memories, I had tried using darkfire and the thing just flickered in my open palms and died a horrible death. When I tried again, it was inconsistent and weak. I had no real control over it. I had wanted to train right away, but they had told me to take it easy for one day. Maybe in that one day, my memories would come back and then I wouldn't need to train, because according to them, I had been using darkfire for over a year and I had gotten good at it. The wolf within me had practically gone silent since I dedicated myself to my demon side now.

Honestly, after they told me my pack tried to kill me, that they had killed my mother, and that the injury that had taken my memories away had been caused by them, I didn't mind. Six days ago, a group had found me when I was out on a mission with Ivy and attacked us, intent on finishing the job they started a year ago. Good riddance to my wolf.

I watched as Ivy extended her hands in front of herself, palms turned up. I mirrored her. She called on her darkfire and black flames covered her hands, flickering up past her head.

I took in a deep breath and focused. I opened myself up to my magic. I felt it fill my veins, flooding my chest. I conjured black flames above my palms. They flickered once, twice. I held my breath, knowing they would be out in another second. No, I had to focus. To think about the darkfire, to dive into the magic, to swim in an ocean of darkfire, to breathe and eat its energy. It was part of me; I just had to trust them, trust myself.

The flames held on. I gasped and stared at Ivy.

"Yes! Keep doing whatever you're doing!" She molded the flames in her palms, and they took the shape of a half dozen darts. "Keep your focus and shape them. Whatever you can do. A dart, a stake, a ball, even a worm. I'll take it."

I laughed and lost my concentration. The flames disappeared instantly, and my laughter died as suddenly as it came.

"Shit."

"No, no shit. You did it!" Ivy beamed at me. "Next time, I'll leave the jokes out of it."

"I like your jokes." Ivy was fun, easygoing, friendly, caring. She had been the most patient with me and helped me more than anyone else in this house.

She did a mock curtsy. "I'm glad to be of service."

I laughed again then forced myself to stop.

I had to make this magic thing work. I felt like, if I could reach into my darkfire, remember how to use it, then it would unlock everything else. As soon as I touched the magic, controlled it, an avalanche would ensue and I would be myself again.

Right now, I was a shelf, mostly empty, with no thoughts of my own.

Did I like chocolate, or was that new? What was my favorite color? What was my favorite food? What was my mother like? Did she try protecting me from our pack? Was she good to me? Did she love me? How did Roman and I find out about the mating bond? I guessed I could ask him but I wanted to remember it all by myself. I wanted to feel it.

And for some reason, I was sure I could figure it out if I mastered darkfire.

"All right. All right." I rolled my shoulders and let out a deep, steadying breath. "Let's try this again."

Serious, Ivy nodded and took the same stance as before. Her darkfire came easily to her, and I liked to think it was because she was a full-blooded demon. However, I just wanted to believe that to make me feel better. I wasn't a full-blooded demon, and from the tales I heard, I could rival Ivy in power, regardless.

I wanted that back.

I called on my darkfire and focused on my hands, on my upturned palms. I envisioned the magic, a dark, oily liquid swimming through my veins, flooding every inch of me like my blood, breathing magic into each one of my pores and cells. I could do this. I knew this. It was instinctive. This magic was a part of me.

Flames sparked to life in my hands. I concentrated and visualized them stronger, bigger, brighter. The darkfire expanded from a small flame to a ball enveloping my hand, to a flare that shot up toward the ceiling.

I snickered. "I'm doing it."

"Focus," Ivy said, her voice sharp for once.

I put her out of my mind, focusing on my magic, on my darkfire.

I made the flames even bigger.

A tingling started under my skin, an exciting feeling, a sense of power and belonging. This was it. I was doing it. This was my magic, and I was in total control.

The sensation increased, a powerful force buzzing through my muscles, something exhilarating and scary at the same time. In my mind, I shaped the darkfire like two long pillars jutting out of my palms. Slowly, my hands withdrew, hovering beside the pillars. The pillars expanded, reaching the floor. I pushed and pulled, shaping the darkfire until it could contract and expand at my will.

My toes curled, my stomach lurched, eagerness danced along my skin.

And then it burst. The magic exploded out of me, so strong and sudden, not even Ivy had time to control it.

The pillars blew up around us, sending us flying back. Ivy hit the wall, and I landed on a bench. The pillars disappeared along with any remnants of darkfire, but my side hurt where it had slammed into the hard, metal bench.

"Are you okay?" Ivy's question turned into a cough. She leaned against the wall, a hand over her chest.

Groaning, I pushed to my feet. Shit, I would definitely have a purple bruise on my right hip and waist tomorrow. "I'll live. How about you?"

"I'm fine."

I glanced around. The mat was scorched. The ceiling too.

"Damn it." I had messed up again. Big time. "I could have hurt you for real."

"No, it's okay. I was able to push it back, that's why we still have our hair and clothes intact."

I pointed at her. "See? I'm a menace."

"Don't flatter yourself, Raika. That was barely something. Even if I hadn't contained it, I don't think it would have hurt us that bad. Besides, that's why I'm here. To teach you and to stop things if they get out of control."

"It's hopeless."

"You know, no one is born knowing how to use their magic. Even witches train for years before they are allowed to use their magic in public."

"I'm not a witch."

"But you went through something we have no experience

with." She pressed her lips tight. "I ... Pretend you're learning it for the first time. It'll be easier."

I slapped my hips, then winced in pain. Shit. "It might be easier, but it'll take longer. Doesn't Father have grand plans on how we're going to save the underworld from the current tyrant king? I need my magic *right now* if I'm going to help."

"Getting frustrated won't help."

No, it wouldn't, but I could do little about my emotions. "I want—"

Footsteps sounded from the stairs. A second later, Roman appeared in the doorway. "Hey, hm, Ivy, your father is asking for you."

Ivy frowned. "Just me?"

Roman nodded. "Yeah. Apparently, he found an entrance to the underworld and wants to go scouting."

I stilled. "And he didn't ask for me?"

Roman turned his eyes to me. "Sorry, Raika, but until you can control your darkfire, you're staying here."

That hurt like a bitch.

Once more, I was certain that everything in my life was tied to my magic. If I could touch it, hold it, everything would make sense.

"I'm sorry, sis," Ivy said. "I'll be back as soon as we can so we can continue training, okay?" She didn't wait for a response, simply offered me a tight smile and walked away.

Feelings of not only being lost and empty, but useless wormed through me.

2

RAIKA

After Ivy left, I stayed in the training room a while longer. At first, I wanted to keep training with my darkfire, trying to control it, but Roman reminded me of a very important detail.

"Without Ivy here, if you lose control, there will be no one to make sure you don't harm yourself or burn down the house."

Of course, he was right.

So, to burn off my pent-up frustration, I hopped on the treadmill and ran for thirty minutes. At first, I almost gave up because of the pain in my hips and waist, but as my body warmed, the pain disappeared. I would probably regret it later.

With each step, my body relaxed and my frustration faded away. I was still upset with myself, with my luck in life to have my memories gone like this, but I didn't feel like being reckless anymore.

Roman stayed there with me, doing some weightlifting exercises, but thankfully, he didn't say anything else.

When I got off the treadmill, Roman halted in front of me. "Go take a shower and change. I have a surprise for you."

I frowned. "What surprise?"

"It wouldn't be a surprise if I told you. Now go. I'll be waiting for you in the foyer." He gently grabbed my shoulders and pushed me toward the stairs. But I didn't move. "Come on. You'll like it. I promise."

I rolled my eyes, but did what he asked. I had to admit, the prospect of a good surprise did lighten my mood, and when I finally came downstairs after a nice, warm shower, and changing into clean clothes, I had a spring in my step.

I went down the stairs, but faltered halfway through.

Roman stood in the foyer in gray slacks and a white button-up shirt, the sleeves rolled to his elbows, showing off his forearms. He saw me coming and smiled at me.

I expected my heart to lurch, my breath to catch. It didn't, but I couldn't deny two things: he was caring in a way that made me feel like the most important woman in the world, and he was handsome.

If fate had chosen him to be my mate, I was probably a lucky girl.

He approached the end of the stairs and offered me his hand. "Let's go, princess."

I took his hand and let him help me with the last three steps. "And where are we going?"

He chuckled. "I'm not ruining the surprise."

ROMAN TOOK ME TO PARADISE.

Or almost.

The bookstore he drove us to was small and cozy and had

that sweet smell of old books I loved so much—how did I remember that?—but the only flaw here was that all the books had a price and if I wanted them all, I would have to pay a small fortune.

"You can buy as many books as you want," Roman assured me when we first arrived. "Your father is paying."

I didn't know which shelf or section to browse first. I grabbed one of the big mesh totes the bookstore offered and decided to walk through the shelves. I didn't want to miss any hidden gem.

Roman followed me from a distance, an easy grin on his lips as he watched me go nuts over books.

My cheeks warmed at his attention.

Roman probably knew me better than anyone, seeing as he'd known me since I was a little girl, and we had been mated for years now. And yet ... when I looked at him, I didn't feel what I would have expected from a mating bond. At least, that was how I thought a mating bond should be. Every time mates looked at each other, their breaths caught, they lost all control, and couldn't keep their hands to themselves. That was what I had read in fantasy books.

I halted. How did I remember *that*, when I couldn't even remember the titles of books I had read before? I couldn't even explain how I knew I loved books so much. I just ... felt.

Honestly, this memory stuff was too much for my addled mind.

I continued my way through the bookstore, my finger brushing the spines of books I wasn't even interested in. Books felt like one of the pieces of the puzzle that completed me and I needed to touch them.

Ivy's mansion had a library, but all the books were fake. They were huge encyclopedias with beautiful leather covers, and their only purpose was to look pretty on the shelves.

I had asked to come to a bookstore before, but my father had been worried about me being out when I didn't even remember my own house. But now he had allowed Roman to bring me here and I knew why: to occupy myself while he, Ivy, Dot, and a handful of his demons went on their mission. So I wouldn't be upset about not being able to join them.

I turned into the romance section, and suddenly an image flashed in my mind.

A man whose face I couldn't see, standing at the corner of a bookshelf, wearing nothing but jeans. A powerful tug came from my chest and I pressed a hand over my breast, as if I could soothe the pain that it left behind.

My head snapped toward Roman. Was that him? Had he been with me before while I browsed books somewhere? And why had he been shirtless? And that feeling, that tug ... it could only be the mating bond.

I opened my mouth to ask Roman about it, but then a woman with a little girl walked in the same corridor. As they passed by us, the little girl pulled at her mother's sweater and whispered, "Mommy, she looks like a princess." Then she looked at me again and smiled.

Something tugged inside of me again, different this time, and I smiled back at her, suddenly taken aback. As the girl and her mother walked away, my chest constricted and my eyes watered. I pressed a hand to my chest. What the hell was this about?

"She called you princess," Roman said from behind me.

I inhaled deeply and blinked, pushing the tears away. For some reason, I didn't want him to see this little insane reaction I had just had.

I turned to the books. "She was just being kind."

"No, Raika, she wasn't. She was being honest."

A knot formed between my eyebrows. I knew in real life princesses didn't wear huge ballgowns everywhere they went, but that was how I imagined them. I was dressed up, in a simple but elegant black dress that went down mid-calf, high heeled pumps, and a set of beautiful diamond earrings and a delicate pendant, which I was told had been gifts from my father on my last birthday.

My long black hair was pulled back into a half ponytail that curled in a big wave down my back, and I had a little makeup on.

I looked rich, sophisticated, but certainly not like a princess.

Shaking my head, I continued browsing the shelves. I paused again at the middle grade section, where a bunch of adventure and fantasy called to me. I picked one up and looked at the cover: a young girl holding a sword atop of a mountain.

Suddenly, I saw a little girl in my mind, seated on a rug, surrounded by pillows, and holding this exact book.

I gasped and held the book tighter. I stared at Roman.

"What is it?" He approached me, his hands hovered over my arms. "Are you okay?"

My throat went dry. "Tell me, when we lived with the pack, was there a little girl who liked to read? A place with a large rug and several pillows?"

Roman's lips thinned and his brows slammed down. "Hm, yeah. The rug and pillows were at the library. You loved spending time there. As for the little girl ... she liked books too."

"Was she something to me? My cousin? My friend?" It

would be odd for me to have a little girl as a friend, unless this was an old memory, and I had been a little girl at the time too.

"Raika, I've told you before. You didn't really have any friends there. Just me."

I nodded. He had told me that. He even told me the pack had hated my guts since I was born, even though back then they had no idea what I was. They had always treated me bad.

I let out a long sigh. "I ... I don't know what is happening, but I just had two flashes and I'm certain they are memories."

"Two?"

Giddy, I placed the book I was holding inside the tote and looked around. "I should start picking more books from the shelves. Maybe more memories will come to me."

"Raika." Roman grabbed my wrist, but a second later he let go, probably remembering he had promised not touching me without my consent first. But this hadn't been *that* kind of touch. "I think we should go."

"Why? I'm finally remembering something. You should be glad." I knew I was.

"I am, truly, but maybe now that you've unlocked two memories, you should go see Dot. She might be able to unlock the rest now."

I liked that idea but ... I picked up my phone and glanced at it. It had been only four hours since the others had left for their mission. "Dot's probably not back yet. Who knows how long this mission will take? A full day? Two? A week? Even if they come back today, I think we can spare a couple more hours here." I smiled at Roman, truly happy with the idea of staying in the bookstore and recovering more of my memories if not all. "Please?"

Roman groaned, but nodded. "But only if you let me take you out to dinner later this evening."

I stilled. Dinner with Roman ... alone. We hadn't done that yet since I lost my memories. I bit my lip. What the hell? Wasn't the guy my mate? I should give him a chance to make me fall in love with him all over again.

I dipped my chin once. "Deal."

IN THE END, Roman and I didn't go to dinner. My father, Ivy, Rotgar, and Dot returned as we were about to leave. The maids arranged dinner for us. Meanwhile, we got together at the family room, where the fire sparked in the fireplace and brandy ran amok.

My father sat at one of the large armchairs, looking weary and weak. Seated in another of the armchairs, Dot rubbed her hands as if she had used up all of her magic and now had to warm her fingers before she could cast another spell. Ivy threw herself on the couch beside me, her black leather clothes dirty as if she had been in a muddy war camp. Rotgar stood on the other side of the room, as if he didn't want anything to do with us. The higher demon was always quiet and reserved, but I was told that in battle, he loved to taunt his adversaries.

Roman brought a second glass of brandy to my father after he drained the first, then sat on the couch beside me.

"Stop this suspense, tell us how it went," I said, glancing between them.

Ivy reached down and started unbuckling her boots. "How do you think?"

"I want details," I urged.

"We found one of the portals to the underworld, but it was too well guarded," my father said, his voice thin. "Lots of Blackthorn Demon Hunters crawling around the place."

I frowned as an image came to mind—a huge stone wall in the middle of nowhere and several people dressed in black leather uniforms around it. One of them came to me and—

"Those damn hunters," Ivy muttered, snapping me out of the memory. What the hell was that? "When we saw there too many of them, we decided to just scout and take inventory."

"But one of the patrols saw us," Rotgar finished. I almost jumped, not noticing he was standing closer now.

"We got into a fight," Dot continued with a big smile. "It was fun."

"Fun?" My father scoffed. "Hardly."

"He used too much of his magic," Ivy said, her voice low. "He's weak again."

I frowned, suddenly concerned. "Is there anything we can do to help you? Dot, can you make a potion to restore his energy?"

"We've tried that," she said. "My potions only worked for a short while. He needs to absorb the power of some magical item."

"Or magical being," Ivy added.

"A potion would help for now," my father said. "There's one in my desk, in the top drawer—"

I was up and out before he finished his sentence. I walked to the home office he had made his own and easily found the drawer and the potion vial my father had mentioned. I grabbed from the drawer, and something on the desk caught my attention.

A broken, shimmering dragon scale rested on the corner of my father's desk. He had told me that when my pack found me and attacked me five days ago, Ivy and I had been out, checking on a great power our father had sensed—it had been the dragon waking up. The Nightshade pack had been there for the same reason, but when they saw me, they abandoned the dragon and came for me instead. With the attack, the dragon escaped, but Ivy had caught this scale that had fallen from the dragon. It had been infused with power, and my father had absorbed it, and he felt energized on the spot. A single scale wouldn't fix the problem, but ...

I grabbed the scale and rushed back to the family room.

"The dragon." I stood amid the couches and armchairs and showed them the scale. "The magic in one single scale gave you energy for days. What would happen if you got your hands on an entire dragon?"

My father's eyes widened. "I could absorb his magic ... if that didn't cure me, it would at least give me a nice boost to endure another year."

"Or even maybe another decade," Rotgar said, his voice low.

Ivy cocked her head. "What are you saying?"

My father gestured for me and I handed the potion to him. He drank it in a big gulp and inhaled deeply. He glanced at Ivy. "You're tasked with finding where the dragon is."

Ivy groaned but nodded.

"What about me?" I asked. "Can't I help this time?"

My father frowned. "Prove to me you can use your dark-fire, then I'll let you go dragon hunting with your sister."

3

***

SHANE

There was nothing here but ashes.

My body and mind were numb as I walked through what once was the town where my pack, the Nightshade, resided. The buildings, the houses, the streets, the flowerbeds along the sidewalks ... everything had turned to ash. The scent of burnt rubber hung heavy in the air, made worse by the unusually hot summer afternoon.

I had known what I would or wouldn't find here, but I had wanted to come back. I had to see if there was any way for us to come back to our homes, even if only in the distant future.

Besides, I had once walked away when I thought the town had been completely burned and everyone here had died, and neither of those things had been true. This time, I had to be sure.

But being here was obviously a mistake.

There was no vestige of the poison anymore, but that could be because ashes covered everything. Even the forest around the town had been decimated.

This place—where I had grown up, where I had trained,

where I had fallen in love, where I had lost my mate—was gone now.

I stopped in front of Raika's house. It was now not much more than black half-walls. She had gotten a few things out before we evacuated, but it didn't seem enough. I wanted more things from her, any damn thing I could salvage from this pile of rubble.

Anything from her.

Inhaling deeply, I stepped into her house, the charred floor creaking under my weight. Just like the outside, the inside was unrecognizable and all black. I stepped to where a shelf was before and picked up what once had been a portrait of when she had just turned sixteen, now it was broken glass and a tiny piece of burned paper.

Even so, I tucked that piece of paper in my pocket.

I turned to her bedroom. In my mind, I imagined myself opening the door and stepping into an alternate reality. Raika would be inside her room, tidying up her things or getting dressed after a shower. She would see me and smile at me. Then she would press her body to mine and kiss me.

My heart seized.

The door was gone, now black and fallen to the floor. And her room ... her bed was a charred mess, everything melted or burned into pure ashes. I could see her lying on the mattress as the fire enveloped her body and took her away from me forever.

Breathing hard, I turned away from the room. My heart hammered against my chest and I had to close my eyes and focus. I counted to ten, then to twenty, then to fifty, but my agony and sudden panic kept growing.

I ran from the house and only stopped when I was in the middle of the driveway. I bent forward, my hands on my knees as I took in deep breaths and tried controlling my emotions.

It stirred inside of me anyway. The Shadow Wolf. He moved in my chest, in my gut. He wanted me to turn my agony and panic into rage. He wanted to come out and destroy everything and everyone.

Raika had been cremated a week ago, and the full moon had passed. I had been locked in the same room Killian and Lavinia had prepared for me many months ago, but even now, I could feel the Shadow Wolf. He was stronger than before. In some ways, I wanted to surrender to him. It would be easy to forget what happened and erase this constant pain if he took over. But I couldn't. Not yet. Not until my brother and sister were safe, until my pack was whole again.

Until then, I had to endure this pain, to push the Shadow Wolf down, and just survive.

It was hard, though. Living without her.

My chest hurt again and I rubbed the heel of my hand against the spot right above my heart. It had been doing that since Raika died. I guess it was the depthless hole in my heart, and it wouldn't stop hurting until the day I died.

Slowly, I walked away from the house and into main street.

Killian appeared from around another house and fell into step with me, a melted tablet in his hands.

"There's nothing here," he said, his tone somber. "We can't save one damn thing." He threw the tablet to the side.

"I figured, but I had to come and see."

He nodded. "I know."

We approached the main square, which was now a giant hole in the ground from which the dragon had emerged.

Dom came out of the school, kicking debris out of the way. "Nothing in here is salvageable," he declared.

I let out a sigh. "I apologize for dragging you two here."

Killian put his hand on my shoulder. "I understand why you had to do it."

"To be honest, I had to come and see it too, man," Dom said.

I looked around, my agony growing deeper.

The sound of footsteps crunching over the charred terrain reached our ears and we turned to see four men coming toward us.

My muscles tensed and I was ready to shift if necessary. "Who are you and what are you doing here?"

One of the men took the lead and raised his hands in a peace sign. "We don't want any trouble." He stopped a good fifteen feet from us and gestured to his companions. "We're from the Whitecrest pack. I heard you were back and we wanted to talk."

Whitecrest pack. Nortrix, their former alpha, had been the one who facilitated Paimon's entrance in this town.

"I have nothing to talk to you about," I said through gritted teeth. The Shadow Wolf was under my skin. "Get out of here."

"My pack is in shambles after what happened here," he said in a rush. I took a good look at him. Short, stocky frame, graying hair, weary face. He looked to be in his sixties, which meant he was probably over a hundred and twenty years old. "Most of our able wolves died when the dragon escaped, including our alpha."

I frowned. "I thought Nortrix had a son."

"He has five sons, but they are all too young to lead," the man said. "The oldest is sixteen."

"With a good council backing him up, he should be able to lead."

The man shook his head. "I wish it was that simple. The remaining members of our council don't want to recognize him as the new alpha."

"That's not a matter of want. It's how it goes. Ask the boy to shout a command. Everyone will have no choice but to obey."

"You don't understand. A war is brewing within my broken pack. We are already reduced to almost nothing. If a war breaks out, I'm not sure my pack can endure."

My brows curled down. I knew what he meant. My pack was broken, reduced to almost nothing, but at least I was here to lead them. I didn't want to lead anymore. I felt broken myself without Raika, but I had a duty to fulfill. Once Tyren was old enough, I would let him lead.

But the Whitecrest didn't have that option. "I don't understand what you want from me."

"I want your help," the man said.

"What's your name?"

"Eike."

"Eike, I don't think I can help—"

"Your pack is in just as bad shape as ours," he said, cutting me off. "If we united, in a way, and you helped Jean while he's young, I believe the council wouldn't have a say in it. They would have to bow before the alpha, and the rebels seeking to start a war would think twice before doing so."

Beside me, Dom scoffed and muttered, "You've got to be kidding me."

I stared at Eike. The idea was absurd, but not the worst I had heard. But if I ever considered this course of action, I needed to know more. "The remaining wolves, were they in favor of what Nortrix was doing?"

Dom glared at me. "You can't be considering this."

Eike went on, "Most wolves, even the ones involved, didn't know the details of Nortrix's plans. When the time came, he commanded the wolves to execute to his bidding without a choice."

My nostrils flared. Nortrix had been a terrible alpha. "What about the council?"

Eike hesitated. He stared at me for a beat too long. "The council—"

"They agreed with Nortrix."

"They didn't know the details either, but yes, they agreed with the grand idea Nortrix had painted of a bigger, more powerful pack, with strong allies and resources. They wanted that."

"Which means they won't accept this idea." To be honest, I wasn't too keen on it myself.

"They can be convinced, with a strong hand."

I shook my head. I already had a lot on my plate as it was. I couldn't add problems from the pack that got my mate killed on top of it all. "I'm afraid I can't help you."

I turned to leave.

"Please, Shane. We'll kill ourselves if someone doesn't step in."

I glanced at Eike. "Then ask for help from the other packs."

"The other alphas are as bad as Nortrix. We need someone with a fair, strong heart to guide our alpha."

I wanted to laugh. Fair, strong heart? My heart had a hole the size of the ocean in it. Infinite and depthless. It had shriveled and died along with Raika. There was no fairness or strength in it anymore. My heart was hanging by a thread. As soon as I could take my own pack off my plate, I would give up.

I shook my head again. "I hope you find a better solution for your problem." I resumed walking again. The sooner I left this place, the better.

"At least take my phone number," Eike said, his voice louder, more desperate. "In case you change your mind."

I wouldn't change my mind, but I could at least take the damn phone number. I waved at Dom. He walked toward the Whitecrest wolves, and as I walked away, I heard Eike giving his number to Dom.

Killian turned and followed me.

I inhaled deeply, hating the scent of ashes in the air, but welcoming it as a deserving punishment.

When Dom reached us, I said, "Time to go."

The three of us walked to the edge of town, beyond the burned part of the forest, to where we had parked the rented car.

Then we drove away and a heavy feeling settled in my shoulders. This was probably the last time I would ever see this place.

4

SHANE

"Here." I put a plate in front of Tyren, another in front of Minsi.

Neither of them even looked at me, or said thanks, or anything before they grabbed their forks and dug in to their omelets.

Since we had to flee our home, moved to the DuMoir village, and cremated Raika, Tyren had been moodier and more into his music-slash-video-games world, and Minsi had retreated into her shell even more. In the past nine days, she had had four panic attacks, one of them while I was out visiting our old home two days ago.

Thankfully, Rue, Lavinia, Almae, and Thea were good with her and knew exactly what to do. Even little Aurora had her way with Minsi. The only word my sister had said since we arrived here was a "hi" to Aurora.

I sat down with them with a sigh and forced myself to eat.

For a week, I had let everyone mourn. I had let myself mourn. My pain would never go away, but I had to force myself to keep moving. My siblings and my pack needed me.

Because of that, we started with our new schedule and a new normalcy today.

I shoved a forkful of omelet in my mouth and almost gagged. "Shit," I muttered. I had made this thing and it was horrible. "Stop eating."

Tyren pushed the pepper and the shredded cheese in the center of the table toward me. "Try these. It'll make It taste ... less bad."

I looked at their plates. Lots of pepper and cheese covered both their omelets. I hadn't even seen them adding those. Was I that out of my mind? Groaning, I added the items to my omelet and tried it again. Not the best, but also far from bad.

I had never been a good cook, but there were certain things I could cook—omelets, for one. Simple pasta in a butter sauce. Grilled cheese. Macaroni and cheese. And usually they tasted okay. Edible.

A sigh escaped my lips and that pain above my heart came back. I rubbed at it with the heel of my hand.

Oh, Raika, my love, you were better than me at everything, especially cooking. You made delicious food for my siblings and took care of them like no other.

I shook my head. No, no time to succumb to the pain and sink in that hole again. At least not yet.

I finished eating, took my plate to the sink of the small kitchen, and wiped the counter. Tyren brought his plate and Minsi's over and put them in the dishwasher.

The houses in the DuMoir village were small, but comfortable, and even though they dated back to the 1800s from the outside, they had electricity, plumbing, and all the appliances needed for modern life.

Our house was one of the biggest, because it had three bedrooms, but we shared two bathrooms, and there was only one main area with the family room, dining room, and kitchen. Some of the houses were one-room studios.

A knock came from the front door and Tyren opened it. Rue stood at the entrance, her face sporting a soft smile.

"Good morning," she said. She looked at Minsi, who was still seated at the table, now with a book in her hands. "Who is ready for school?"

Minsi's eyes widened and she looked at me.

"You are, right?" I walked to her. She turned to me as her body started locking down. If I didn't avert this in two seconds, she would have another panic attack. I pulled a chair back and sat beside her, but angled my body to face hers. "Hey, pretty girl. You like school, especially when it's Rue teaching, because ..." I cupped my mouth and whispered, "She lets you read a lot. Right?" Minsi blinked and the tension deescalated by a millimeter. "How about you go with Rue? After class, she'll take you to the library and let you pick any book you want. Then you can bring it home and tell me about it."

Her eyes widened, but this time it wasn't with fear, but eagerness. She glanced at Rue, who chuckled. "We can go to the library in DuMoir Castle with Aurora. Would you like that?"

Minsi nodded.

Rue extended her hand. "Then come or we'll be late for class."

Minsi shot to her feet. I stood, pressing a kiss to the top of her head before she slipped away from me. With small steps, she made her way to Rue. I met Rue's eyes above her head.

"Thank you," I whispered.

She nodded at me. "I'll take good care of her."

I knew she would.

Minsi waved at me then disappeared with Rue. My heart squeezed. I didn't know what to do with Minsi, and I felt so freaking lost. For now, the Silverblood witches had made a potion we could give her when the panic attacks began, but I hated it because I felt like we were numbing her.

I didn't want this for her.

I didn't want this for anyone.

A moment later, Tyren showed up back in the living room wearing shorts, a T-shirt, and sneakers. "I'm off for training," he said as he walked to the door.

"Sure. Hm, Tyren ..."

He halted by the door and looked at me. "What?"

I stared at him. I didn't even know what to say to him. I felt like everything was falling apart, but everything had already fallen apart, and I had no idea how to fix it.

"Nothing," I told him. "Have a good training."

He nodded at me before walking away. Out he went, with Hugh and the other male wolf shifters to train with Killian and Dom. I had promised to join them and oversee training myself.

As much as I wanted to believe we would have peace now that I could practically retire, hanging on to the memories I had of Raika, I wasn't that naive. The world wasn't black and white, and I was sure there was more to come.

What, I had no idea. But before we were caught by surprise, I wanted everyone in this damn pack to be trained. Even the females. Lucille had wanted to practice with the males before. She got it. She and the others were probably headed to the training grounds right now.

I walked out into backyard and looked at the small garden behind our house. The sun was already halfway up in the sky and its warmth felt nice against my skin. I closed my eyes and tilted my head up, soaking it in. If only life was this simple.

With a grunt, I sat on the small porch steps and looked at the new red rosebush right in the yard's center. After Raika's cremation, Minsi was hysterical. To try to calm her down, Thea told Aurora to bring Minsi a present. The seven-year-old half-witch, half-vampire had brought a green stem, but nothing more. Holding hands, the two of them had come to the backyard, and Aurora had magicked the stem to come "alive." It floated between them, planted itself, grew larger and wider, and eight bright red roses blossomed in a few minutes.

"For Raika," Aurora said in her mature voice.

Minsi watched over the rosebush like a hawk.

And I did too.

The rosebush had nothing to do with Raika, besides the fact that it had been a gift to comfort Minsi after Raika's death. And yet, I often came back here and stared at the rosebush.

Because it comforted me.

I rubbed at my chest as the constant pain there increased.

All I wanted to do was lie down and think about Raika. Remember her. Remember her pretty face, her smile, the gleam in her blue eyes when she was happy. Her soft lips, her arduous kisses, her delicious scent, and her hot body, especially when it was pressed to mine.

I missed her. I missed her more than I missed the air when I stopped breathing.

My eyes stung and I blinked fast.

I didn't want to cry anymore. I wanted to honor Raika, her love, and her life, by doing the best I could for the pack she had worked so hard for. Somehow, I would give the pack a better life. Somehow, I would break the curse and stop frightening everyone each time the full moon came. Somehow, I would avenge Raika.

I had no idea how, or when, but one day, even if it was in a hundred years, I would find a way to kill Paimon.

Until then, I had duties to attend.

I exhaled as I rose from the porch step, got ready, and left for the building in the town center, which now housed our administrative sector: my office and the council meeting room.

When I stepped inside the large, rectangular conference room, the few remaining council members were already there, seated in chairs forming a circle: Hamill, Rue, and Killian, who was still an honorary member.

Serge had been a member, but he had left us, betrayed us, and now I had no idea where he was or what he was doing. And that was good, because that one also deserved to be killed in the most painful way.

"Morning," I said, approaching them. I looked at Hamill. "Feeling better?"

"Yes," he answered.

Hamill had been our first poison victim a little over a week ago. He had fallen ill, and looked as good as dead with pale skin, sunken eyes, and black fingers. Now, despite his age, he looked healthy.

"Good." Nodding, I sat on one of the chairs. "So, what's the latest?"

Rue started. She told me about how the kids were having fun with their new school—which often included field trips to DuMoir Castle or the Silver Moon Academy. A couple of witches helped Vianna and her keep the kids and teenagers entertained until we decided what to do. Would we stay here?

Would I find us someplace else? But where? And how? Just go around and claim some land for us? Land had owners, and if we set up camp anywhere, we would be exposed, open to attacks, and the moon knew we'd had too many of those.

Hamill was next. He told me about the rest of the pack. Most wolves were still wary of everything that had happened in the last ten days. Hell, in the last year. They weren't happy about losing the crystals, fleeing our town, hiding with the vampires, about having an alpha who was cursed to become an uncontrollable Shadow Wolf during the full moon, and even though they hadn't approved of Raika being my mate and the fact that she was half-demon, they missed her. They wished she was here, because, according to Hamill, she had soothed them and stayed in control of everything before. They wanted that from her again.

By the moon, didn't I want that too?

But I couldn't bring back the dead.

I pressed a hand to my chest, where the pain forcefully reminded me of that each second of each day.

Then it was Killian's turn. Usually, he and Dom took turns coming to the daily meetings—while one was here, the other was training with the rest of the wolves.

"The wolves haven't been talking much during training," Killian said. "At least, not while I'm there. Most didn't seem open to Lavinia and me. Now it's worse."

I let out a long sigh.

There was no easy fix for any of this. What I had to do was come up with ideas, give them purpose; that way they would feel a part of a community again, their time would be well spent, and maybe they would start seeing the vampires —and the witches—in a new light.

Because as much as I liked to think we wouldn't stay there

forever, the truth was, I didn't know if leaving the place was feasible. For now and for the unforeseeable future, we were living alongside vampires and witches, and the sooner everyone got along, the better.

I opened my mouth but I shut it again when Killian's phone rang. He fished it from his blazer's pocket and glanced at the screen.

He frowned as he answered it. "Lord Drake." He nodded, his eyes on me. "Yes, my lord." He lowered the phone. "Drake needs to see us."

<hr>

5

SHANE

RUE WENT BACK TO VIANNA, MINSI, AND THE OTHER KIDS; Hamill went to train with Dom, Tyren, and the other wolves; and Killian and I set off to DuMoir Castle. Though the castle was a short distance from the village, Killian had one of his cars parked beside the assembly building—a brand new McLaren.

He told me he had one twenty years ago, and it was totaled when the warlocks attacked him and locked him inside a box that was actually a door to another realm.

When he got back, the first thing he did was to buy another one, and now he drove the thing to and from the castle, since he had nowhere else to drive it.

"What's the problem this time?" I voiced my thoughts as Killian drove us into the garage at the back of the castle.

"Why do you think there's a problem?"

"From the tone in his voice." I had heard him through the call. "And because he usually doesn't ask for us like that if there isn't a problem."

Lord Drake had weekly meetings with all the castle's

princes and other high-ranked vampires. When I lived here, I was sometimes included in those meetings. I had even participated in several missions, which had been great to fill my time and my head, since I believed my entire pack had been killed and I was the sole survivor.

Killian and I entered the castle, walking through the wide hallways, greeting the vampires and witches. Besides the DuMoir vampires and the Silverblood witches residing in the castle, there was also an angel, Zadkiel, who was mated to Elisa, Thea's right hand. I had also seen other species coming and going: fae, warlocks, demon hunters, and more.

I had spent most of my life isolated inside the Nightshade lands, tucked in deep into northern Canada, and surrounded by other wolf packs, so I didn't really know much about supernaturals' history and affairs, but from what I had heard, our world had changed a lot in the last five to eight years.

Before, all species fended for themselves. There was rarely an occasion when two or more species worked together, and inter-species relationships were frowned upon if not forbidden. Couples of mixed species usually had to hide their affairs so their mates or lovers weren't killed. Alliances like the one the Nightshade pack had with the Nightmist coven had been considered treason and shameful. Now, some covens or packs still preferred to remain true to their heritage, but friendships and alliances were strong and sometimes necessary.

Killian and I passed Lyra on the stairs. Lord Drake favored the female vampire and planned to make her a princess—the first in DuMoir's history. She waved at us and we nodded at her.

Reaching the top of the stairs, Killian and I halted at Lord Drake's office door and Killian raised his hand to knock, but the door opened before he could. Prince Cain stepped aside and let us in.

"Did you need us?" Killian asked as we entered the room.

Drake's office was large and elegant, and right now almost full. Thea, all the princes—Dorian, Aston, Gray, Cain, and Killian—and I were here.

Seated behind his desk, Drake met our eyes. "I did."

Lord Drake didn't look much older than me. Twenty-five, twenty-six maybe? But I knew he was over five hundred years old. He had been a prince of DuMoir Castle for hundreds of years, and had become the lord about eight years ago, when the previous lord was assassinated and Drake was framed for his murder. That was when he met his mate, the witch Thea, the current queen of the Silverblood coven.

Aurora was their daughter and said to be the next Queen of All Witches—a witch whose power was so great, she commanded all witches and all covens.

Killian and I stood beside Cain, Aston, and Gray behind the two chairs occupied by Thea and Dorian.

"What is it?" I asked, knowing this involved me or my pack.

"I received word from the Blackthorn Demon Hunters." Drake's eyes met Cain's, which told me it was probably Norah who had called Drake. Then, he looked at me. "Yesterday, Paimon and a handful of demons were at the underworld gate outside of Winnipeg."

I went still.

"He's trying to go into the underworld," Thea said, her voice low. "We always thought the princes wouldn't just hide after having the underworld taken from them, but I didn't expect Paimon to be this direct."

Drake nodded. "I've talked to Hadrian and Rey." Hadrian

was the new leader of the Blackthorn Hunters, and Rey was the headmaster of the Blackthorn Academy. "And we've come to the same conclusion: Paimon is likely to be assembling an army to attack the underworld."

"So he was scouting." Cain crossed his arms. "But doesn't it sound odd to you? If we were getting ready for a war, you wouldn't go scouting the terrain yourself."

"Not unless the open war was plan B," Drake said. "His plan A might have been to sneak inside the underworld and attack the source. If he took Tanner down, along with his sisters, he wouldn't need a war. The underworld would be his."

"But the gate was too well guarded," I said, my voice strained.

"Exactly," Drake said. "He didn't expect that. But now he knows all gates might be like that and he won't risk coming again unless he has the army to attack and win."

"You're saying we should get ready for a war?" Dorian asked. He was older than Drake and had a shorter temper.

Drake stared at Thea. I always had the impression that these two could read each other's thoughts, probably because of their mating bond.

"It's the demon hunters' call, as this is their fight," Drake said.

"But if the underworld is attacked and falls again, it'll be everyone's fight," Aston said. There were a few agreeing murmurs around the room.

Drake nodded. "I agree, but for now, we should proceed with caution." My nostrils flared and my rage spiked at that. Caution? Did that make sense? "The demon hunters are currently searching for Paimon. Gray, you're to take a handful there and help." He paused. "And report to me whenever possible."

Gray lowered his head. "Yes, my lord."

"The rest of you, be ready. If the demon hunters call for a war, we'll take our entire army to them and make sure our side wins." Drake sighed. "You can go now." Everyone started moving, me included. "Shane."

Shit. I turned and faced Drake, who was now standing behind his desk. "Yes?"

He looked at Thea as she was the last to walk out of the room. She offered me a soft smile before closing the door behind her.

Then his eyes turned to me. "I know hearing about Paimon and learning he was spotted must be difficult to you. I also know you're probably plotting how to go after him yourself."

For a half second, I thought about denying. I had heard stories about all Thea and Drake had gone through, all he had done for her. At least his mate was still alive. Mine ... I inhaled deeply.

"I want to kill him myself," I confessed. "I don't care if it's now, if it's tomorrow, or in ten years. If this war happens, if Paimon is really starting this, I want to be there."

Drake's dark brows curled down. "What about your pack? Don't you think they need you? Shouldn't you be taking care of them instead of chasing a higher demon?"

My hands closed into fists. "My pack can survive without me."

"I'm sure they can. But what about your brother and sister?"

A snarl started low in my chest. "Leave them out of this."

"I'm not trying to play the bad guy here, Shane. I'm laying out all the cards in the game before you choose your next move. I know I'm saying this and yet, I would probably jump in head-first if I had the opportunity to avenge my mate, consequences be damned. But when the odds were stacked against Thea and me, I didn't have someone with a little more experience trying to help me. And that's what I'm trying to do. I want to help you."

"Then promise me that when the time comes, I'll be the one to kill Paimon."

Drake shook his head. "I can't promise you that, because the demon hunters will lead this one, but I can ask them to include you in their plans, if it comes to that."

That wasn't what I wanted, but I would take it. At least for now. "That's fine," I said it through gritted teeth.

Drake pressed his lips tight. "I'm really sorry, Shane. I heard Raika was an amazing woman. You have every right to avenge her, and I'll help you with what I can."

Something caught in my throat. "Thank you."

Without another word, I left his office. Thankfully, Killian wasn't waiting for me outside. Everyone was busy with possible war preparations.

Great, because I had preparations of my own.

6

RAIKA

SMALL BALLS OF DARKFIRE DANCED IN MY HANDS. THEY WERE little, the size of my closed fists, but they were all mine. I focused on them, molding them with my thoughts: a twister, darts, and I even united them to create a beautiful dark dagger. I picked up the dagger, tangible in my hands, and threw it at one of the targets along the wall.

The dagger hit the target the wrong way and I lost my grip on my magic. The dagger became a cloud of smoke before hitting the ground.

I groaned and Ivy pressed her hand over her mouth, hiding her laughter.

"Just laugh, evil woman, that's what you want."

Ivy took a deep breath, trying to calm down. I rolled my eyes at her.

It had been five days since my father had challenged me to finally get a grip on my darkfire. I had been practicing in the basement for at least eight hours per day, and I could feel myself gaining ground, though it wasn't as fast as I wished.

I still couldn't cast waves or giant walls or throw three

hundred bolts of darkfire like Ivy could, but this was something. I was doing it. I was controlling my darkfire.

The bad part was I had thought when I got to this point, something would snap inside of me and my memories would rush in and everything would go back to normal.

No such luck.

"Patience, Raika," the witch told me. "They will come back at the right time. You'll see."

If only it were that simple.

"What about a break?" Ivy asked.

She had been practicing with me, even though she had to find the dragon. She had sent a group of demons out to do the job instead—with Rotgar, of course. He didn't seem happy about it, but he had to do what she told him to.

I picked up my phone from the mat and looked at the time. "No, I can still train for another hour without a break."

Ivy let out a sigh that sounded like a groan. "Come on! You're doing great. You'll be annihilating entire armies soon enough."

I cringed at that. They talked about killing and fighting as if was like breathing air—something we did without even thinking about. But each time I thought about killing, my stomach tensed with knots.

I knew we were getting ready for a war. I just hoped my memories returned before that; otherwise, how was I supposed to fight?

I shook my head, clearing those thoughts from my mind. I didn't need any doubt in there right now.

"If you don't want to train, I understand, but I am."

Rotgar climbed down the stairs, his steps fast, and he halted at the edge of the mat. He looked at her from head to toe and back, as if she was a bug in his path.

"What is it?" Ivy asked.

"There's a bounty hunter," Rotgar said. He sounded bored.

Ivy frowned. "A bounty hunter?"

"He claims he specializes in big creatures, even dragons."

Ivy's eyes widened. "Dragons? But this is the first one in almost a thousand years. His advertising needs work."

"That might be, but if he gets the job done, who cares?" Rotgar shrugged. "I've asked him to meet with us."

Without waiting for a response, the higher demon turned and raced up the stairs.

I stared at her. "This is progress, right?"

"If this bounty hunter is real, then yes, I guess." She wrinkled her nose. "I'm going to take a shower." She turned to the stairs. "Aren't you meeting him with me?"

I looked around at the gym. I needed to train more, but curiosity got the best of me. "Wait for me!"

IN THE END, there had been no need to rush. After I took a shower and changed into a dark purple cocktail dress, I met Ivy in the living room just to learn the bounty hunter would arrive in two hours.

I was in no mood to change into training clothes, just to have to take another shower and change again in two hours, so I stayed in the living room with Ivy. She put on some music, served us red wine, asked the maid to bring us snacks, and sat down on the couch.

I picked up some of the books I had bought at the bookstore a few days ago, piled them up on one of the side tables, sat on the couch right beside them, and browsed through them.

"Are we having a party?"

I glanced up. Roman entered the living room, cutting a dashing figure in a dark suit. He smiled at me. I smiled back, though I wished that my heart had lurched at the sight of him. He might be my mate, but my memories were all so banged up, the bond seemed to be lost in there too.

"If Ivy had her way, we'd have a party at least twice a day."

"What? No. At least three times." She winked at me.

Roman sat beside me, eyeing the books on the table and the one in my hand. "How many have you finished?"

"None, to be honest."

He mocked gasped. "Raika isn't reading a book per day? That's impossible. Are you sick?"

I hit his arm with the book. "I've been busy with training."

"And keeping me busy," Ivy said.

"What, would you rather be out looking for the dragon yourself?"

"Oh goodness, no. That's why we have soldiers. They do the dirty work for us."

I laughed, grabbing the next book in the pile. It was a middle-grade fantasy book about a warrior girl. What was this doing here? I wasn't into middle grade, was I? Maybe in the past, when I was their age. For some reason, I felt like adult fantasy suited me better ... but this one. I turned the book in my hand, puzzled.

"Is there something wrong?" Roman asked. "You seemed to like that book in the bookstore."

I did? I thought back to our time at the bookstore. It felt hazy, as if I couldn't recall the trip. I inhaled sharply. Oh no, what if I lost even my new memories? What if I had one of those memory problems where the person could only remember the last hour or day, or whatever.

My heart pounded against my rib cage. I needed Dot. She could look into this, into my mind. And—

The sound of the front door opening echoed outside the living room. We all stood as footsteps neared us. A maid appeared in the doorway and gestured for someone to come forward.

A man walked into the living room. I stared, taken aback by his appearance. He was tall, probably six-three, with broad shoulders, and strong arms, mostly apparent from underneath the sleeveless leather vest he wore, along with matching pants and combat boots. A large crossbow peeked out from across his back. He regarded us with his dark green eyes before running a hand over the top of his head. His light brown hair was longer, the side shaved short. However, the most intriguing part of him was the deep, light red scar across his left eye and eyebrow. It didn't take one bit away from the beauty of his face and the sharpness of his features.

Ivy stood. "You must be the bounty hunter."

The man inclined his head in agreement. "Kaz, at your service." His voice was deep and rough.

"Come." She beckoned him forward. "My father will join us shortly and—"

"I'm here."

I snapped my head at the sound of his voice. My father marched through the entrance from the dining room, Rotgar close at his heels. My father wore a nice suit and looked slightly better. Dot's potion must have done the trick, for now.

I stood to meet him, but he waved me off.

Rotgar stood by the wall again, while my father took his usual armchair and gestured for Kaz to take a seat. The bounty hunter didn't hesitate. He slipped his crossbow from his back. Ivy and Roman tensed. Knowing Ivy, she had her darkfire at her fingertips, ready to blast the stranger if he as much as looked at our father the wrong away.

I frowned, realizing I hadn't had the same reaction. I sat there, watching everything as if it was a movie playing on the TV.

The bounty hunter rested the crossbow beside the armchair right across from my father and sat down, facing him fully. Didn't he know who he was dealing with, or was he always this brazen?

Shooting a veiled looked at me, Ivy sat too.

My father narrowed his eyes at Kaz. "We heard you're the one to hire to capture big creatures."

"Yes, sir. Anything you need."

My father rubbed at his chin. "What about dragons?"

"Even dragons."

"Have you ever hunted dragons, Kaz?" Ivy asked. "I thought dragons had been extinct for a long time."

"People believe whatever they want." Kaz looked at Ivy. "Yes, I have hunted one dragon before, the only one I had ever heard about. Though, that seems to have changed."

My father nodded. "A dragon awoke from a magical slumber in northern Canada, but now we don't know where he is."

"Interesting."

"How much for you to capture him and keep him alive until I get to him?"

Kaz seemed to consider this. "Capturing but not killing will be harder. Half a million to start." Ivy sucked in a sharp breath. "Another half million when I deliver him to you."

"That's too—"

"Deal." My father extended his hand toward the bounty hunter, ignoring whatever Ivy was about to say.

Kaz shook my father's hand. "Would you have anything from the dragon, or maybe a weapon used against him, or even the clothes you were wearing the last time you encountered him? It'll help me track him."

"The scale," I said.

"Ah, yes." My father jerked his chin and Rotgar walked out of the room. Two minutes later, he strolled back in, taking his sweet time, the scale in his hands. He handed it to my father. "Will this do?"

"May I?" Kaz reached forward. My father placed the broken dragon scale in the bounty hunter's hand. He wrapped a hand around it, closed his eyes, and inhaled deeply. When he opened again, a lopsided grin adorned his lips. "Yes, this will do."

"Excellent. When can you start?"

"As soon as you make the first payment."

My father smiled. "Of course." He pulled out his phone and started messing with it. "Just one more thing. My demons will go with you."

Kaz's gaze hardened. "I work alone."

My father held Kaz's stare, impassive. "Not this time. My demons go with you."

Kaz's jaw worked overtime. Something about that tickled my mind, as if a memory wanted to come forward, to blast through whatever wall was holding it back, but when I tried grasping at it, it slipped between my fingers.

"Fine. But if they slow me down, I'll leave them behind."

"They won't slow you down." He shot a look at Ivy, one that said you-better-not-mess-this-up. Wait, what about me?

While my father and Kaz exchanged account numbers, I scooted closer to Ivy and whispered, "What was that look?"

"What look?"

"The one he gave you. Like he was telling you that you're in charge, but he didn't even look at me. He won't let me go?"

"I don't know. He hasn't said anything."

"But I'm able to control the darkfire. I might not be able to do all you can, but I can defend myself. If he says I can't go, you have to help me."

Ivy's brows curled. "I don't—"

"Promise me you'll help me. You'll ask for me to go with you." I needed this. I didn't know why—I wasn't even that excited about hunting a dragon—but I had to go. Finding my darkfire and being able to use it hadn't worked to bring my memories back, but maybe being outside this house would. I couldn't explain it, but I knew I had to do this. "Please."

She sighed. "I'll try."

My father and Kaz continued talking about what Kaz needed: supplies for the tracking and the trip, an off-road truck or SUV, and time.

"How long until you capture the dragon?" my father asked.

"It'll depend on where he is," Kaz said, his tone flat. "If the dragon is already on the other side of the world, it could take up to a month. If it's close by, then maybe a week."

My father nodded and pointed to Ivy. "My daughter, Ivy, is a higher demon and she'll be going with you. Whatever supplies you need, tell her, and she'll make sure you have everything."

Ivy opened her mouth to speak, but I was faster. "I'm going too."

My father's hard eyes found mine. "Is that so?"

I puffed up my chest. "I've been training nonstop, and I have control over my darkfire."

He glanced at Ivy. "Is this true?"

She nodded.

The fact that he didn't believe me right away, that he had to ask Ivy, hurt.

He looked at me. Really looked at me, as if he could feel my magic inside me. Perhaps he could. "Very well. You can go with them, but you follow Ivy's orders. Understood?"

Eagerness filled my chest and it was all I could not to bounce on my toes. "Yes, sir."

"Just ... go see Dot before you go," he said. "It'll be good to do a meditation session beforehand." He turned to Kaz. "She'll need a few minutes."

Kaz didn't seem bothered by that. He had been stoic and closed off since he arrived, so that didn't say much. "We leave in one hour."

7

SHANE

Killian had stayed at the castle to talk to his vampires about the possible war and what that meant. For now, they would send scouts out and increase training, to make sure everyone was prepared.

Alone, I went back to the village. Right now, everyone was busy with their tasks: the kids were in school, the others were either training or helping around the village, and Jay was setting up our new infirmary. The vampires were providing everything he might need.

At my house, I grabbed a duffel bag from inside my closet and started packing. It was an odd sense of déjà vu. A little over a month ago, I had done the same when I found out Raika was still alive—

The pain stabbed me in the chest like a knife, cutting true and deep. I rubbed at it with my closed fist.

Now, it was different. Now, Raika was gone. Now, I would avenge her.

Before, I had left without telling anyone, but this time I

couldn't do that. I wasn't alone here, though I felt like I was most of the time. So when my bag was ready, I texted Rue.

She replied a couple of minutes later, letting me know she was in a clearing behind the village with Vianna and the kids.

I'll see you in five, I texted back.

When I stepped into the clearing, my heart squeezed. The kids ran around, laughing and yelling. Some played tag, others sat on a large blanket and played instruments, while others ate snacks spread over another blanket.

Minsi sat alone on a blanket, with her nose stuck in a book.

How I wished she would break through that shell and play with the other kids, even if for a moment. I didn't wish for her to stop reading, to go out and be the most extroverted kid I had ever met, but ... I sighed. It couldn't be good for her to be this isolated. She was among a dozen other wolves, and yet, she stayed in her world the entire time.

Rue saw me standing there and walked up to me. "You have me worried."

I frowned. "Why is that?"

"It isn't common for you to want to talk to me in the middle of the day."

I nodded. "I wanted to inform you of my plans, because I owe you that much, and because I'll need your help, even more than what you already offer me. Us."

Rue tilted her head, her long gray braid moving with it. "What is going on?"

I told her about my plan and asked, "Could you watch over my siblings while I'm away? Especially Minsi?"

Rue pressed her lips tight. I knew she wanted to argue with me, but nothing she or anyone else could say would change my mind. "Of course I will. Just ... please, come back."

"I will," I said automatically.

She rested her hand on my arm. "I know how it is to lose your mate, Shane. The constant pain inside your chest. The renewed grief when you wake up in the middle of the night and suddenly remember they are gone. The nonexistent will to live. But you're not just another wolf in our pack. You're our alpha. You need to be strong for all of us, for Tyren and Minsi too. Tyren is too young to become alpha, and Minsi ..." She sighed. "Minsi needs you more than anyone else."

I nodded. I didn't want to live on, but I had to do it. "Thanks."

After a pat on my arm, Rue returned to the kids. I felt torn about walking up to Minsi and giving her a hug before leaving, but what if I did that and she realized something was wrong? She was alone, but she was peaceful. I didn't want to disturb that peace.

On my way back to my house, I grabbed my phone and texted Dom.

Where are you?

Finishing up training. Why?

I started typing my answer. I didn't want to face him or argue about my choice. I wanted him to read my response and just follow my orders.

"Shane."

I stopped walking, looking in the direction of the voice.

Lucille walked out of her house and jogged to me. The sun reflected off her blond hair, and for a moment, her beauty struck me. It was a shame she didn't seem able to move on from our past relationship. She really deserved to find a mate and be happy with him.

"What is it?" I asked, pocketing my phone again.

"Nothing." She shrugged as she fell into step with me. "I just ... saw you and wanted to talk to you. How are you?"

"Good." Another automatic answer and a complete lie.

She cocked her head to the side. "Shane, I've known you since we were little kids. You can't lie to me."

I shook my head. "What do you want me to say, Lucille? I've been feeling wretched and in agony every second of every day since Raika's been gone. Is that what you want to hear?"

"If that's the truth, then yes."

A knot formed between my brows. "No one else needs to live in misery with me."

"Shane, we're all living in misery. Everyone here has lost loved ones, lived as slaves, and then lost our home. We're now forced to shelter with vampires. Besides, Raika made her mark on us. Everyone misses her."

A lump rose to my throat.

Finally, after a week of forcing myself to get up in the mornings, to breathe and keep going, I had a reason to live, even if brief: I was going to find Paimon and I was going to kill the bastard.

And I was going to make him suffer.

I wanted to focus on that and only that because it was better to hang on to my anger than my sorrow.

"I appreciate the concern, Lucille, but I'm fine." I halted in front of my house. "You should go."

Lucille's face fell. "Of course." Without another word, she left. I was about to head inside my house when I caught sight of Dom running this way.

For a moment, I froze. What was wrong?

But then he stopped a few feet from me and took a deep breath, his expression neutral. "You didn't reply to my text. I was worried there was something wrong."

"Sorry. Lucille found me." I gestured toward where she went. "I was about to reply now."

Dom crossed his arms. "I'm here now. Just tell me."

I groaned. I really didn't want to do this face-to-face. I didn't want to have to explain myself or argue with my friends. They didn't feel the pain I did. But Lucille was right. They were all in agony and miserable, just as I was. It wasn't fair of me to think I was the only one suffering here.

"Drake got word that Paimon is plotting to take the underworld back," I told Dom.

His eyes widened. "But that would mean a war."

I nodded. "Precisely. However, I won't let that happen."

"What do you mean?"

"I'm leaving. Right now. I'm going after him. I'll kill him myself."

Dom stared at me. "You do realize he is more than a higher demon? He's a former prince. His power is unheard of, and with all due respect, I don't think you're up to par to take him down."

I sighed. "Maybe not me, but my Shadow Wolf. I'll let him out and he might be what we need to take him down." If not that, then I could at least do some good damage, until the demon hunters came and helped me finish the job.

"The full moon was a few days ago. If you let the Shadow Wolf out now, it'll be harder to control him."

I scoffed. "I can't control him. Once he takes over, my consciousness is gone."

"Isn't he taking more and more of you?" Dom's voice rose. He was upset with me. "Do you want to risk letting him out now and losing yourself to him?"

"If I'm not near my pack, I'm not afraid. Just promise one thing, if I do lose it, you'll find me and you'll kill me before I kill innocent people." Dom closed his eyes for a moment and cursed under his breath. "Dom, please."

He cursed some more. "Fine. I promise." He extended his hand to me. I clasped his forearm in a tight grip. "Don't make me do it, though. Don't lose to the Shadow Wolf. And come back to us."

I nodded. "Keep everyone safe while I'm gone."

"I'll do my best."

I let go of his arm and stepped inside my house. I grabbed my duffel bag from my bed, slung it over my shoulder, and went back out. Thankfully, Dom didn't wait for another awkward goodbye and I was able to run to DuMoir Castle without anyone bothering me.

I found Prince Gray in front of the castle. He and ten vampires checked their bags and supplies.

A frown curved his lips when he saw me coming.

"Where do you think you're going?"

"Where do you think?"

"That's not what Lord Drake ordered."

I stood a foot from him and gave him my best I-don't-fucking-care glare. "I'm going with or without your help. So why don't you make this easy for the both of us and let me hitch a ride?"

Gray stared at me, clearly not pleased. "Fine. Come along. But I'm reporting this to Drake."

I shrugged. "Do whatever you have to."

WE DIDN'T DRIVE to Winnipeg. That was a twenty-five-hour trip, and even though vampires slept a lot less than most species, we would need to take too many breaks, making the trip even longer.

Instead, a portal opened and a warlock walked out from it. Aspen worked directly with Keeran, who was good friends with Lord Drake. Keeran was Almae's son and Lavinia's cousin.

Aspen guided us through the portal. We walked through and appeared outside the underworld gates in Winnipeg.

The situation here was much different from a couple weeks ago.

There had been a lot of demon hunters protecting the portal before. That was nothing compared with the number of demon hunters swarming now. It was a dark sea of movement and flashing weapons.

A group of demon hunters came over to greet us, including Norah.

"Prince Gray," she said, shaking the vampire's hand. She shot me a glance. "I thought only the vampires were coming to aid us."

I cocked an eyebrow. "I have a tab to settle with Paimon."

Her face fell. "I heard about Raika. I'm so sorry."

I nodded.

"But if you're here for revenge, I'm afraid it won't be so simple," Norah went on.

"What do you mean?" Gray asked.

"Come with me." She gestured for us to follow her through the crowd.

Beside the portal was a dark green tent with open sides. Underneath it, a large dark green rug, a long table, and several chairs had been erected, and a handful of demon hunters filled the space.

I recognized a couple of faces at the table: Rey Lowe, the

academy's headmaster, and his partner, Erin Belmont, princess of the underworld and a famous demon hunter.

They greeted Gray, the other vampires, and me.

"I wish we were meeting under better circumstances," Rey said.

"We can celebrate when we kill Paimon," Gray said.

Rey nodded. "Please sit."

"Before we start, I have a request," I said. I had no time to waste. If they were working on plans, I wanted to be included in them. "I want to be the one to kill Paimon."

Rey frowned. "No offense, Shane, but I'm not sure a wolf shifter, even an alpha, can take a former prince of the underworld alone."

"I'm not asking to do this alone, I'm asking to deliver the killing blow."

Erin put a hand over Rey's. "I understand why you're asking. We're still trying to navigate away from a full-blown war, and there are many moving pieces on the board, but I promise you, I'll do my best to include you in our plans."

I would take whatever they could get me. For now. "Thank you."

***

THE MEETING DRAGGED on for hours. Demon hunters came and went. King Tanner and Princess Jasmin joined the party, but everyone was so worried about Tanner's security, it was agreed he should remain inside his castle, which was also swarming with demon hunters.

My phone kept blowing up with calls and texts from Killian and Drake. I ignored them all.

Half of the demon hunters here were divided into small

groups, along with our vampires and me, and sent to scout the area around the portal, until possibly finding Paimon or his allies. The same was being done with the other portals to the underworld, in case Paimon planned to enter the underworld from another entrance.

I was paired with Doreen and Thierry, two experienced demon hunters, older than I was. Though I had met Doreen before, I wasn't happy about being included in a scouting party, but it was a lot better than sitting back at home and waiting for news.

I slung my bag across my shoulders, grabbed another pack of food, and set off with my companions into the forest.

8

SHANE

After an hour of trekking in the forest without any real direction, one thing became clear to me: the demon hunters weren't sure where to look for Paimon and they were grasping at straws. I would definitely have done the same thing if I suddenly hadn't remembered one detail. I knew a certain fallen angel who had been around a lot of demons in the past couple of years.

I called Ariella.

She didn't answer right away, but I left a voice message. An hour later, when the sun was setting and the chill of the night blew around the forest, Ariella called me back. Thankfully, I still had a cell signal.

I explained to Ariella what was going on and asked if she had heard anything about Paimon and his allies.

"Actually, I have," she said, her tone clipped.

My breath caught. "You did?"

"Where are you?"

"Around Winnipeg."

"Shit. Can you come to Denver in about an hour?"

That wouldn't work. "Give me two and I'll be there."

"Great. See you then."

I turned to Doreen and Thierry. "I might have a lead."

They both stared at me as if I was speaking another language.

"What do you mean?" Thierry asked. He had short black hair and brown eyes.

"We need one of the warlocks to open a portal for us," I said.

"A portal to where?" Doreen said. The wind ruffled her red-orange hair.

"Denver." I started walking back.

"Shane, wait." Thierry caught up with me. "Our orders are to search for Paimon."

"That's exactly what we will be doing, but more efficiently." I halted and faced them. "Believe me when I say this: no one wants to catch this demon more than I do. I'm not joking around. Come with me and see it for yourself."

"Fine place," Doreen said, eyeing the dilapidated barn with peeling brown paint, a rickety porch, and a hanging sign twisting in the breeze by one chain.

"I didn't choose it." I walked past her and Thierry, entering the place. I bet Ariella had chosen it because it looked like an abandoned shack in the middle of nowhere.

After we crossed the portal into Denver, Ariella texted us the address to this bar. It was just outside of Denver, but to get there we had to rent a car. While we drove there, Doreen told me how supernaturals borrowed cars instead of renting them. I guess I would have done that if I was trying to hide.

As soon as I stepped through the door, the scent of cheap beer, cigars, sweat, and sweet perfume hit my nostrils. I wrinkled my nose, choking on the foul air. That was what I got for having a wolf's sense of smell. There were games to the right —pool tables, foosball, and darts—counter-height tables and stool chairs to the left, and a bar at the back. Behind it, we could peek at a kitchen where smoke curled up from the order pass-through.

There were a few patrons, looking just as raggedy and decaying as the bar. Low country music played in the speakers and a couple danced beside the bar.

Ariella waved at us from a table in a dark corner.

Despite everything going on, I walked to her with a smile on my lips. I hadn't had much contact with the fallen angel, but she had been a pretty good friend to pretty good friends of mine. I had seen and spoken to her a handful of times, and every time, she seemed a little uptight and focused on her mission—to find her stolen wings. Without them, she couldn't go back to the place we called heaven.

For many years now, she had been on Earth, searching, fighting demons, tracking them, trying to find the ones who had stolen her wings in the first place, without any success.

She stood from her chair and embraced me. "It's good to see you." She patted my back. "I'm sorry about Raika."

I pulled back, looking at her. She looked the same—a head shorter than me, with a lean frame, silver-gray eyes, and white-blond hair. She wore leather pants and a blouse, and looked way too well-dressed for a shanty dive bar.

"Thanks," I whispered. "And thanks for meeting me."

She turned to Doreen. "Nice to see you again." Then to Thierry. "Nice to meet you."

"Same," Doreen said at the same time Thierry said, "You too."

We sat down around the table and a waitress halted beside us. "What can I get for you?"

I didn't want anything, but ... "A beer for me."

Thierry asked for the same, and Ariella and Doreen ordered wine. We also asked for two portions of fries to be shared.

Once the waitress was out of earshot, Doreen leaned over the table, her eyes on Ariella. "So, what do you have for us?"

"I met a demon who was in hiding," Ariella started. "I wanted information from him, so I made an attractive offer. In the end, he confessed he had been deep in business with Paimon, but he had done something wrong and was now in hiding."

"He's not in Paimon's good graces, then," Thierry said.

"No, but that doesn't matter as long as he can point you in Paimon's direction, right?"

"Right," I said. "Where do we find him?"

"Here," Ariella said with a proud grin. "I told him to meet me here in ..." She looked at her phone for the time. "In ten minutes."

"Won't he expect to see you alone?" Doreen asked.

The waitress placed our order on the table, then put a hand on Thierry's shoulders. "Can I get you all anything else?"

Thierry stiffened.

"No, thank you," Doreen said without even looking at the woman.

With a huff, the waitress walked away.

"To answer your question," Ariella continued, "I'll take my drink to another table."

"And then?" Thierry asked. "You're going to ask him where we can find Paimon and you think he will tell you?"

"He will tell me, one way or another." She grabbed her wineglass and sat at a table right in the middle of the place, at least fifteen feet from ours. And I realized, if the demon didn't turn back to take in the entire bar, he wouldn't see us here in the corner at first, which gave us an advantage.

I hoped this went smoothly, but nothing was that simple, not in the supernatural world.

Ariella sipped from her wine, her gaze fixed on the entrance. Thierry drank two gulps of his beer before setting it aside, but Doreen and I didn't touch our drinks. But I nibbled at the fries—they were mushy and cold, but I needed something to occupy my hands and my mind.

"I heard what Paimon did to your pack," Doreen said, catching my attention. I stilled, a french fry halfway to my lips. "I'm sorry."

I flinched at her words. I was sick and tired of everyone saying they were sorry. I didn't want their pity. I wanted action.

I shoved the fry in my mouth. "We'll get through this."

"I know the DuMoir vampires can provide anything you might need, but know that the Blackthorn Hunters would also help, if given the chance."

"Right now, I want to help you take Paimon down. That's all I want."

Doreen nodded. "You know, revenge won't bring her back."

"Doreen!" Thierry hissed.

"What? He has to understand." She leaned over the table again. "My brother was a hunter and he was killed by demons. All I wanted was to avenge him, but in doing that, I was pulling away from my family, from Kayleen, my younger sister, who needed me more than ever."

I pushed the rest of the fries away, turning to the side to see Ariella and the entrance better. Curses and rage bubbled in my chest, traveled up to my throat, burning like the freaking sun, but I swallowed them down. I was here on a mission, and I wouldn't let anyone or anything distract me.

"Doreen, drop it," Thierry said again.

"No, listen—"

She shut up when the front doors opened and a man entered the bar. I turned back to the table and held on my warm beer, as if I was interested in the two people sitting across from me, who were now engaged in small talk.

From the corner of my eye, I followed as the man glanced side to side, and dragged his feet to Ariella. He was short for a male, but with broad shoulders, clad in a heavy black jacket and dark pants. He pulled the hood down as he sat across from Ariella, revealing a buzz cut and matching stubble all over his face. He had a nasty scar on his cheek and down his neck, giving him a badass and dangerous air.

I focused my hearing.

"What do you want?" the demon barked.

"Nice to see you too, Soghen." Ariella gestured for the waitress. The woman didn't seem happy to have more customers as she made her way to their table and asked what they wanted. "My friend here wants to order something."

He glared at Ariella, but he then said, "A burger and a beer."

"And you?" the waitress asked.

Ariella pointed to her untouched wineglass. "I'm good for now. Thanks."

The waitress left.

"What is your game?" Soghen asked.

"No games. It's simple, actually. I want an answer to a question, and you will provide it to me."

He crossed his arms. "What if I don't?"

"Remember last time we met? I kicked your ass. Do you want to repeat that?"

"You said this would be worth my time," he mumbled.

Ariella grabbed something from her back pocket and placed it on the table. A thick white envelope.

The demon's eyes widened, and he snatched the envelope and hid it inside his jacket. He peeked inside and his eyes rounded some more. "What could you possibly want?"

"Where can I find Paimon?"

He cursed and stood. "No."

"Just answer the question."

Soghen shook his head and turned to walk away. I got up from my seat and put myself between him and the doorway.

"Shit," he muttered.

I shifted my hands into claws and let him see them. "Answer her question, or I'll be the one kicking your ass."

Cursing, he feinted to the left, but went to the right ... right into Doreen and Thierry. The demon was surrounded.

"You've got to be kidding me." He turned to Ariella. "Now you're resorting to this."

She shrugged. "If that gets me what I want."

He shook his head. "I can't tell you. He'll kill me."

Ariella rose to her feet. "And I'll kill you now If you don't answer the question. What do you prefer?"

"Die now, or get out of here and hide, hoping Paimon wouldn't find me." Thierry rubbed at his chin. "I think I would take option two."

"What's going on?" the waitress asked. She had Soghen's burger and beer in her hands.

"Nothing that concerns you," I snarled.

She dropped the burger and the beer on the nearest table and dashed to the bar in the back. I was sure she was now calling the police or something like that. We didn't have much time if we wanted to avoid more trouble.

Ariella took two steps closer to Soghen. "Where's Paimon?"

The demon shook his head. "I don't deal directly with him. I deal with his second in command, Rotgar."

Ariella frowned. "I heard his second in command is a woman."

Soghen snorted. "Ivy? Paimon favors her because she's his daughter, but he pretends to give her control. At least, that's what Rotgar says."

"That's enough bullshit," I snapped.

Ariella nodded. "Just tell us where to find Paimon. I'll settle for Rotgar."

"I-I can't."

Losing my patience, I grabbed the demon's throat and squeezed, pulling him up. He grabbed at my forearms and rose on his tiptoes.

"Answer the lady," I snarled.

"I ... said ... no!"

In a flash, the demon shifted. His human form melted away, giving way to gray, rough skin, a shaved skull, two curling horns, black eyes, and razor-sharp teeth. His neck became twice as large and I lost my grip on him.

I gaped at him. He was still short, but he looked ugly and built like a bull.

And just like a bull, he charged me.

I shifted my arm and swiped at his face. He ducked under my strike and twisted away, avoiding Ariella but facing the demon hunters and their Dawnblades.

Around us, the patrons screamed and fled. The waitress disappeared inside the kitchen and closed the door.

The demon called upon darkfire, the magic wrapping around his arms. I felt the familiarity of his magic tugging at my Shadow Wolf. No, I wouldn't lose control now.

Ariella lifted her hand and flashed a bright light at Soghen's face. He blinked and stood still. Thierry and Doreen grabbed his arms, holding him in place.

I loomed close to him and he pushed off the floor, hitting me in the stomach with both his feet. I stumbled back three steps, bumped into a chair. With the force of the impact, Soghen took Doreen and Thierry down with him, over two tables and a few chairs, breaking most of them.

Groaning, Doreen and Thierry let go of the demon and he ran.

I jumped and shifted midair, my clothes ripping apart in the process. The demon ran from the bar and I followed. He was ten steps out when I jumped and landed right on his back. The force took us down, but I stayed on top of him. When he tried to turn, I bit down on his neck and pressed my teeth around his throat.

He stilled.

Two seconds later, Doreen and Thierry were by our side, their Dawnblades pointed to the demon's head. I backed away, snarling at him. Slowly, Soghen turned around. He sat up on the rough ground, his hands raised.

Ariella walked toward him, her fingers poised with dancing light. "Now, tell us where the hell Paimon is hiding?"

9

RAIKA

IT TOOK US MORE THAN AN HOUR TO LEAVE.

First, because Dot couldn't see me right away, and when she did, we spent at least thirty minutes meditating together —and she used her magic to do whatever she did with my mind to find my memories.

Obviously, this session was as hopeless as the previous ones.

Then, our bounty hunter said the dragon scale had been depleted of its power and he couldn't use it to track the dragon. He needed to do a small magical ritual to reactivate the scale, so he could tap into its magic. Otherwise, he would be flying blind.

The ritual was done in the mansion's back garden, and Kaz had asked us to stay away. Of course, we watched from a second-floor window, but he had either created a glamour so we couldn't see it well, or he wasn't doing anything.

"What species is he?" I asked, suddenly curious.

Kaz sat in the back garden, his legs folded underneath

him, his eyes closed, the scale on the grass in front of him. And that was all we saw.

Beside me, Ivy shrugged. "I honestly don't know. A warlock, maybe?"

"What are the species that can look like humans?" Roman asked. "Wolf shifters, demons, warlocks …"

"Fae, if they use glamour," Ivy said.

"Though, he's probably a demon hunter," Roman said.

Ivy nodded. "That would make perfect sense."

When Kaz was done with his ritual, he grabbed the scale from the ground and entered the house. We met him in the sunroom downstairs, and he announced. "The dragon is in Maine."

Since it was already late afternoon, my father suggested we stay for the night, but Kaz wasn't having it.

"By tomorrow morning, the dragon might have crossed the Atlantic."

He was the expert, so we followed his advice.

Ivy met Rotgar to talk about their plans, but my father told us Rotgar had left to work on another piece of the plan. Ivy seemed hurt that the higher demon was being sent away, and she didn't even know what that was about, but she wiped the disappointment from her face as fast as it came.

Because of the distance, we chartered a flight to Maine, then rented an off-road truck that was the size of a small house.

The flight had taken ten hours, and we slept most of the time. When awake, Ivy tried engaging in small talk with Kaz but he shut her off every time.

"This guy is ridiculous," she complained as we walked to the truck in the rental place parking lot.

I looked up at the sky. Gray clouds covered the sky, but otherwise, it was a warm morning. I sighed. "Just let him be."

She opened the truck's door and took the backseat. "It's like talking to a brick wall." I rolled my eyes and sat beside her. She went on, "It's bothering me."

Kaz opened the driver's door and I nudged Ivy to stop. We didn't know what species he was, but most supernaturals had enhanced hearing. Even from outside, he might have heard her, and the last thing we needed was our guide to be mad at us and ditch us.

Kaz slipped behind the wheel, while Roman sat on the passenger side, and off we went. Every twenty to thirty minutes, Kaz stopped the truck and did some tracking. He sat there, with the dragon scale in his hands and his eyes closed. Suddenly, he opened his eyes and drove again with purpose.

Kaz dropped the scale and brought the truck back to the road.

"What are you doing with the scale?" Roman asked. After my father allowed me to join the party, Roman insisted he had to come too. As he had said it, he couldn't be away from his mate. If only I felt it like that …

"The scale points me in the dragon's general direction," he said.

Ivy leaned forward between the front seats. "Why so often?"

"Dragons are big creatures and they are fast when flying," Kaz said, his tone flat. "He can change directions and go toward New Hampshire at any time."

"You check to make sure we're still on the dragon's tail," I said.

Kaz's eyes met mine through the rearview mirror and he gave me a curt nod.

We stopped around noon to eat, then we kept going. A couple of times we moved from northeast to northwest, then north. The dragon kept moving, but Kaz told us that he felt we were getting closer.

"It won't be as easy or as fast as you believe," he said.

No kidding.

Around six in the evening, we stopped for gas and dinner. While Kaz filled up the tank, the rest of us went into the convenience store to buy some burgers.

"Should we get a burger for Kaz?" Ivy asked.

I stared at her.

Roman didn't seem to notice it. "Who doesn't like burgers? Order one for him. If he doesn't like it, he can buy whatever he wants."

Roman grabbed some chocolate bars from the shelves and went to the fridges in the back, and Ivy ordered four burgers from the server behind the counter.

I kept staring at her.

"What?" she snapped.

"What is going on?" I asked. She shook her head, as if telling me she had no idea what I was talking about. "Kaz. You've been talking about him since he first showed up. Are you ...?" I lowered my voice. "Are you into him?"

"What? No!" Then a small smile graced her lips. "Well, not really, but he's hot, and this brooding mood of his is getting to me."

I put a hand over my open mouth. "Holy shit, you like him!"

"Wait up a minute! No, I don't. I barely know the guy." She leaned into me and whispered, "But if he wanted to meet me in the bed of that truck and have his way with me, I wouldn't stop him."

I slapped her arm and laughed. "You're so into him."

She shrugged. "Can't a girl just want sex because the guy is hot? No feelings involved?"

I chuckled. "Of course she can." And I truly believed that.

My eyes wandered to Roman, who reached inside one of the fridges and grabbed some sodas.

"What about you?"

I snapped my gaze back to her. "W-what?"

Ivy leaned on the counter while we waited for the burgers. "You haven't remembered anything about him?" She jutted her chin in Roman's direction. "What do you feel when you look at him? Horny?"

My cheeks flamed. "No." I sneaked a quick peek at him. He had a basketful of chocolate, chips, soda, and water. "I mean ... he's hot."

But that was it. I didn't feel like I wanted to rush to him and rip his clothes off. Like I needed him to look at me, to touch me all the time. I wondered ... I was twenty years old, he was a little older, and we had been together for a long time. We probably had sex before, didn't we? I wanted to remember how it was, how it felt ... how everything about him with me had been.

Having a mate for life and not remembering one bit of our past together sucked big time.

"And?" Ivy prompted.

I shrugged. "I don't know."

"Pretend you don't know him. Pretend we're having a girls' night out and you see this hottie and he wants to take you back to his place. Wouldn't you go with him?"

I ... I wasn't so sure I would. I didn't know why. He was my mate, wasn't he? Should I feel the attraction, the pull toward him even without knowing who he was? Once more I wondered if having my memories damaged had also damaged the bond. Maybe I should ask Dot.

I sighed. "I'll take a raincheck. We should talk about this when I have my memories back."

She scoffed. "You're no fun."

The lady behind the counter came back with a bag and our burgers, and we met Roman at the cashier to pay for our stuff. Ivy handled the money part, while I stared at the truck parked beside the pump and Kaz leaning on the side of the truck. His arms crossed.

A silver sedan stopped right behind the truck and a young couple hopped out. The girl pointed to Kaz and asked him something. He shook his head, said something back, and looked at us.

The girl followed his gaze.

"Shit." Roman jumped in front of me and lowered his head, his back to the front of the store.

I looked at him, at his strange behavior. "What happened?"

Roman grabbed my hand and pulled toward the back. "Ivy, take care of this."

Ivy cursed under her breath. "Just go." She pushed us behind her.

"What's going on?" I asked, confused and anxious. Holding tight to my hand, Roman guided us to the back of the convenience store. We entered an employee-only area and he didn't stop. In the middle of what looked like a storage room, I halted and tugged hard on his hand. "Roman, what's going on?"

He turned to me, his eyes wild. "Those two ... they are from our pack. They're here to kill you."

My knees weakened. "W-what?"

He held tighter to my hand. "Now do what I tell you, so we can get out of here safely. Understood?"

I nodded, though I felt like I couldn't move.

A boom came from the front of the store and the walls shook.

Roman rushed through the storage room, and we stopped again before another door. He opened it a little and spied out. He put a finger over his mouth and I nodded again. Slowly, we walked out, at the back of the gas station, and kept low around a white van.

Another boom sounded, louder now that we were outside, and I covered my ears. Was it always like this? The fights, the chases, the missions? Running, loud sounds, the heart pumping so fast it felt like it would burst from the chest?

Maybe I wasn't cut out for this, not without my memories, not without knowing how to fight and how to use my darkfire properly.

If I was here and chickening out, it was my own damn fault! I had been the one who insisted on coming. I wanted to be a part of this. Now I was here. And I wouldn't chicken out.

I closed my eyes and inhaled deeply. A scream, a grunt, and the sound of metal scraping against concrete came from the other side of the building. My insides knotted again, but I told myself I couldn't do this. I couldn't allow fear and apprehension to win.

I exhaled and shook my shoulders, trying to calm down. *Could* one calm down in a situation like this?

The sound of screeching wheels rounded the corner and the truck appeared right beside us.

"Get in!" Ivy yelled, half her body hanging from the passenger's window and darkfire dancing in her hands.

Roman jumped to his feet and pulled me with him. We ran to the truck and hopped in the backseat. The door wasn't even closed yet when Kaz sped off and away.

I looked back at the couple standing in the middle of a half-destroyed gas station. Why was the man holding a sword? Wasn't he a wolf shifter too?

I frowned. They probably couldn't see me now, but I could see them, and they looked around my age. We could have been friends, but Roman told me I didn't have any friends. It was just him.

When the two of them became little specks in the distance, I turned and sank into the seat.

Kaz glanced at the rearview mirror, his brows knotted.

"What happened back there?" Ivy asked. "Who were those two?"

Roman grunted. "They are from our old pack. I think they were here to kill Raika." Kaz snorted. Roman frowned. "What?"

"They weren't wolf shifters," he said, his tone flat.

I stared at Roman. "Not wolf shifters?"

He shook his head, dismissing Kaz words. "Of course they are," he said in a low voice.

Kaz probably didn't hear what Roman said as he went on, "And they're here for the dragon."

"What? How do you know?" Ivy asked.

"Because the girl said I reeked of dragon, probably from the tracking spell I've been doing with the scale," he said simply. "And she confessed to tracking the dragon."

"Shit," Ivy muttered. "This means, we have competition."

Kaz nodded once. "It does."

"Then what are you waiting for?" Ivy gestured to his legs. "Floor it!"

Kaz stepped on it. He was already driving over the speed limit. Now it felt reckless, but I wouldn't be the one to say anything.

I looked out the window, the world speeding by me, and a sense of confusion and loneliness wrapped over me like a heavy blanket. I was missing something; I just didn't know what.

10

SHANE

"The demon lives well," Doreen observed.

"I expected more," Ariella said.

"I expected more doom and gloom," Thierry commented. "Like, maybe a dark mansion or even a large cave. But not this."

I suppressed a groan. What did it matter where the demon lived? As long as we were able to get to him, it didn't.

After extracting the information from Soghen, Doreen killed the bastard anyway. She said he had a file with the Blackthorn Hunters and she couldn't let him go, even if he wasn't in trouble at that moment.

He told us Prince Paimon had an office in a building in the business district in Vancouver. Once more, we had asked a warlock to portal us here. He seemed pissed, but Doreen had a high rank with the demon hunters and he was supposed to collaborate with anything the demon hunters needed right now.

The building was a modern high-rise with glass sides,

where many suited men and elegantly dressed women came to and from.

We parked our car in a parking area close by and watched from the bus stop on the other side of the street. I had a newspaper in my hands, Thierry and Doreen had earbuds, though nothing was playing, and Ariella messed with her phone. We looked like four random people waiting for the bus. Though, if we stayed here for more than a few minutes, then we could draw attention.

Ariella stiffed. "I smell demons."

I sniffed the air and didn't pick up anything but pollution, gas, and other city scents. "I don't."

She tapped her nose. "Special angel power."

"Which ones?" I asked, eyeing the building's main entrance.

"I can't tell."

"What if you got closer?"

"The scent would be stronger."

I folded the newspaper and left it on the wooden bench. "Then let's go."

"Wait ..."

I didn't. I looked both ways and crossed the busy street in the coming traffic. Ariella rushed after me. I was dressed in jeans and a Henley shirt, and Ariella had the same pants from last night with a gray blouse. We weren't dressed for this kind of place, but hopefully, we could sneak in anyway.

The building lobby was a huge room with white tiles for floors, high ceilings, and a handful of guards. Right in the center was a round counter with three ladies behind a welcome desk. Behind them was a line of badge gates and beyond that, the hallways, elevators, and stairs.

Shit, how would we get past that?

Ariella grabbed my arm and stopped me. "Two of the guards are watching us."

I looked over her shoulder and saw them. "How's the scent now?"

"Stronger, but leading back there." She jutted her chin to the back. "I can't tell where they went from here."

"Then we need to get you back there."

"Unless we want to start another fight, I don't see how."

I took stock of all that was around us. The place was well lit from the glass walls, but there were plenty of lights in the ceiling and the internal walls.

"Could you use your magic to cause a short circuit in the electricity? Make the light bulbs burst, or maybe even fry the computers."

She frowned. "My magic isn't electricity, Shane. But I think I can do it with the lights if I touch a switch or outlet that is connected with the rest. As for the computers ... it should be the same principle, right?"

Ariella walked up to the welcome desk and one of the ladies turned and smiled at her. "Welcome to Empire Terrace. How can I help you?"

"Hi. I think I'm lost." Ariella rested her hands and her phone on the counter. "I'm supposed to have a meeting with Attorney Douglas Ashley. He's a divorce lawyer." She cupped her mouth, leaned forward and whispered, "I'm trying to get rid of that big guy right there."

Pretending I hadn't heard anything, I stood there. The receptionist took a good look at me. "I'm afraid there's no Dr. Douglas Ashley here."

"Are you sure? Could you check your system for me? Please."

The receptionist hesitated. "Sure." She turned around

and reached for a clipboard from the top drawer chest behind her.

Ariella pushed her phone down and it fell on the inside desk. "Oops." She reached for it, but first, she placed her hand over the outlet installed on the desk and sent a spark of her magic.

Instantly, all the lights flickered. Some even burst, sending shards of glass everywhere. The computers were down too. Everyone in the lobby cowered, and some people ran, as if there had been an explosion.

In the middle of the confusion, Ariella and I sneaked past the crowd, through the gates, and into the nearest hallway.

She sniffed the air again. "This way."

We raced down the first-floor hallway and stopped right in front of a closed door. The sign on the door read: Dr. P. Mont, Tax and Legal Consultant.

"If I had seen this before, I would have never guessed," I said.

"Me neither." Ariella pushed the door open and we arrived in a small reception with a waiting area and a check-in desk along a wall.

The lights here were working fine, as were the computers. She must have sent a small spark of light through the lines, only enough to take down the lobby and nothing else. How she had been able to control that was beyond me, though.

An old woman was seated behind the check-in desk. "How may I help you?"

"Hm." Ariella looked at me.

"We have business with Paimon."

The old woman frowned. "I think you're in the wrong place. There's no one with that name here."

Ariella extended her hand and light shot out from her

palm. It traveled to the old lady, wrapped around her neck, and pulled her up. "I know you're a demon and this is where Paimon conducts his business. Where is he?"

The old lady shed her human skin.

A creature who was at least eight feet tall appeared in her place. With slick skin, long thick limbs, a huge square head, big black eyes, and a mouth that rivaled that of a shark, the demon bared his sharp teeth.

Ariella's magic snapped from around the creature's thick neck.

"Do you want to see Prince Paimon?" the demon asked, his voice otherworldly. "I shall grant your wish."

I moved my feet wide and Ariella brought both her hands up, covered in light. We were ready for a fight. Suddenly, the two doors in the reception area burst open and a throng of demons surrounded us.

All right. This had been a little irresponsible. We should have thought this out. Nevertheless, I wouldn't go down without a fight.

I began changing, but I never finished.

The old-lady demon appeared by my side and punched me square in the chest. Pain flared everywhere as I flew to the wall.

I groaned as another round of pain took over me.

I slid to the ground, and then darkness surrounded me.

A JOLT RAN through my face and I startled awake. Panic rose in my lungs as I realized I was tied to a chair and I was ... I looked around, puzzled. In a house?

I groaned as a full bout of pain irradiated through my

body—my face, my back, my chest. Ariella and I had gone into Paimon's office, and we were attacked by a demon army. The old-lady demon threw me at the wall and I blacked out.

And now here I was.

I looked around—I was tied to a dining chair in the middle of a large living room. The place looked expensive with modern furniture, smooth hardwood floors, full glass walls, metal decorations, and chandeliers. I had to say, the modern fireplace that cut through the wall in a simple, long rectangle with the fire running along it in a single line was a nice touch.

I frowned. Wasn't Ariella with me? Where was she now?

I wasn't alone, though. There were at least ten demons standing in the room's corners and openings, and probably more behind me, where I couldn't see them.

From the corner of my eyes, I saw two demons talking, then one left the room.

A moment later, I heard footsteps approaching and stiffened.

This couldn't be good.

My heart seized when the man who had been in front of Raika, who had pierced her heart with a shadow sword, now stood not five feet from me.

Paimon.

"Ah, I see you're awake." The demon smiled at me. I jerked in the chair, but the ropes tightened and dug into my skin. Paimon tsked. "Enchanted ropes. The more you move, the more they tighten."

I exhaled heavily. It took all of my restraint to stop moving, but I did. "I will kill you," I said through gritted teeth.

"You have no idea how many times I've heard that throughout the centuries. How about you, Rotgar?"

One of the demons who had been talking before approached. So this was Rotgar—he looked like a regular human with unimpressive features and a nice black suit.

One corner of Rotgar's mouth tilted up. "Too many too count."

"Same." Paimon opened his arms wide. "And yet, here I am."

I stared at him, wanting nothing more than to jump over him, to punch that smug smile off his pretty face. He seemed sophisticated and rich in his suit, but I knew the truth. This demon was evil, pure and simple. He was the worst of the worst, and for that, he had to die.

"You killed my mate." The words I didn't plan on saying tumbled out of my lips.

I hadn't been there when Paimon appeared in the main square with Nortrix. My friends told me about his short monologue. The demon revealed being Raika's father, and he was there to take the crystals because he needed their magic, and to take Raika too. He wanted her by his side, for whatever reason.

Paimon nodded. "Yes, you're Shane, right? Nightshade alpha and my daughter's mate."

His daughter ...

Rage filled my veins and I acted. I jumped off the chair, ropes and all. I let my fangs out and shifted my arms. The ropes dug into my skin a little more, but I didn't care. I opened my mouth and jumped at Paimon's throat.

He lifted his hand and sent a blast of darkfire to me. It exploded in my chest and I fell back, over the chair, and onto the floor. But Paimon wasn't done. He wrapped darkfire around my neck and shoulders and pulled me up.

"Impressive," he said, looking genuinely amazed. "But not enough. I'm too strong for you, even when I'm at my weakest." He set me down on the chair again.

I breathed hard, my muscles trembling. I might not be strong enough to take him out now, but I would find a way to end him.

Paimon glanced to the left. "Did I forget anything?"

I followed his gaze, and for the second time in less than five minutes, my heart stopped again.

Dot.

Dot was here.

The Nightmist witch smiled at me. She turned her gaze to Paimon. "There's one more thing."

The rage started inside me like a small stream, but grew into a river going down the hill and preparing for the waterfall. It came unbound and strong, if I had been standing, it would have brought me to my knees.

My chest heaved and the Shadow Wolf tickled the back of my mind.

"He's cursed." Dot pointed at me, and a spark of dark magic flew to my chest. Like a shock, it spread through my body, numbing me.

My head lolled forward and I inhaled a ragged breath.

"The Shadow Wolf," Paimon said. "You told me about that. Won't that be a problem?"

Dot shook her head. "I can keep it under control."

"Splendid." Paimon walked to me and leaned closer. He grasped my chin and made me look at him. "I'll keep you locked in my prison until the next full moon. When you shift into your Shadow Wolf, I'll kill you."

I frowned. "Why wait until the full moon?"

"That's when the Shadow Wolf will be stronger," Dot said.

I shook my head. Wouldn't that be worse for them? That didn't make sense.

"Take him to the prison," Paimon ordered.

Rotgar advanced on me along with another demon. Hands wrapped around my arms and pulled me up. The ropes, still enchanted and strong, never let out as the demons dragged me away from the living room—two held my arms, while another four surrounded me. Dazed from Dot's spell, I couldn't focus on my surroundings, but I did my best. We went through a hallway and past a door to the outside. A short set of steps followed, and I tripped over one of the demons carrying me. I fell back on the stairs and took a deep breath. I needed to think clearly, to pay attention, but this damn spell was making me feel like I had drunk too much.

A voice came from the top of the stairs. "We've got a report, sir." The voice was faint, probably from being so far, but despite my drunkenness, my hearing was still good. "They are closing in on the dragon."

The dragon? The same dragon that had been sleeping underneath my pack lands for centuries?

"Where are they now?"

"Northeastern Maine."

"Excellent," Paimon said. "I'll be ready to travel when they call me. The sooner we kill this dragon and I absorb his power, the better."

Paimon was weak, and he weakened easily. He lived on small bursts of magic and sacrifice from others. I gulped. That was why he wanted to wait until the full moon to kill me. Because my Shadow Wolf would be stronger. He could absorb more magic.

And now it seemed he was after the dragon.

Dragons were powerful creatures, by far the most powerful of all supernaturals. If he absorbed the dragon's powers, it was likely Paimon would recover from whatever ailment afflicted him.

The demons tugged at my arms, and we continued our trek outside. We passed a pool and a pool house, and into the woods beyond. Where were they taking me?

The terrain was uneven, and a short mound covered half of two big trees. In that mound was a metal door. One of the demons opened the door, the others pushed through it. We went down a flight of stairs, through another reinforced door, and into a long, dark, and cold corridor with several doors.

The prison cells.

Rotgar pushed me into one of the dark, humid cells. I tripped on the uneven floor and almost fell face-first. Once the door was locked behind me, the ropes around my wrists and torso disappeared. I stared at my free hands, then at the door.

Rotgar's impassive face showed up in the small window at the top half of the door. "Don't even think about it. The doors are reinforced with magic. You would have to be Prince Paimon to be able to escape them."

I rammed against the door.

The demon took a large step back, his eyes wide. The door shook, but didn't give. He was right. I could try to escape, but there was no getting out of here. At least not this way.

Resigned, I sat down on the rough floor and closed my eyes.

Let them think I had given up.

When they least expected, I would get out of here. And

then I would go after a freaking dragon. Because if I couldn't kill a former demon prince by myself, then I would at least take away the one thing that could make him whole again.

Without his powers back, Paimon wouldn't be able to fight.

Without his powers, he would weaken more and more.

And when he was at his weakest, I would strike.

I would kill him.

11

SHANE

Despite the pain and exhaustion assaulting every inch of my body, I stayed focused and alert. My wolf healing kicked in and in a couple of hours, I would be feeling a lot better.

That was the physical side of me.

As for the mental ... a rising panic started deep in my chest. I had been in a cell before, for freaking six months. I had no way of escaping; the witches had made sure of that.

But this time, I had to.

I hoped Dot hadn't remembered the wards she and the other witches had put in places when I was in the lodge with them, or that she alone couldn't do the spells.

I took a long breath. If I was going to escape this place, it wouldn't be while I panicked or slept, and I didn't plan on escaping next week.

I was going to escape today.

I also didn't want to think about Dot. Here was a witch who could undo my damn curse, but I couldn't take her with me and killing her wasn't an option as she was the only one who could reverse the curse.

I would deal with her another time.

Hours passed and no one came to check on me. I could hear them, though. Several demons were beyond the door, walking up and down the corridor and the stairs, keeping guard.

Eight hours after I had been put in here, just after sunset, two demons opened my cell door. One stayed put, in case I acted, and the other placed a tray with food on the floor.

My stomach growled. I hadn't eaten since breakfast, but my hunger could wait.

I held on to my anger and let my Shadow Wolf take over.

In a second, I had shifted.

All I could think of was destruction. I needed to destroy, to maim, to kill. But a spark of something surged—I needed to flee. More than anything, I knew I needed to escape.

The demons scurried back, their faces pale. One tried closing the door, but I shoved my arm out and grabbed the door. I ripped off its hinges as if it was paper, and threw it aside. The door broke against the wall with a loud boom.

The demons shifted into their ugly forms and attacked me.

I ripped through those two as more came through the next door. Some demons came at me hand in hand; others threw their darkfire at me.

With a growl, I swiped my paw at one of the ugliest demons, opening three big gashes on his neck and chest. He folded at my feet and I stomped over his body.

A larger darkfire bolt hit me square in the chest, sending me back a few feet. I roared as rage filled my veins. I charged ahead, taking several demons down.

Escape.

Kill.

Escape.

Kill.

It was a war inside me.

I kept on moving, taking as many demons as I could along the way, but always advancing. Making my way to the second door, up the stairs, then through the outer door and into the forest.

Here, more demons surrounded the prison entrance, their backs to me, and they were fighting someone on the other side.

I didn't care. All I cared about was killing.

Escape!

I advanced on the back of several demons before they knew what was happening. I ripped out their throats, pulled off their heads, and broke their backs. We advanced into the forest and into the back garden, behind the pool house.

Among the chaos, I saw the three figures fighting the demons—two females and a male. Did I know them? It didn't matter, I had to kill them.

Kill.

Escape!

A power like no other hit me in the side. I skidded several feet and growled at the demon who had struck me.

"Don't kill him!" the demon told the others. "I need him alive."

I turned to the demon and charged at him. He threw his hand out and a big bolt of darkfire flew out of his fingers. It exploded against me, pushing me back into the air and back several feet. I fell on my side and groaned, a little dazed.

Kill.

Kill!

While I was down, demons surrounded me, but I killed a

handful of them and turned to the demon whose blood I craved. Beside him, a witch laughed. She threw her dark magic at me. I jumped to the side, escaped her strike, and snarled at her. I knew her. Somehow, I knew her and I loathed her.

Destroy! Kill!

I wanted to get to her, to him. I wanted to rip their chests open, to eat their hearts—

"Shane," someone said.

Who was Shane? I didn't care. I had to kill. I had to flee.

I ripped through half a dozen of demons, then saw an opening through the woods. I fell on all fours and ran.

Escape.

I zoomed past the trees and bushes and thorns. I could hear the fighting behind me, and I wanted to turn back and kill.

No, escape!

Several times, I hesitated. My steps faltered.

Kill.

But I kept moving forward. To where? I didn't know. It didn't matter. I just had to go.

Go back.

Destroy.

Kill.

I stopped in a small clearing and let out a painful howl.

"Shane."

I turned in the voice's direction. The two females and one male I had seen fighting the demons stepped into the clearing. They had their hands up and kept their distance.

Kill.

I snarled at them.

They shouldn't be here. They shouldn't have come. My

mouth salivated with the need to jump on them, to close my mouth around their necks—

Kill!

I rushed them.

Three steps in and a bright light flashed before my eyes. I blinked and turned away from the light, but then it was everywhere. The light surrounded me like a bubble. I howled in pain, in agony.

"Shane, come back," someone said beyond the light. "We need you."

I blinked, but the light only grew stronger. It pushed beyond my fur, against my skin, until it was in my nostrils, in my pores. I screamed.

I lay on the cold grass, curling into myself.

"Shane," the voice came again.

But this time, when I looked, I recognized the woman kneeling beside me. "Ariella."

She nodded. "Welcome back."

Thierry and Doreen stepped closer, and Thierry threw me a jacket.

"Thanks." I slipped it around my arms and zipped it up. It was tight on my shoulders and went down to my mid-thigh. I felt ridiculous in it, but it would serve for now. I looked up at my companions. "Not just for the jacket." Ariella stood up. "They didn't get you?"

She shook her head. "They tried, but they wanted you. I decided to pull back so we could rescue you."

Doreen put her hand on her waist. "Pretty bold of you to escape Paimon's house by yourself. Didn't you think we were coming to get you?"

"I hoped you three were smarter than to risk your neck for me."

Thierry shook his head. "When we work together, we work together, no questions asked."

"We should go," Ariella said. "We outran the demons, but they won't stop searching until they find us."

We started the long trek through the forest. Fifteen minutes into it, I grew tired of how slow it was going. They told me where they had hidden the car; another shifted into my normal black wolf and raced there.

A handful of times, I had to take a detour to avoid the demons searching the forest, but I found the car a lot quicker than we would have if coming on human legs. I shifted back, put on clothes, and drove down the road to the closest point where the others could get to me.

They were beyond the tree line, hiding and waiting for me.

Once Ariella was in the passenger seat, and Thierry and Doreen in the backseat, I stepped on it.

"I'm still amazed Paimon didn't kill you right away," Thierry said, breaking the silence in the truck.

"About that." I told them what Paimon had planned on doing with me, and that he was after the dragon. "I listened to half a conversation, but I believe he plans to find the dragon and use his magic to power his own."

"With a power like that, he might be too strong for any of us," Ariella observed.

Doreen inhaled deeply. "We can't let him get the dragon."

"My thoughts exactly," I said. "The good news is that I heard where the hunting party is right now."

"You want to go after them?" Ariella asked.

"I want to go after the dragon."

"Wait." Doreen raised a finger. "You want to kill the dragon?"

I pressed my lips tight. "I ... No, I don't. I want to protect it or put it to sleep, but if it comes between that and letting Paimon get his hands on him, then yes, I will kill the dragon."

"Dragons aren't easy to kill," Thierry said.

I looked at him through the rearview mirror. "I know that, and that's why I need your help."

Doreen and Thierry exchanged a look.

"Shane, what you're planning makes sense, but I think there's one more pressing thing to do," Doreen said. "We now know where Paimon is hiding, and because of that, he'll certainly move and fast. We need to warn the demon hunters and get ready for an attack *right now*."

I understood her point, but ... "By the time the demon hunters get there, he'll have already moved."

"We'll take those chances," Thierry said.

"You want to go back?" I asked.

Both of them nodded. We spoke little while I drove to the nearest town and left them at a rental car place.

When I stopped the car in front of the store, Doreen looked at me. "Are you sure you don't want to come with us? You wanted to have your shot at Paimon."

I shook my head. I was certain they would find the mansion empty by the time their army got there. Paimon would be in hiding, and the only way to stop him, even if only temporarily, was to catch that dragon. "No, I'll stay."

Doreen nodded. "Thank you for your help."

"Right," Thierry agreed. "If it weren't for you, we wouldn't have known where Paimon was. Now we at least have a hot lead."

I nodded. "Thank you for letting me tag along."

Doreen patted my shoulder before exiting the car. Thierry offered me an army salute and followed her. Ariella and I watched as the two of them entered the rental car place and talked to a sales associate.

Ariella looked at me. "Are we going to catch a dragon now?"

A lopsided grin spread through my lips. "We sure are."

12

SHANE

Ariella and I got an overnight flight to Maine and rented a jeep at the airport. The only thing we knew was that we were looking for a dragon in northeastern Maine. But damn, a giant dragon couldn't be hard to spot, could it?

We drove north, always on the lookout for things flying in the gray sky, among the clouds, or disturbance on the landscape—an angry dragon being chased could burn down the place as easily as it had burned my pack lands.

As the hours passed, we saw nothing. A handful of times, we stopped at gas stations or rest areas along the highway and asked if anyone had seen something unusual. But without us explaining exactly what we were looking for, it was hard to get direct answers.

Another gas station approached ahead, but we had stopped at a previous one not thirty minutes ago.

"Look." Ariella pointed at the gas station.

Half of the roof had collapsed, smoke rose from one of the pumps, a car was overturned, and the doors to the convenience store were gone. A handful of people gathered away from the gas station, beside a police car and a firetruck.

Could this have been the dragon?

I exited the road and drove to the gas station. I stopped my Jeep beside the humans.

Ariella and I hopped out of the car and approached the humans. "What happened?" I asked them. There were three people who had the gas station's vest over their clothes, an old man whose truck seemed intact, and a younger couple who whined about their totaled car.

The policemen and the firefighters were close to the structure, probably searching for anyone who could have been hurt, or trying to assess the damage.

The old man glanced at me. "Gang fight, I think."

I frowned. Gang fight? That wasn't what we were looking for. "Are you sure? A gang fight did this?"

A woman who worked here nodded. "A group arrived. One filled up the tank, the others came inside the store to buy food. I served them burgers. Then another group arrived. They talked to the guy at the pumps, and a fight broke out."

"But they had insane weapons," a male with the gas station's vest said. "I don't know how they did it, but their weapons shot out bright and dark lights. It must be some kind of prototype or special effect." He shook his head. "Or I'm in shock and imagined things."

"No, I saw it too," the woman said.

Ariella and I exchanged a glance. Two groups with magic fighting. Here, close to the dragons? Who could—? I inhaled deeply as I remembered something.

Walking away from the small crowd, I grabbed my phone from my back pocket and called a saved number.

"Shane?" Evelyn answered after two rings. "Something wrong?"

"I should ask you that. Did you just destroy a gas station in Maine?"

She was silent for three seconds. "How do you know that?"

Bingo. "Because I'm right in front of it."

"Wait. You're in Maine?"

I nodded, even though she couldn't see me. "I am, and I think we should meet."

"Hm, sure. We'll stop at the next town and I'll text you the address."

"That works."

I pocketed my phone and turned to Ariella. "We should go."

We hopped back into the Jeep and Ariella asked, "So, are you going to tell me what you found out?"

"Friends of mine are tracking the dragon," I said. "They want to help him get to safety. So the two gangs are Paimon's demons and my friends. We're meeting them, and hopefully, they will let us help them. We'll be stronger together."

I PARKED beside a silver sedan outside a fast-food restaurant, and Ariella and I got out of the Jeep.

She stared at the empty car. "This is their car?"

"I believe so." I looked to the restaurant's door. "Let's go see if—"

The door opened and Evelyn and Ash walked out, carrying a paper bag with their lunches.

Evelyn's eyes widened at the fallen angel beside me. "Ariella?"

"Evelyn?" Ariella said, matching Evelyn's disbelief.

"Wait, you two know each other?" I asked, confused.

The girls smiled at each other.

"Yeah, Ariella came to my shop over a year ago, I think," Evelyn said. "She had been attacked by some demons and was in pretty bad shape."

Ariella nodded. "She helped me once when I got injured."

"Right. It was right when I met Ash too." She gestured to her boyfriend. "Ash this is Ariella, Ariella, this is Ash."

The two of them shook hands. "I've heard about you," Ash said. "Evie didn't know much about you, but she said you were one badass angel."

Ariella rolled her eyes and grimaced. "If I was really badass, I would have already caught the demons who stole my wings."

Evelyn shook her head. "You are badass. Just ... since the new king took over the underworld, things have been crazy. There are more demons topside, and also a lot of them in complete hiding. But I believe in you. You'll find your wings."

Ariella waved her hand. "Okay, but that's not why we are here."

"Right," Ash said, facing me. "What are you two doing here?"

I looked around, to see if there were any bystanders. We were standing between our two cars, in front of an old fast-food restaurant, in a town that didn't seem to have a lot of movement, if any at all. Still, I wanted to be sure.

"The group you met at the gas station? That's Paimon's demons coming after the dragon."

Evelyn frowned. "So now Paimon is after the dragon?" I

nodded and explained to them why. Evelyn gasped. "We need to help this dragon ASAP!"

I would do my best to help Evelyn and the dragon, to get him away from here and Paimon somehow, but if we sent the dragon across the ocean and Paimon followed him ... I didn't see many options other than killing the dragon. But I didn't say that to Evelyn. If I did, she wouldn't let me tag along.

I nodded. "Exactly. We came to protect the dragon from them."

"Great." Evelyn opened their car's door. "Then we stick together. It'll be easier to fight the demons if it comes to that."

After some logistics, we agreed it was better if we all took the Jeep, since it was sturdier than the sedan, and could probably go off-road. Ariella and I bought us lunch, and the four of us resumed our trip.

This time, though, we had Evelyn: She could sense dragon magic and she told me which direction to go.

13

RAIKA

WE DROVE NORTHEAST FOR A COUPLE OF HOURS, THEN WE moved straight north. Soon, we would be driving into Canada.

At some point, I rested my head back and napped. When I woke up, my head was on Roman's shoulder and my hand on his over my lap.

I quickly stiffened and straightened, pulling my hand from his.

Roman smiled at me. "Sleep well?"

"Yeah," I mumbled. "Sorry for leaning on you."

He frowned. "Sorry? Why? I'm your mate, Raika. You don't need to apologize for that." He patted his shoulder. "If you want, this spot is now available."

"I'm good," I said quickly.

I picked up my phone and opened up the internet browser. I didn't have any social media, and other than books, no real interests—not that I could remember. There wasn't much for me to do, other than searching about memory loss, which I already had done many, many times.

Finally, in the middle of the afternoon, Kaz said, "We're close."

Not long after that, we drove by a farm on fire.

"This can't be a coincidence," Ivy observed.

"No, it can't," Kaz agreed.

He drove onto the farm's entry road and stopped the car a safe distance from the fire. We ran toward the handful of people working together to save the cattle and everything else around it.

"What happened?" Ivy asked.

Feeling like I couldn't just stand there and watch as they desperately tried to save their farm, I sprang into action. I joined an older woman as she tried to usher the cows to go through a gate and into a small pen, away from the burning field. In the distance, a truck with a water tank drove beside the fire, sprinkling water.

A man with graying hair turned to us. "I-I don't know. I couldn't say. Because ... it sounds crazy."

"Was it a dragon?" Kaz went right for the jugular.

The man's face paled. "Yes, it was. How do you know?"

"Where did the dragon go?" Ivy asked.

The man pointed to the horizon, beyond his farm and field, where a forest extended before a bulky mountain.

A spark of fire burst from the middle of the field, billowing to the sky. It was advancing fast.

"Did you call 911 ?" I asked.

The man nodded. "The fire station is a little ways from here. It'll take them a while to get here." He pointed to the truck watering the field. "That's why I've got my son doing what we can."

That wouldn't be enough. In a few minutes, this fire would consume everything around it.

I turned to Ivy. "Is there anything you can do? Use your magic to contain the fire? Snuff it out?"

Ivy frowned and shook her head. "Use my magic in front of humans?"

"They already saw a dragon!" I snapped. "Will it be worse if they see some magic?"

Ivy blinked. "No, I supposed not." She exhaled a long breath. "I'm not sure this will work, though."

"Just ... try it. Please."

She nodded. "Sir, you and your family should back away a little."

He looked confused. "B-but we need to get the cattle out, and my son needs to contain the fire."

I held the man's arm and pulled him back gently. "Sir, trust us. We'll help you." At least, I hoped we would.

Numb, the man nodded and let me take him back. He called his family, and he also called his son's phone and told him to back out a little.

Ivy closed her eyes and focused. I felt her magic as it built up inside her, then reached out, brushing against me. Damn, she was a powerful higher demon.

She sent a ball of darkfire to the center of the field. It hovered above the fire, and slowly, it changed. It stretched little by little, becoming a dark cloud over the fire.

Ivy groaned, the magic's demand too high even for her.

I placed my hand on her arm. "Use mine too."

She didn't hesitate. I gasped as her magic called to mine. Because we were half sisters, it was easy for her to tap into my magic. She had done it before during training, when she was trying to show me how to do it, and how to feel for it.

And now my magic moved along with hers like an avalanche. My knees wobbled, my breathing grew shallow, but I hung in there. This had been my idea, and I would see it through.

I just hoped it worked.

The cloud stretched faster over the fire now that Ivy could access my magic. It stretched as wide as the fire had. I half focused on not passing out, and half watched the sight in front of me. What was Ivy doing? Would she make the clouds rain now? How?

Groaning, Ivy lifted her hands a few inches ... then she brought her arms down, fast. The clouds descended over the fire, smothering it.

A wave of smoke washed over us and everything around the field, but when we were able to see again, I laughed.

Ivy had done it! The fire was gone!

I squeezed her hand. "You did it!"

She looked from the scorched field to her hands. "Yes, I did."

The farm owner and his family rejoiced for a minute. They embraced a dazed Ivy, thanked her profusely. The son even gave her a quick peck on the lips.

But then they grew serious and stared at us as if we were aliens.

"We were hoping you won't say anything about this to anyone," I said, my voice gentle.

"The firefighters will be here soon," the man said. "What will I tell them?"

I shrugged. "I can't help you with that." I looked at my friends. "We should go before they arrive."

Everyone nodded and turned to our truck. My heart tugged as the family looked at the field ... it would probably cost a fortune for them to recover this, but at least they hadn't lost more, and they were all alive.

I was the last one to enter the truck and Kaz drove out as soon as I closed the door.

Kaz threw us a side glance. "I thought you were all demons."

"We are," I said. Well, I was half, and Roman was by association. "Sort of. Why?"

"Demons usually don't help others if it doesn't benefit them," he said simply.

My brows curled down. I didn't like that. "Not all demons are equal."

I looked at Ivy in the front seat. She still stared at her hands, in shock. Was she surprised she had created such a massive spell?

She shook her hands, took a deep breath, and looked at the mountain in the distance. "Are we hunting a dragon or not?"

Kaz sped up. He took us past the farm and into the forest, toward the mountain.

"The mountain," I whispered suddenly. "Dragons like hiding in caves and tunnels."

Kaz spared a quick look through the rearview mirror. "That's true."

Which meant our dragon had gone for the mountain. How did I know that? Had I read it before? Studied it? As with everything, I couldn't remember.

And that frustrated me like nothing else.

The terrain in the woods was bumpy, but the truck could take it for now. We would have to leave the truck behind and trek to the mountain on foot.

I wasn't eager for that.

14

SHANE

WITH EVELYN'S GUIDANCE, WE EASILY FOUND THE DRAGON.

First, we actually found a farm that had been burned beyond recognition. I stopped there because Evelyn sensed an enormous amount of dragon magic around the field.

The police and firefighters swarmed the place, asking the farm owner what had happened, but the man shook his head and didn't answer. I grabbed one of the closed water bottles from our Jeep and took it to the man.

"He needs a break, gentleman," I said to the two police officers questioning him.

The two officers glanced at the water, then at me. "Let's talk to the son," one grumbled.

They walked off and I offered the water bottle to the farm owner. "Here you go."

The man took the bottle from me. "Thank you."

I crossed my arms. "Funny, right, how the field was burned so completely, and yet there's no fire anymore. It seems almost like ... magic."

The man's eyes rounded. "N-no. There's no such th—"

"It was a dragon, wasn't it?" I could see it in his eyes. He knew it; he was afraid of confessing. Everyone else would think he was crazy. "I wonder, though, how the fire was extinguished. It wouldn't just simply go out. Someone really powerful must have used a spell to contain the fire."

The man's eyes darted side to side. "It ... there was a group here. Two men, and two women. The women did something ... I can't explain. I've never seen anything like it."

"They used magic." I bit the inside of my cheek. That was unusual. The demons working for Paimon wouldn't stop to extinguish the fire. They would gather the information they needed, and they would probably add firewood to the fire, if they had time for that.

The man nodded. "But ... they told me to not tell anyone."

"Don't worry. I also want the world of dragons and magic to stay hidden." I paused for effect. "The people who were just here, they are my friends. Can you tell me where they went?"

The man gestured to the woods behind the farm—and the mountain beyond it. "That way."

I patted his shoulder. "Thank you. And I'm sorry for your farm."

The man sighed and drank from the water.

I walked back to the Jeep, where Ariella, Evelyn, and Ash waited for me. "He said the dragon and *my friends* went that way." I pointed to the mountain.

"Of course," Evelyn said with a nod. "Dragons like mountains."

I turned on the engine and glanced at my real friends. "We need to get ready. We'll be walking into a battle."

"With demons and a dragon," Ariella said.

I clicked my tongue. "With demons and a dragon."

I drove into the woods, the Jeep taking the rough terrain pretty well. Halfway to the mountain, we had to abandon the Jeep because the trees were too close together, and the trenches carved by erosion too deep.

We armed ourselves with our bags, checked our shoes, and started the trek to the mountain.

The sun edged closer to the horizon, making the gray day even darker, and it was taking too damn long.

I handed my bag to Ash. "I'll scout ahead."

"Don't eng—"

"I won't," I said, cutting Ariella off. "I'll see if I can spot the demons or the dragon. I'll come back soon."

I let them walk past me while I took my clothes off. I threw them at Asher's back and shifted. It felt good to be in my black wolf's skin and in control. In this form, there was no bloodlust.

I raced past my friends, zooming through the trees and up the mountain. I slowed down when the trees thinned and I could see the mountain's base below.

And something unexpected caught my attention. A narrow trail led around the side of the mountain. A few wisps of smoke rose to the sky. The mountain had some residents.

I ignored those—as long as they didn't want the dragon, I didn't care about them—and continued along the mountain's base.

I looked up and saw figures bobbing up and down the mountainside. I could see ... four? Even with my wolf sight, I couldn't see them well.

A roar sounded and the dark green dragon appeared in the sky.

On instinct, I lowered myself to the ground and watched in awe as the beautiful creature flapped his humongous wings and dove toward the mountain.

Then, he disappeared into the mountain's side.

The group of demons sped up, going toward the cave the dragon had flown into.

Shit, they were too far ahead.

I raced back to my friends. Thankfully, they had sped up and were close by. I shifted back. "We've gotta go," I said as Ash threw me my clothes back. I shoved on the pants and shoes, and ran while still putting my shirt back on.

"What happened?" Evelyn asked, trying to keep up with me.

"The dragon flew inside the mountain, and the demons are right at the entrance," I told them.

"Shit," Ash muttered.

"If you can run faster, then go!" Ariella urged.

I could run faster, but ... "If I arrive alone to fight four demons, it will get me nowhere. We go together."

"They probably won't kill the dragon right away," Evelyn said. "If Paimon wants the dragon to absorb his powers, then the dragon needs to be alive."

"Right," I said.

We emerged through the trees and ran up the mountain. Time seemed to slow down as we made our way through the loose rocks, dry vegetation, and a few dragon scales. The dark gray clouds rumbled above us.

Shit. All we needed was to get rained on right now.

A faint scent hit my nostrils and I faltered.

Jasmine. I looked around. Was there jasmine growing around here? I couldn't see them. With my sense of smell, they could be on the other side of the mountain and the wind brought it over.

I shook my head.

The huge cave opening came into view, giving us renewed energy, and we sprinted forward.

We emerged inside a long, dark tunnel, and the first thing I noticed was the jasmine scent was stronger here. I frowned. I didn't understand anything about flowers ... did jasmine grow inside mountains? That couldn't be.

Or I was going crazy.

Ariella cast several balls of light and sent them floating above and ahead of us. We ran through the tunnel and more than once I sniffed the jasmine in the air.

Then, just before the end of the tunnel, the pain in my chest surged hard, like a hand squeezing my heart. I almost doubled over.

Ariella slowed down when she saw me. "Shane, are you okay?"

I rubbed my hand over my heart, the scent of jasmines stronger now. "I ... I don't know."

Evelyn and Asher disappeared from the tunnel, and Ariella and I followed.

We emerged into a huge cavern with another six tunnels on the perimeter—and our enemies right in the center.

They held flashlights and faced the other tunnels, but when Ariella's lights flooded the room, they turned to us.

My heart stopped.

My breath caught.

My knees gave out.

"Raika," I whispered, clearly delirious. The pull of the mating bond tugged deep in my chest. "I'm seeing things."

She stared at me with her brilliant blue eyes as if she had

spotted a dead rat in a corner.

"No, you're not," Evelyn said, just as shocked as I was.

It couldn't be.

A man stepped in front of her. Roman. What the ... rage filled my veins. "What is going on here?" I snarled.

"Ivy!" Roman shouted.

A fight broke out.

I watched, baffled, as darkfire covered Raika's hand and she threw her magic at me.

At me!

Ariella cast a light shield in front of us. Bolts of darkfire exploded against it, shaking the cave.

"Something is going on here," Ariella said. "If that's Raika, she's brainwashed."

"Don't ..." I inhaled deeply. My mind, my emotions—I couldn't make sense of anything. All I knew was that Raika ... my Raika, my mate, the woman I thought was dead, the woman I had held dead in my arms, the one I had cremated and put to rest was here. She was here. She was alive. And so was Roman. "Don't hurt her."

Dark magic covered Evelyn's hands. Ash held his sword, ready to fight. They nodded.

Ariella pushed the shield out, like a wave, but with the amount of magic being thrown against it, the shield broke— and the mountain shook.

Evelyn went for the other male in their group, Ariella faced the one called Ivy, Ash turned to Roman, and I dove for Raika.

"Raika, what's going on?" I asked, my voice trembling. She threw a dark bolt at me and I dodged it easily.

"Don't listen to him, Raika!" Roman shouted. He shifted his arms only. "He'll tell you lies!"

My Shadow Wolf stirred inside me, asking for release. It would be so easy to let it out now, but I couldn't. I gritted my teeth and hung in there.

Ash thrust his sword for Roman's chest, but Roman was agile too. He ducked and then used his wolf arms and strength to slap at the sword. It flew away several feet.

Raika retreated, throwing darkfire at me. "Stay back!"

"Raika—"

"No!" Roman stepped between us.

I hesitated. What the hell was he doing? How was he alive? "Shut the fuck up, Roman!" I would deal with him later.

Ivy and Ariella's fight crossed over ours, their dark and light magic firing at all angles, and most of it exploding against the cavern's walls. Each time, the mountain shook a little.

I rushed past Ivy and Ariella, and looked at Raika, my hands up, my palms out. "Raika, I don't know what is going on, but—"

Roman growled. He grabbed her wrist and ran with her toward one of the tunnels.

The mountain shook again, a lot harder than before, and began to fall.

"Watch out!" someone yelled.

I didn't think. I ran after Raika and Roman. Bigger rocks fell. Shit, this would be bad. I caught up with them as they reached the mouth of a tunnel. With all my strength, I dove at Raika as a smaller rock fell right on top of her. I wrapped my arms around her waist and pushed us farther inside the tunnel. The flashlight she was holding fell from her hands.

In midair, I did my best to turn us around, but there was no time. We landed hard on the rough ground, on our sides.

A moment later, the mountain stopped shaking and the rock stopped falling.

I sat up. I couldn't see anything since it was dark, but I could feel Raika's body still half over me.

"Here," I said, holding her arm to help her sit up, but she didn't come with me. "Raika?" I called. No answer. Panic bloomed in my chest. No, no, not again. By the moon, I couldn't take this.

I patted down the ground beside us, making sure it wasn't too rough, then I gently rolled her off me and laid her down. I scurried away, running my hands on the ground, searching for the flashlight Raika had been holding before.

I found the flashlight and turned it on. Light illuminated what was once the tunnel's entrance—it was now covered by giant boulders.

Shit.

Then I scooted back to Raika and pointed the flashlight to her. I panicked for a second, when I saw the blood trickling along her pretty face, but then her chest moved up and down, and relief washed over me.

She had fainted, thank the moon.

I pointed the flashlight to her head. There was a nasty scratch right on her hairline, probably where that small stone fell, and that was what knocked her out. I examined the scratch and decided it was a little worse than I first thought. If she didn't have wolf healing, she would've needed a stitch or two to close it.

I moved the flashlight along Raika's body to make sure she was all right. She had a few scrapes along her arm, her pants were ripped on the side, but that was it.

I returned the flashlight to her face.

She put a hand over her eyes. "Turn that thing away."

15

RAIKA

THAT DAMN LIGHT IN MY HEAD. OH, MY HEAD. I BROUGHT THE hand shielding my eyes to my head and winced in pain when I touched something wet.

The man averted the flashlight. "Careful."

I frowned. Who was he? I stared at him in the dim light coming from the flashlight, and something in me stirred. Something I didn't understand, something I had no name for, but something full, and strong, and pure. It was a force to be reckoned with and it made me breathless.

This something tugged at my chest, as if it had cast a line and now it had caught a fish.

I stared at this man.

He was a stranger. I had never seen him before. And yet there was something about him. He was handsome, I had to give him that. He had light bronze skin, broad shoulders that stretched the fabric of his shirt, dark hair that framed a beautifully set face with dark eyes, high cheekbones, thick eyebrows, and sharp chin and jaw.

"Are you okay?" he asked, reaching for me.

"Stay back!" I scooted away, and the movement sent a jolt of pain through my head. I groaned. I must have hit my head when this brute threw me back. But glancing now at the rocks covering the side of the tunnels, I would say he had also saved my life.

The man raised his hands, the flashlight pointing up. "Raika, I don't know what is going on, but we need to talk."

"Talk?" I scooted away a little more, until I could rest my back on the side of the wide tunnel. I felt dizzy and tired. But when I leaned over the rocks, sharp pain jolted through my back and I yelped.

The man advanced toward me, worry etched in the gleam of his eyes and the knot of his brows. "What is it?"

"Stay back!" I yelled, a finger raised.

He stopped, but didn't retreat.

Good enough ... for now.

I reached to my back and found my shirt was ripped on the left side. When I peeled the fabric back a little, I found another wet patch. I hissed as a new wave of pain rippled through my side. Probably a deep scratch, but now that I knew of this one, it hurt more than my head.

"Raika ... you need to let me see those cuts." He glanced to the side, to where my bag had dropped off my shoulders when I fell. "Do you have a first aid kit there?"

Funny thing was, I did. But I wasn't going to tell him that. Besides, didn't he want to kill me? From what Roman had told me in that gas station, this brute and his friends were part of my former pack. They had found me and they had followed me here.

They were here to kill me.

Why did he need the first aid kit for that? With his size and visible strength, all he had to do was pin me down and squeeze my neck. I probably wouldn't even be able to move or scream.

I shook my head—and another pang of pain bounced around my skull.

I groaned.

"Raika, talk to me."

"What's there to talk about? Do you like to taunt your victims?"

He balked. "Victims? Wait, I'm confused. What is going on? Why are you running from me? Why aren't you letting me help you? Hold you?"

"Hold me?" I scoffed. "I don't even know you—"

"What?" He ran a hand through his hair, and his bicep contracted. Damn, he really was ripped. I blinked. What the hell was I thinking? "Raika ... you don't remember me?"

I lifted my chin. "When you and your pack tried to kill me two weeks ago, I lost my memories."

"I tried to kill you? My pack? *Our* pack, Raika, and we would never try to kill you!"

"Stop, stop!" I searched for an exit. There was only one way to go, and from the little I could see in this barely illuminated place, it seemed to be a long tunnel. Then I remembered ... "Where's Roman?"

The man shook his head. "I don't know. I'm hoping he is on the other side of those rocks—" He gestured to the pile of boulders blocking the tunnel's entrance. "—and not under them."

I flinched. I hoped so too. "I need to get to him." I braced myself against the wall and pushed up. "He told me he feels pain when I'm hurting. I don't want him to suffer." My head grew dizzier.

"Why would he feel pain when you're hurt?"

"He's ... he's my mate." Darkness swam at the corners of my eyes.

The man advanced on me so fast, I didn't even see him coming. He put his hands on either side of my head, caging me against the rocky wall.

He bared his teeth, his eyes yellow. "*He's* your mate? No, Raika. He's not."

He lowered his head and looked right into my eyes. I tried melting into the stone behind me, but there was nowhere to go.

An image flashed in my mind. This man in this same position, but shirtless and holding me against a rock like now.

And me ... wanting him. A force too strong for words pulling me to him.

Just like I felt now.

I blinked, confused and dazed, and pushed hard against his chest. He didn't budge. "Get off me!" I yelled.

He took a small step back.

I made to turn and walk away, wherever this tunnel led me, but the dizziness and the pain won. I tried catching myself on the rocks, but my hand slid past them as I fell back and blacked out.

A WARM HAND cupped my face, and I turned my head toward it. This hand, this warmth, this touch ... it was welcome and familiar.

I miss it.

I snapped my eyes open and stilled. I was seated against the rocks, and the man leaned over me, his face so, so close.

One of his hands was on my face, tilting it up, and the other on my head. He pressed something to the cut there. I hissed.

"Welcome back," he said, his voice deep, but soft. "Brace yourself."

For—I gritted my teeth as a burning sensation started at the cut. "W-what are you doing?"

"I've found your first aid kit. I'm applying an antibiotic cream to your cut. Your healing will speed this up, but this and a small bandage should hold it for now."

He pulled back and reached for something beside him— the first aid kit. I stared at him, not understanding a thing.

"Why are you helping me?"

His eyes found mine and he looked at me as if I was crazy. "While you were out, I thought about your situation. I don't know exactly what happened or how, but I'm convinced your memories were erased and that you've been told something completely different from the truth."

I scoffed. "Does that even make sense?"

"After everything we lived through this last year, I would say it could."

We ... he said *we*.

I crossed my arms, which pulled at the cut in my back and made me wince in pain. I ignored it as best as I could. "Then tell me what you know."

His brows curled down. "What's my name?"

I stared at him. "I don't know."

The pull inside my chest tugged harder. *Yes*, it said, *you know*. Maybe I did know, when I was part of his pack, before they had tried to kill me and I ran away.

He let out a sigh. "My name is Shane." He shifted his position, coming to sit right by my side, his torso facing my side.

I leaned to the other side. "What are you doing?"

"I'm going to tell you what I know while you let me look at this cut."

It wasn't a question. I bit down on my cheek, wanting to tell him no, but the damn thing was hurting. If he could put some healing salve on it and bandage it well enough so I could then fight my way out of here, great.

"Fine." I twisted a little bit, giving him better access to my back.

"This will be long," Shane said and then he launched into a crazy tale.

According to him, he and I found out we were mates when witches who were once allies to our pack, the Nightmist coven—Dot's former coven—attacked after his little sister's birthday party. We went into a fissure inside a rock formation to hide from them, and that was when the bond snapped.

He pressed a hand to his chest right when I felt the tug pressing against my own.

Shane said that a few days later, a half-demon, half-wolf shifter named Conri invaded the pack with his demons and the witches, and massacred our pack. Or most of it. He was taken away, believing we were all dead, while we thought he had balked at the challenge and fled, leaving us to die.

Conri treated me well and allowed me perks the other wolves didn't have because Conri wasn't working alone. He was working with Paimon, my father, and Paimon had ordered Conri to not hurt me.

Conri was there to find the crystals that powered the barrier around the pack lands and kept enemies out. However, we had recently learned the crystals were powered by something else too: the dragon we were now hunting.

Shane found out we were alive and came back for us. He

killed Conri and claimed his title—the pack's alpha. However, two of the crystals had been stolen, the barrier was gone, the Whitecrest pack had been threatening us, and so many other little things that didn't matter now.

Shane tugged at my shirt and I nodded. I helped him fold the lower half of my shirt up over my breasts and I held it in place with my arms. "Paimon had Nortrix challenge me away from the pack lands, but Nortrix never showed up. Meanwhile, he was in our town to open a portal and allow Paimon to come over and take the other crystals." He applied some antiseptic to the cut, and I tensed and gritted my teeth as it burned. "Sorry."

"Just ... go on." I didn't want to listen to him. So far, everything he had told me made no sense whatsoever, but it was something to keep my mind off the wound on my back.

"The town was supposed to be deserted, but some wolves refused to leave, so you went there to convince them to come with you ... and Nortrix and Paimon caught you. It seemed Paimon had planned on going after you anyway." His tone was hard, angry. He smeared some cream on the cut, and I bit my tongue so I wouldn't scream. "Without meaning to, Paimon released the dragon and he burned our town. In the confusion, Roman took you aside ... and right into Paimon's arms. It was then I arrived, and I was looking for you. And then I saw it." He placed a full hand on the center of my shoulder blades. My breath caught. "Paimon killed you with a sword right in front of me." His voice broke. "Then he was gone. You fell in my arms and ... died." He leaned forward and rested his forehead on my shoulder.

My head told me to push him away, to not let him do this. He couldn't touch me like this while telling me all these lies, but my heart and that insane pull coming from it told me something else, something so crazy, I didn't dare to listen.

But I also couldn't pull away.

"I took your body, Raika," he whispered. "I cremated you." His lips touched my shoulder and I shivered. "I don't know how it's possible. I thought you were gone. Do you know how it feels to see you again? To have you here with me?" I closed my eyes and leaned into him. "I have you back now and—"

Clarity filled my head and I scooted away from him. "You have nothing, no one." I pulled my shirt down. "But a story full of lies."

"Look me in the eye and tell me you feel nothing for me." His voice was hard, hurt.

I looked at him, and my emotions rose from my chest, fast and hot, and oh, by the moon, this man ... I averted my eyes. "That doesn't mean anything."

He crossed his arms. "Then tell me your version of the story. Who am I? Who's that blonde woman, that other guy? And how did you lose your memories?"

Not wanting to talk to this brute, I reached for the bandages, lifted my shirt again, and applied it to my cut myself. Though, when I pulled my shirt down, the bandage stuck to it, and crumpled at the hem. "Shit."

"Give it to me." He extended his hand. I eyed his hand as if it could bite me. "I'll behave ... for now."

I didn't like that. Lies—my body liked that very much. I could feel my heart thumping faster just thinking of him coming closer.

This was crazy.

Without another option, I handed him the bandage and turned my side to him again. Then I told him the truth: a little over a year ago, his pack attacked me when they found out I was a half-demon. They killed my mother, but Roman, who was my mate, helped me escape the pack. We ran into my father, who took me to live with him and Ivy, my half sister—I didn't tell him about Paimon's plan for the future, because he didn't need to know that.

"About two weeks ago, I was out with Ivy on a mission when your pack found us again and they attacked," I said. Shane pressed the bandage against my skin and pulled my shirt back down. "I almost died in that battle, and ended up losing my memories."

I turned again, making sure I kept at least a good foot between us. The look on his face caught me by surprise. His brows were curled, his jaw worked hard, I thought he would break a tooth, and his hands were clenched by his side.

This was the alpha of my former pack. A pack who wanted me dead for what I was. And here I was, trapped with him without any chance of a quick escape.

I moved another foot back.

"What can I do to prove to you what I'm telling you is the truth?"

"Nothing. Though I would appreciate it if you don't kill me."

He let out a hollow chuckle. "Raika, you're my mate, the woman I've been in love with since you were five years old. I've lost you twice already, and I thought I would die in agony and pain both times. My body, my heart, and my soul are yours. Do you really think I could ever hurt you?"

The intensity of his gaze made me uncomfortable. Bothered. Hot.

Shit, I needed to get away from here.

I put a hand on the wall and stood slowly. Shane jumped to my side and held my elbow, keeping me steady. His warm hand on my skin, I—a wave of dizziness hit me and everything went dark for two seconds.

As soon as I recovered, I pulled my arm from his grip.

"Raika, if I wanted you dead, I could have done it three hundred times already." He picked up his bag and mine from the ground, never losing grip on the flashlight.

I gave him a side glance. That was true enough, I guess.

But then what? Why would he spin such an elaborate tale? To trick me? Again, why? Did he want something from me? Maybe he hoped if I fell for his story, I would reveal my father's plans, and he would use that knowledge to defeat my father.

That had to be it. That was the only reason I could see.

Right now, I didn't have a choice. I would have to go with this brute. My only hope was that this tunnel led outside, or to a tunnel where the others were, so I could get rid of him fast.

For some reason, being around him made me uncomfortable.

Also ... hot and bothered.

16

SHANE

I POINTED THE FLASHLIGHT FORWARD, ILLUMINATING THE endless tunnel. It narrowed at times, then became so wide, I was sure the dragon could pass through here. But it never ended. How big was this damn mountain?

After almost two hours of walking, I said, "We should take a break."

Raika didn't protest it. She leaned on the rocky wall and pressed a hand to her back, where the cut was. I grabbed some water from my bag and offered it to her.

She hesitated but took it. "Thanks." She winced when she lifted the bottle to drink.

"Want me to take a look at it?"

She returned the bottle to me. "What?"

"The cut. On your back. I see it's bothering you. Want me to take a look?"

"Oh, no." She shook her head vehemently. "It's just tugging a little, nothing much."

Her face was the same, her voice was the same, but the

wariness in her bright blue eyes, and the way she spoke were different. Not Raika. At least, not my Raika.

By the moon ... what had they done to her?

My fingers itched to reach to her, to touch her, to pull her to me, to embrace her, to wrap my arms around her, secure her against me, take a good lungful of her scent, make sure she was really here and this wasn't a freaking hallucination.

"Are you hungry?" I opened my bag and started searching for food.

"No, I'm good."

I stopped and looked at her. This was definitely not my Raika. One, she had never refused food before, and two, she had never spoken to me like that.

Another whiplash of anger struck me, and I marched past her before I did something stupid.

Like kiss her senseless ...

With a soft groan, Raika pushed off the wall and followed me. I faltered then, my instincts telling me to go after her, to check if she was okay.

But I needed a minute.

Being around her and not being around her true self was messing with my mind and feelings big time.

I didn't know what to think, what to do.

On one hand, I wanted to push her against the wall, press my body to hers, kiss her until the mating bond's call was stronger than anything else and she remembered me, remembered us. I wanted to show her how much I missed her.

On the other hand, I didn't want to scare her. She seemed lost and confused, and she didn't believe me. Rage sparked inside of me, and the Shadow Wolf stirred ... what had Paimon and Dot done to her? Was this some kind of spell that blocked her memories? How did I undo it? I needed to talk to Lavinia.

As we walked through the long tunnel, I wondered how Paimon had gotten away with this. I had seen him kill her. I had held her body. I had felt her life leaving her. I had taken her away, prepared her body, laid her in that pyre, and lit it. I saw her beautiful body become ashes right in front of my eyes. I had gathered her ashes and put them in a vase and stored them away.

How was she here, a few steps in front of me?

I was grateful beyond words. Seeing her like this was enough to bring me to my knees, but I still had to make sense of it. How had she died, and then not?

I would worry about that answer later. Right now, I wanted to get us out of here. Find a way out of this mountain.

And then what? Would we fight? Would we still go after the dragon? All I could think of was taking Raika away from everyone and everything, dragon be damned.

But if we left the dragon, then Paimon would get it and become stronger. And even if he hadn't killed Raika, he still had to pay for all the suffering he had brought upon me and my pack. Since the beginning when Conri invaded and massacred the pack and had the witches take me away, it was Paimon's doing.

He would suffer for it all.

Paimon and Roman.

I gritted my teeth and clenched my hand around the flashlight. It creaked under my grip, and I realized I almost broke it. I released my iron-clad hold and let out a long breath.

The anger didn't fade.

I would like to think I was the better man and would give

him the benefit of the doubt, but from where I was standing, there was no doubt. Roman had helped Paimon take Raika that night, to fake her death. He disappeared that night, and we assumed he had died in the fire along with so many of the Whitecrest wolves. And now he was pretending to be her mate.

The motherfucker.

Jealousy burned white hot in my veins.

"Have you kissed Roman?" I hadn't intended to ask, but the words flew out of my mouth.

Raika halted suddenly and turned her wide eyes at me. "That's none of your business."

"The hell it isn't." I stalked to her. "You're my mate. If—"

"No, I'm not," she snapped. "Roman is my mat—"

I growled and pushed her to the wall. "I'll prove you're *mine*." She gasped and raised her hands, pushing against my chest. But I was stronger than her. I splayed my hands on the wall on either side of her head and leaned into her. "Tell me you don't feel this."

"I ..."

I pressed my body onto hers slowly. If she protested this time, I would let go. I would never, ever take her by force, even if she was mine and mine alone. Raika's body reacted to me. She gasped again and arched her back, gluing her breasts to my chest. Dear moon ...

"I know you feel it. I can see it." I lowered my head to her shoulder, and she stretched her neck. I smiled as I grazed my nose along her throat. She inhaled sharply, her hands closing around my shoulders, her nails sinking into my skin. Her sweet jasmine scent mixed with her arousal, and I growled again. "I can smell it." I shifted my weight and pressed a little more against her, so she could feel my desire for her. A little moan escaped her lips and I almost lost it. It took everything in me to not rip her clothes off and take her right here, right now.

But next time I was inside her, she would know who I was.

With great effort, I stepped back and stared at her.

She looked halfway undone with her eyes half-closed, her lips parted, and her body tight. My hard-on was having trouble fitting in my pants.

Raika blinked. "What ...?"

I crossed my arms. "Don't bother denying it because I saw, I felt, and I smelled the desire on you." Shit, I was still seeing and feeling and smelling all of that. "Tell me you felt like that with any other man, and I won't insist you're my mate again."

She opened her mouth. Closed it. Standing straight, she smoothed down her clothes, ran a hand through her long hair. "I ... I have no memories of the past, only of the last two weeks or so. I don't know how I felt for Roman before."

I shook my head. "This is not about remembering. You don't remember me, but tell me what you felt just now? Wasn't there something here—" I pointed right in the center of my chest, beside my heart. "—pulling you toward me? A force you couldn't explain, but couldn't deny?"

She averted her eyes.

Good.

She chewed on her cheek. "That doesn't mean anything."

I scoffed. "Right. Keep telling yourself that." Suddenly, an idea popped in my mind. I didn't know why I hadn't thought of that before. I picked up my phone. "Here." I opened the picture library and handed my phone to her.

With wary eyes, Raika took the phone from me. The knot

between her brows only deepened as she flipped from picture to picture.

There weren't many, but there were several of her. Hell, the majority of my pictures were of her, her with Minsi, or with both my siblings. But there was a handful of the two of us together.

Slowly, the knot in her forehead smoothed, and her eyes widened. Tears brimmed in her eyes. Shit, I hadn't wanted to make her cry. I had wanted her to see.

"Raika, I—"

She raised a hand to stop me. Then she pressed that hand to her mouth. "I can't." She pushed the phone to me. "I can't." She took off.

"Raika!" I yelled.

I glanced at the phone. It was a selfie I had taken of the four of us—me, her, Minsi, and Tyren. All of us smooshed together and smiling wide, like a happy family.

I shoved my phone in my pocket and ran after her, pointing the flashlight ahead of us before Raika ran into a wall or a cliff.

I didn't have to run more than fifteen seconds to catch up with her as she had halted where the tunnel widened into a bigger cavern—full of shiny blue flowers. Their odd glow illuminated the entire place.

"What the ...?"

Raika inhaled deeply. "They smell so good."

They did. Like a mix of cinnamon and mint and warmth. It was odd, but it went well together.

Raika started forward, but I held her arm. "Have you seen these flowers before? I haven't. We don't know if they are poisonous."

She frowned, and I let go of her arm.

Just then, a small brown bird flew in from another tunnel across the room. I stilled. If a bird was in here, it had either got lost inside the tunnels, or it meant an opening couldn't be too far away.

"Look." Raika pointed to the bird.

It dove into the flowers, then surged up again, unharmed. The bird perched on a crevice in the cavern's side and we watched him for a moment. Nothing happened.

"I think it's safe," she said before tiptoeing among the flowers.

They seemed okay, but I was still wary as I followed her into this meadow, doing my best to not step on the flowers.

What were these flowers? How did they bloom in here? I could only guess they were magical. I plucked one and looked at it. It didn't seem much different from a rose, but the petals were pointier and smoother, like velvet, and the center had a small yellow center. I put it in my bag. I would give this to Lavinia later so she could figure out if these flowers were useful or not.

Raika knelt in the center of the meadow and ran her hand over the flowers. "They're so smooth."

The bird flew away and into one of the tunnels.

"We should follow the bird," I said. "It must know the exit."

"Right." Raika stood and walked toward the tunnel.

Then she halted, pressed a hand to her neck, faltered two steps to the side, and went down.

My heart stopped. "Raika!"

I ran to her.

But I never made it.

Something pinched my neck. I stumbled forward, my vision darkened, my limbs grew heavy.

And down I went.

A POUNDING pain shook my skull and I woke up with a groan.

It all returned to me in a second—Raika and I went down in the flower meadow—and I sat up with a start.

Where was Raika?

I glanced around. The first thing that registered was the handful of naked lightbulbs hanging from the ceiling, and the three narrow windows with wooden bars cut through the top of the opposite wall—it was dark outside.

I was in some sort of wooden cell, clearly not made for someone as big as me, in a room with at least five cells like this one. One of the prison walls was the rocky side of the mountain. So we were probably in a bigger cavern inside the mountain, or we were at its side. That must have been the chimney smoke I had seen earlier.

Raika rested on the rough ground of the cell next to mine. I scooted closer to her and reached through the wooden bars. "Raika?" I touched her arm.

She groaned and her eyes fluttered open. Then she promptly pressed them closed again. "Ow, my head."

"Yeah, I know. Whatever they gave us to knock us out has lingering effects."

Raika pushed up until she was sitting in the center of her cell. She looked around as I had done, taking everything in. "Who are they?"

I shrugged. I hadn't seen anyone before blacking out, and so far I couldn't tell where we were. It would be easy to let panic call the shots now, but I wasn't going to give in. I had escaped from worse situations, and I would make sure Raika and I got out of this one too.

I reached for my phone, but of course, it wasn't on me. I looked for it and found our bags across the room, in another empty cell. Shit, calling Ariella or Evelyn and Ash was out of question.

I grabbed the thick wooden posts and gave them a nice tug. "I think I could break these."

"But we don't know what we're up against. What if you break these down and once we run out there, we face a hundred minotaurs or something?" I stared at her and chuckled. She crossed her arms. "What's so funny?"

"You read a lot and it shows."

She bit down on her cheek again. "I don't remember reading, but I know I love books."

"You have probably read thousands of books," I told her. "Each time I saw you when we were growing up, and it was almost every day, you had a different book in your hands."

She looked down, the knot returning to her forehead. She had run from me after looking at the pictures on my phone, she had almost cried, and I desperately wanted to know what she had felt, if she had remembered anything. But I could see how bringing up the past was bothering her.

I would dial it down a little for her, but I wouldn't give up. At some point, a gesture or my words had to break through the spell Paimon and Dot had placed in her mind, and she would remember everything.

"I still think we should wait to see what we're up against," she said, her voice low. "Then we can make a better escape plan."

I nodded. "Agreed."

It didn't take long for us to find out who had captured us.

The prison door opened and three creatures walked in—they were short and the tallest of them probably didn't come up to the middle of my chest. They had pale-green skin, huge, pointed ears, flimsy dark hair, and scrunched, ugly faces.

Goblins.

I had heard of them before, but I had never seen them.

Dressed in crude leather outfits and with rough axes and maces hanging from their belts, the three goblins halted before our cells.

"What were ye doin' with our flowers?" the tallest one asked.

"Your flowers?" I shook my head. "We were passing through. We don't want any flowers. We were after the dragon."

"Ya, that pesky dragon," the one on the right said. He had a thick golden hoop in the tip of his long ear. "Were ye tryin' to capture the dragon, or kill it?"

"Capture him," Raika said at the same time I said, "Kill him."

The goblins exchanged a wary glance.

"The dragon has been bad for us," the third goblin said. He had a nasty scar across one of his eyes. Instead of brown, this eye was white. "It keeps movin' inside the mountain and it doesn't care about our flowers."

"Look," I started. I wanted to stand up, but in this tiny cell, I could barely kneel. "Release us. We'll find our friends and we'll take care of the dragon. We'll either capture or kill him, but he won't be a problem to you anymore."

The goblins didn't look happy with that idea.

"We mean no harm to you or your flowers," Raika added. "We got lost inside the tunnels, but all we want is the dragon."

"Hm." The tall one scratched his chin. "We'll think about it."

They walked out of the prison and closed the door with a loud thud.

"We could take them," I said to Raika.

"The three of them, yes, but we don't know how many are out there." She frowned. "Besides, I don't want to hurt anyone unnecessarily."

Her heart was always the purest and the kindest, and I admired that. It was one of the reasons I loved her so much.

"All right, we'll wait and see what they decide," I told her. "But we also can't wait forever. And if they decide they won't let us go ..."

She let out a sigh. "Then we'll talk about another plan."

I rested my back on the wooden posts and stared at her.

She averted her eyes, a slight red color tinting her cheeks.

I didn't know if I should laugh or shout. This situation, it was all crazy and twisted. About a week ago, if anyone told me I would find my mate alive, chase down a dragon, and be held captive by a group of goblins, I would say they were insane.

But here we were.

One hour passed. The golden hoop goblin returned with a female goblin and brought us some food. A weird looking porridge, burnt bread, and water. We thanked them and ate only the bread and drank the water.

Then another hour passed.

Then another.

Light started slowly filtering through the windows.

I groaned, restless. I needed to stretch my legs, to stand tall, to do something. Staying in this cell, pretending it could hold me and not talking to Raika, was killing me right now.

"Those pictures," she finally said, her voice soft. She lifted her eyes to meet mine. "Those aren't photoshopped, are they?"

My brows curled down. "You were told I wanted you dead. If I did, why would I waste my time photoshopping all of those?"

She pressed her fingertips to her temples. "It doesn't make sense."

"Of course it does. Dot spelled you. She made you forget your entire past, your entire life, so they could manipulate you." The question was why? What did Paimon want with Raika? Why had he faked her death and brought her to his side? Paimon being a doting father and wanting his beloved daughter with him when he conquered the underworld? I didn't buy it.

"That's ridiculous."

"As is me lying about you being my mate." This subject was riling me up.

"Who were the other two in the pictures? The girl and the boy?"

It broke my heart that she had to ask about them. "My siblings, Minsi and Tyren."

Raika put a hand over her chest. "I—"

The prison door opened and someone marched in.

A different goblin, taller than the other three, but just as slim. He had an even more rugged face, a big, bald head, and thick eyebrows. He stared with the authority only a leader had.

"Ye sayin' ye can slay the dragon, uh?" he asked, his voice deep.

I puffed out my chest as best as I could in this tiny cell. "Yes, we can."

Raika glared at me. I would say anything this guy wanted to hear as long as it took us out of here.

"Why do ye want to slay the dragon?"

"There's an evil higher demon who wants to kill the dragon and absorbs his powers, so he'll grow stronger."

The goblin snorted. "All demons are evil."

"That's not true!" Raika stood in the cell, the top of her head half an inch from the top wooden beams.

The goblin spat on the ground and repeated, "All demons are evil."

"Regardless," I said, my voice louder. I threw Raika a look that said please-let-me-handle-this-one. If she really was my Raika, she would know what I meant. "This demon needs to be stopped." Raika groaned and turned her back to us. "If he grows more powerful, he'll try to take back the underworld."

The goblin pursed his lips. "Maybe that isn't a bad idea."

I wasn't expecting that. "Why?"

His dark eyes fixed on mine, and he seemed to consider if he should tell me or not. "We live at the base of the mountain, and now that demons aren't welcomed in the underworld anymore, they come crawling into our village and claim our mountain. We wouldn't care if they didn't destroy our flowers or attack our people."

The wheels in my brain turned fast. "I'm an honorary member of DuMoir Castle."

"Those pompous vampires have a werewolf in their midst?"

"Wolf shifter, and yes, they do." And also several witches and an angel. Soon, it would be the whole zoo in there. "I can talk to Lord Drake. He's dedicated to keeping the peace and helping supernaturals. If I ask, I'm sure he'll send a team of vampires and they will deal with the demons for you."

The goblin narrowed his eyes. "A vampire would never care for goblins."

"Lord Drake is different. I assure you, he'll listen to me and he'll help."

All of a sudden, the prison door opened and the goblin with a gold hoop rushed in.

"What is it, Etyx?"

"Sloz, I know ye didn't want to be disturbed, but ... it's Dalk."

Without sparing another look at us, Sloz ran out of the prison. Etyx went after him.

I watched as the door closed, and Raika and I were left alone in the prison as if we hadn't been negotiating a way out of here. I turned to talk to Raika about it and found her fuming at me.

"What the hell was that?"

"What?"

"An evil higher demon? Are you kidding me?"

I didn't know what to say to her. I crossed my arms. "Then tell me your version of the story." Or the version that she had been told because it wasn't her story. She had been lied to and she couldn't see it. Damn, how I wish Lavinia was here right now. Even if she couldn't break the spell, she could at least confirm my story.

She bristled. "Why would I? You're my enemy and—"

I leaned into the wooden beams separating our cells and stared right into her eyes. "I'm not your enemy, Raika. I'm your fucking mate!"

The door opened again and Etyx walked back in. "Don't stop because of me. I'm just here to keep an eye on ye."

I didn't want to talk about that anymore, because if I did, I would break something. Instead, I wanted to know something else. "What was that all about?"

Etyx clasped his hands behind his back. "I'm not supposed to talk about it."

"Come on, how bad can it be? We're stuck in here and have nowhere to go." Let them believe they could keep me locked in this shitty cell. "Tell us something juicy."

Etyx glanced at the closed prison door, then sighed. "It's Dalk, Sloz's son." He lowered his voice and said, "He's half-human, half-goblin, and since being abandoned by his mother and having to come live with us about two years ago, he has been suffering from severe panic attacks."

I froze. Panic attacks. I knew what to do, but I wasn't good at it. But there was someone else who was. I looked at Raika. "She can help."

Her eyes bugged. "What?"

17

RAIKA

SHANE WAS DRUNK OR JOKING. I HAD NO IDEA HOW TO HELP someone with panic attacks. "Are you crazy?" I whispered.

"My sister, Minsi, suffers from panic attacks all the time, and Raika is the only one who can calm her down," Shane told Etyx.

The goblin turned his gaze to me. "Is that true?"

I stared at Shane. He nodded his head. Shit. I knew what he was doing. He was lying so we would be let out of these cells.

I gulped down and said, "Yes. Yes, it's true."

"I'll be right back." Etyx marched out of the prison.

Instantly, I turned to Shane. "What the hell? Why did you lie?"

I expected him to argue with me on this, but his eyes softened. "Raika, I didn't lie. Minsi really has panic attacks and you're her healing balm. You taught me how to deal with her, but really, you're the only one who can calm her down."

I huffed. "If that's true, then what? Your sister is suffering right now?"

He looked at me, no words, no gestures. Shit. He meant Minsi was really suffering *right now*? I averted my gaze, my mind reeling, my feelings raw and twisted in knots.

When I looked at the pictures in Shane's phone, the tug in my chest had intensified tenfold. It was like I could feel it, all of it, behind a thin but unbreakable wall. It was right there, and I couldn't reach it. Those people, the feeling behind the smiles in the pictures, the way they looked at each other, that they hugged and touched.

And that little girl. Minsi. It was like ... I knew her, but I didn't. I couldn't remember.

The agony had grown so deep, I shoved his phone back to him and ran as if I could get away from it all.

I didn't understand what was going on; I couldn't make sense of any of this. Shane said that if he wanted me dead as the others told me, then he would have killed me already, and I believed him. I mean, look at his size! He was *a lot* stronger than me. Even with my darkfire, I bet I was no match for him in a fight.

He had said that if he wanted me dead, he wouldn't be showing me these pictures and telling me I was his mate.

I touched the center of my chest, right between my breasts, where a crazy pull had started the moment my eyes met his. When he had pushed me to the wall, when he had touched me, the tug beat as fast as my traitor heart, and it was like I couldn't control myself. In that moment, I had never wanted or needed anything or anyone else in my life. Despite not remembering 99 percent of my life, I knew that, just as I knew I needed air to live.

"Raika," he whispered.

My breath caught and I closed my eyes. My name on his

lips. The rough edge to his voice, the almost possessive tone. It sent a shiver up my spine. Holy shit, what was happening?

The sound of the prison door saved me. Etyx rushed in, followed by the two other goblins who had first talked to us.

The tallest one fumbled with keys and reached for my cell. "Sloz agreed to let ye talk to Dalk."

Shane grabbed two of the wooden beams in his cell. "You're taking her?"

"Yes," Etyx said.

Shane's grip tightened and the wood cracked under his hands. "You take me with you, or you bring this kid here. Either way, you can't take her from my sight."

"Ye're the one in the cell, mate," the one with the scar and the white eye said.

Shane's eyes turned brighter and his arms shifted into furry claws. He growled and swiped at the wooden beams before him, severing them in half.

The goblins jumped back several feet, and even I plastered myself to the farthest side of my cell.

"I've been quietly standing here, being courteous and patient," he said through his fangs, his voice deep, almost unnatural. "But if you try taking her away from me, I'll wreak havoc on your entire village."

I blinked. I wanted to yell at him for being sexist and possessive, especially of a person who was not his, but that wasn't my body's response. Instead, my core warmed up and something like desire whipped through me hard and fast. For a delirious second, I wished he had broken down the beams that separated our cells so I could kiss him.

I shook my head. What?

The goblins exchanged nervous looks. Etyx ran out of the

prison again, while the other two reached for the weapons at their waists and pointed them at Shane.

"Stay where you are," the tallest one said.

Shane's eyes, teeth, and arms went back to normal. "I don't want any trouble."

A moment later, Etyx came back. Sloz was right behind him, and so were two more people—a small and old female pushed a crude wheelchair where a screaming kid sat.

My heart tugged at the sight.

Sloz halted right in front of my cell. "Etyx told me ye can help my son."

I stared at him. Desperation was etched in each of his features. He loved this kid, and I wanted to help.

I nodded, even if I didn't really know anything. Just had to try. Hug him, maybe. Comfort him. Do something.

My cell door was unlocked and weapons were raised, their tips pointed at me.

"Try anything funny, and we'll kill ye," Etyx said.

I walked out of the cell and approached the boy. He stared at me, but he didn't see me. His screaming seized for two seconds, just to start again. He rocked back and forth, his hands closed into fists in his temples.

I knelt beside his chair and took a good look at him. He seemed taller than the other goblins, probably because of his human side. His skin was a smooth green-grayish tone, his face wasn't as wrinkly, his ears weren't as long—but they were just as pointy. If I had to guess, I would say he was nine, maybe eight, but he was small for his age.

Just like someone I know.

My eyes bugged. Who? Who did I know?

I reached for the boy and rested my hand on his arm gently. "Hi, Dalk." He didn't move or flinch or acknowledge me. He was lost in his own world. "It's okay. Everything will be okay."

Not really sure what I was doing, I started singing. Some random lullaby I wasn't even sure how I knew. My voice wasn't the greatest, but I could carry a tune, especially if I didn't try anything too crazy with it. I kept my voice low and mellow as I smoothed my hand up and down Dalk's arm, always singing.

Slowly, the boy's screams lowered in volume. When he lowered his hands and glanced at me, I smiled. He flinched from my touch, so I retreated my hand, but I kept singing. I stayed there, smiling at him, looking at him, not touching, not pushing, but a support, a pillar if he needed one.

The screams stopped, but his body still shook.

I didn't say anything, but took a deep breath, held for two seconds, then let it slowly out. I did again. And again. On the fifth time, Dalk joined me. With shallow breaths first, but then he was copying me beat by beat, and even his trembling stopped.

His eyes were locked on mine now.

"Can we play a game?" I asked. Dalk nodded once. "Can you name five things you can see?"

Dalk hesitated. "A pretty woman. A big man. My father. His friends. The cells."

"Good job! How about four things you can touch?"

He nodded and listed the four things.

Just then an image popped in mind. A little girl and me in her bed, me holding her tight while I asked her these same questions and the shaking in her body slowly went away.

Minsi.

A pang cut through my heart, and when I spoke next, my voice broke. "Now, three things you can hear."

We went on until this game, which I had no idea I knew, ended. By then, Dalk wasn't screaming or shaking anymore. He still looked confused and alarmed, but we had stopped the panic attack.

After saying thanks, the female goblin took him away.

I watched until he disappeared past the door, a smile on my lips. I turned to my cell, but first found Shane with a lopsided grin, his eyes on me. His gaze was half I-told-you-so and half I'm-proud-of-you, and I had no idea what to do about that.

I reached for my cell, but the door was closed.

"Ye're not going back there," Sloz said. I turned to face him. "Dalk has had a hard time all of his life. He didn't fit in the human world, so his mother abandoned him here as if he was the plague." There was anger and sadness in his voice. "But he doesn't really fit here either. He's been havin' trouble adaptin', and others have trouble acceptin' him. His mother told me he had anxiety since he could walk, but the panic disorder started after movin' here. And I had no idea how to deal with it. But you just changed that. And for that, you have my eternal gratitude."

My heart swelled for them. I was so freaking glad for being able to give them this, even if it was a brief moment of peace. "You're very welcome."

"Because of that, I'll let you two go," Sloz said.

Etyx unlocked Shane's broken door, as if he needed that to get out of it now.

"I offered to send my vampire friends to help you with the demons if you let us go," Shane started. "I know that is not why you're releasing us, but if that's okay with you, I'll send them anyway."

"I wouldn't be opposed to that," Sloz said. "Though I won't be holdin' my breath."

Shane nodded.

Etyx handed us our bags and gestured for the doors. "I'll escort ye out of the village."

We walked out of the prison building, and I squinted under the rising sun. Though there had been light inside the prison, it had been faint compared to natural light. The clouds from yesterday were long gone.

I stared at the small village in front of us. Several wooden houses with roofs made of hay along the side of the mountain, and many curious goblins peeking from their half-open doors at the two strangers.

Etyx didn't pay them any attention while he walked through the narrow path between the houses, closer and closer to the mountain. When we walked past the last house, a wall of thick wood with sharpened tips came into view.

He halted right at the small gate and pointed up, to the mountain. "We found you through a tunnel up there. Just keep going and you'll see it."

Shane frowned. "While we've been here, have you heard or seen the dragon?"

Etyx nodded. "The dragon went out once, but he returned a couple of hours ago and hasn't left since."

"And the people who were with us?" I asked, eager to know what happened to them. "Have you seen anyone else around the mountain?"

Etyx shook his head. "Ye're the only two we've seen around here."

"Oh, okay."

"Thanks, Etyx," Shane said, shaking the goblin's hand. "You'll be hearing from some vampires soon."

Etyx let out a snort. "Yeh, right. Take care, ye two." And just like that, he closed the gate at our backs.

Shane and I exchanged a glance. I resumed walking and made my way toward where Etyx had pointed. Though I wasn't sure what to do. We were outside the mountain, not lost in its tunnels. I could try ditching Shane now and go back to the bounty hunter, my sister, and my m—

I couldn't say it. I couldn't even think it.

No, because someone else pulled at my strings, made me hot and bothered with one look, and holy shit ... I walked faster before he could hear the rapid thump of my heart or the scent of my desire.

Traitor body.

This couldn't be happening.

But what if it was? What if it meant something? Since meeting Shane, everything had changed. My feelings, my thoughts, even my memories. I felt a connection to him, and I had seen things in my mind that hadn't been there before. Memories I had forgotten.

Or that had been erased.

Oh, gosh, no, this was confusing.

Almost thirty minutes up the side of the mountain, we found the tunnel's entrance.

I halted right at the edge of the darkness within. "Question now is, should we go in and search for them, and risk getting lost? Or should we skirt the mountain and look for them from the outside?"

Five feet from me, Shane ran a hand through his hair. He grunted, then looked at me, his eyes intense. "Not long ago, I promised you I would never lie to you again, so here it is: I don't want to go back and find the others. By the moon, I don't even want the dragon anymore. I was hunting the dragon so Paimon couldn't use him for himself. But then ..." He stalked forward until he was a foot from me.

I inhaled sharply, my body locked, my mind torn between backing away or leaning into him.

"Then I found you again. Alive and well. And my instinct now is screaming at me to take you out of here while I can."

This time, I took a step back. "Shane, I—"

A shadow moved inside the tunnel and I stilled. Shane noticed it too and turned to the tunnel's mouth. "There's something in there," he whispered.

I could feel it too.

Suddenly, shadows spilled out of the tunnel and surrounded us.

The shadows shaped into tall and lean humanoids with pitch-black skin, skeletal faces, and horns on their bald heads. Their eyes sockets were hollow, and their mouths were a long slit from side to side, filled with sharp fangs.

The blood drained from my face.

Shane grabbed my arm and pulled me close to him. "We'll—"

"I'm Prince Paimon's daughter," I practically shouted. "Don't attack. We're on the same side!"

The demons struck. I raised a wall of darkfire in front of us, but more demons were behind us. One snatched for me but I ducked under his lengthy arm. I threw a bolt of darkfire at the side of his head. He dissipated into shadows again, and disappeared.

Something told me he wasn't really gone.

As I dodged the attacks and threw my own, I counted the demons—ten against the two of us.

Once more, I told them who I was, but they either didn't listen to me, or they didn't care. One came for my throat, but I moved out of the way and sent darts of darkfire to him.

Meanwhile, Shane had turned into his wolf and ripped through the demons as if they were made of paper.

A demon feigned an attack and I fell for it. Then two more appeared behind me and grabbed my arms. I screamed and jerked against their hold.

Shane turned to look at me, and that cost him. The demon he had been fighting struck him hard on the side, making Shane stumble to the side and fall to his knees.

My heart squeezed.

Get up.

The demons holding me dragged me inside the tunnel. I screamed again and conjured my darkfire. I cast two big-ass bolts over my hands and—

The demons snuffed it out as if it was nothing.

A third demon, his body mostly shadows now, passed right through me. I felt like swimming in syrup. Nausea assaulted my stomach, and my head spun.

What the hell?

I tried catching my feet on the rough tunnel ground, to slow down the demons, to do anything, but there was nothing to grab hold.

Then I heard a growl that sent a shudder through my body. At the tunnel's mouth, Shane snarled at the demons dragging me away.

And he shifted.

But not to his human form.

To another wolf. A bigger one, darker, with red eyes, and who stood on two legs.

Shadow Wolf.

The words simply came into my mind.

He charged, and fear sliced through me. He was faster and stronger, and he cut through the demons who appeared between us in five seconds flat.

He lunged and closed his mouth around the throat of one of the demons holding me, his sharp teeth coming inches from my throat. I yelped and yanked back. The other demon held me tighter, but I used my free hand to throw darkfire at him. It exploded against his chest, pushing him back a foot or so and making him release me.

I called my magic, but before I could kill the bastard, Shane jumped at him. In two seconds, the demon was gone.

Then Shane turned to me.

His mouth peeled back, his teeth bared, his red eyes shining, and his body poised for another attack.

I lifted my hands. "Shane."

A memory came to me fast and unbidden.

Shane, just like this, with blood dripping from his mouth, and me in this same position, with my hands up like this, and telling him, "It's okay. We won. You're okay now. I'm okay now." He'd snarled and charged at me. I thought it would be my end, but instead, he had stopped in front of me, leaned into me, and changed into his human form, while both of us folded to the ground.

It had worked before, so it had to work again. I took a step closer to him and said, "It's me. You know me, right? It's fine now. We're fine. You can come back."

Shane howled. His powerful body shivered, and then he shifted.

Back to his human, and very naked form.

Heat spread over my cheeks and I turned my back to him. "Hm, you could—Hm." I gasped as his strong arms wrapped around me and his warm chest glued to my back. His head lolled forward, to my shoulder.

"When they dragged you away, I lost it." He turned his face to my neck and placed a soft peck on my skin. My body came alive, and I melted into him. I shouldn't, I couldn't. Why? I didn't remember. All I wanted was this man who set my blood on fire. He grazed his lips up my neck and whispered in my ear, "I can't lose you again, Raika. I can't survive that."

I didn't know what to say. I didn't even know why and how, but I felt the same. I turned my face to his.

He pulled back an inch to look into my eyes. "I want to kiss you, but you don't remember me, and—"

"Just shut up and kiss me," I whispered, breathless.

He chuckled. "You'll never change." He grew serious again and pressed his lips to mine.

"There you are!"

18

SHANE

"OH, OH!" ARIELLA PUT A HAND OVER HER EYES, TURNING around. "Bad timing for that, don't you think?"

With a groan, I let go of Raika. "Just ..." I found my bag, put on some pants, and said, "You can turn back now."

Ariella spun on her heel, her silver-blue eyes amused. "So, Raika, I would say nice to meet you, but first I would like to know what you were doing with the bad guys."

Raika looked at Ariella but didn't say anything. Instead, she picked up her bag and slung it over her shoulder. She walked past us, toward the tunnel's mouth.

I sighed and shoved a T-shirt on, socks, and my shoes. "She doesn't remember anything."

"What do you mean?"

I told her that Raika only remembered things from two weeks ago—after Paimon had killed her right in front of my eyes. And that all she knew had been twisted and she was living a lie.

"I think it's a spell," I said.

Ariella nodded. "It sounds like it. I'm sure Thea, Almae,

or Lavinia can undo it." I nodded, hoping that was true. "Am I the first one you encountered?"

"Yeah." I rehashed our time in the caves, except for the parts where I had almost kissed Raika.

Ariella stared from Raika to me, her eyes wide. "What the hell? It took me hours to finally make it through the tunnels and out of the mountain, but I didn't see any other living soul. Or demon. And you guys found two different kinds?"

I looked at Raika, still standing at the tunnel's mouth. She hadn't glanced in my direction since Ariella found us.

"We should go," I said, still unsure if I should stay and help Evelyn and Ash, or if I should take Raika and bolt before the others found us.

We took two steps toward the exit. Roman and Ivy appeared beside Raika. The three of them faced us.

My muscles locked up and I let out a snarl.

"Thank you for rescuing my mate," Roman said with a grin. He placed an arm over Raika's shoulder—and she flinched.

"You're a traitor," I said through gritted teeth. I could feel the Shadow Wolf asking for release again. He had killed demons, but he still wanted more violence. And I was *so* inclined to let him have it. "When I get my hands on you, I'll rip you apart limb by limb."

Roman's grin faltered. "It's a good thing you won't, then."

Ivy lifted her hands and shot darkfire bolts at the tunnel's mouth.

"No!" Raika yelled.

The tunnel shook and rocks slid down and blocked the exit.

My Shadow Wolf surged forward. I started shifting, consumed by rage.

"Shane, no!" Ariella created a bubble of light around me. I closed my eyes against the brightness. "Listen to me. You have to calm down. Don't lose yourself to the darkness. We'll fix this mess. I promise."

Easier said than done.

But I knew she was right. If I lost it now, I could end up hurting my friends and it would only delay everything else.

I inhaled deeply and focused my mind on getting out of here and rescuing Raika. For that, I needed a clear head. I took another deep breath and the Shadow Wolf stepped back. He was never gone, but for now, I could keep him at bay.

When I opened my eyes, the light bubble was gone and smaller light balls floated around the tunnel like lanterns.

"We need to get out of here." I stomped to the rock wall, ready to punch my way through somehow.

"Then step back." Ariella stood in the middle of the tunnel, her hands raised. "This is how I got out the first time."

I stepped back, watching. Ariella closed her hands. Light surged from within two rocks. It spread fast until the rocks seemed made of pure light. They imploded with a muffled boom and became dust.

She kept going and I paced behind her, my impatience taking a new high. This certainly was a more effective way than manually removing rocks, especially the bigger ones, which I wasn't sure I could lift. But all we needed to do was open a space big enough for us to squeeze through.

As the rocks disappeared, sounds from the other side reached my ears. I shifted my arms into claws. "There's someone on the other side. Be ready."

Ariella imploded two larger rocks, making smaller ones move and slide down. For a moment, I thought she had made a mistake and more were falling into place, and we would still be trapped here, but then it all stopped.

A hole big enough for me appeared in the rockslide, and I lunged through it, ready to shift. I halted in front of two figures, my claws raised to strike.

I stepped back as Evelyn and Ash raised their hands and sword at me.

"Shit, sorry." I let go of my wolf and my arms went back to normal.

Ariella climbed through the hole.

"What happened?" Evelyn asked.

I told them about Raika, the goblins, the demons, then Roman and Ivy taking Raika.

"I need—"

Movement to my right had me calling on my wolf again. My fangs bared and I snarled at the newcomer—the man who had been with Raika and the others when we first arrived.

He appeared from the side of the mountain, his hands raised, a crossbow neatly resting behind his back. "I'm not here to fight."

"Aren't you working for Paimon?" I asked, a bite to my words.

He stopped a good ways from us and lowered his hands. "I don't care about him or the others. I just needed this." He pulled out a broken dragon scale from the inside of his jacket. "With this scale, I can track the dragon."

Evelyn frowned. "What do you want with the dragon?"

"To set her free. To help her escape to a place where she can hide in peace."

"She?" Ariella asked.

"Yes, the dragon is female," the man said. "My plans were thwarted, though, when Paimon sent the others with me. I had hoped to come alone. Alas, I was going to get rid of them one way or the other." He gestured down the mountain. "Apparently, I don't need to worry about them anymore."

I snarled again. "Perhaps you need to worry about us now."

"You can try," the man said, matching my glare. "But I don't care about any of you either. But if you stop me from saving the dragon, I'll end you."

I advanced a step, ready to take him head on.

"Wait." Evelyn lifted a hand. "Are you saying you can keep the dragon safe from Paimon or anyone else?"

The man nodded. "Yes. If I can get to her, I can take her away from here, to a place no one will be able to find her."

Evelyn crossed her arms. "And what is that place?"

He shook his head. "I can't tell you that."

"Then how do I know you're not lying? That you won't take the dragon and kill her?"

His eyes hardened. "What you think or don't think doesn't matter to me, but the dragon does. Dragons are the purest magical beings in all the realms, and it's my duty to keep them safe."

"What are you?" Ash asked. "A dragon protector or something?"

"Or something."

I grunted. "Honestly, I planned on killing the dragon so Paimon couldn't use her magic." Evelyn shot me a glare. "But if you can take the dragon and keep her away from him, then better. Meanwhile, I have to rescue my mate." I turned to leave.

"Wait," Ariella said. She looked at the stranger. "What's your name?"

He hesitated. "Kaz."

"Kaz," she started. "Your quest is noble and we'll either get out of your way or help with it, if you want, but first, we might need your help."

He frowned.

I clenched my fists. "Why is that?"

One corner of her lips curled up. "I think I have a plan."

19

RAIKA

THE MOMENT IVY CAUSED ANOTHER CAVE-IN, TRAPPING SHANE and that other woman inside the tunnel, my heart wrenched and the pain almost brought me to my knees. For a good two minutes, I stared at the rocks as they created a new wall, my mind blank, but my feelings on steroids.

My chest hurt and I could barely breathe.

Shane.

"Come on." Ivy hooked her arm with mine and pulled me back.

"Wait," I finally said, my voice frail.

"We need to find Kaz and the dragon," she said.

I yanked my arm free of her grip, turning to her. "I'm not going."

She blinked. "What are you talking about?"

"I …" I looked at Roman. I didn't know what was happening, why, and how, I just knew something was wrong here. "I can't remember the details, but I know you're not my mate. Shane is, and I can't leave him."

"Shit," he muttered. He looked at Ivy. "She's remembering."

Ivy nodded, a knot between her brows. "The spell is wearing off."

"I knew staying far from Dot would cause problems," Roman said.

I gasped. "What the hell are you talking about?"

Ivy shook her head and turned to me. "I'm sorry." She pressed her hand to my chest and her darkfire hit me hard, wrenching my gut and twisting my insides.

I fought against it. I tried breathing through the heavy sensation spreading through my limbs, but I couldn't win.

I blinked once, twice, then my eyes didn't open again.

I CAME TO SLOWLY, my head pounding. I felt like I was in a rocking boat, and I was terribly seasick. I sat up, my eyes adjusting, and I reached up to rub my temple, but both my arms came together. I blinked and stared at my hands. I was seated on a comfortable couch, and my hands and feet were bound by thick ropes.

Desperation clawed its way through my chest.

"What ...?"

"How are you feeling?"

I looked up and found Ivy seated in an armchair across a coffee table. I stared at her, confused. "Where are we?" This wasn't our house.

"While we were away, our father was found out. He had to move."

What ...

Then it came all rushing to me.

The mountain, the dragon, meeting Shane, getting lost with him, feeling things I didn't remember but couldn't deny.

And finally, Ivy trapping Shane inside the tunnel, and she and Roman talking about me as if I wasn't there.

"What is going on?" I asked, my throat raw. "Why am I tied up?"

Ivy's brows curled down. "He's mad at me for bringing you here instead of going after the dragon, you know? Actually, he's mad that I told him you were ready to go with me. This is all my fault."

I frowned. "What are you talking about?"

"What do you remember?"

"What do you mean?"

"Don't play dumb with me, Raika. Tell me what you remember."

I bit down hard before saying, "You mentioned a spell wearing off before putting me under."

She nodded. "What else? Anything from before that? From before the spell?"

I shook my head. "So it is true? I haven't had an injury that caused memory loss? It was a spell. Dot cast a spell to make me forget everything from before? But ... why?"

My father appeared to my right. "Because I want all my children with me." He walked closer. "You see, King Brikan's demise was his children. He had sired so many powerful children, some of them got together and destroyed him."

"There was also the prophecy," Ivy said.

He waved her off. "That came from having so many children. I don't have as many, but I thought that instead of ignoring my children only to have them turn against me one day, why not bring them together and make them my most trusted allies." He halted beside Ivy, placing a hand on her shoulder. "Ivy wasn't the first I found, but she was the only one who stuck around."

I gulped. "What happened to the others?"

"Three refused to join me are now in the underworld, just not in the way I hoped for," he said matter-of-factly. My gut twisted. "There are two more, but they are too young. When they get older, I'll have them join us."

I frowned. "You killed the ones who didn't want to join you. What happened to me? You asked, I refused, but instead of killing me, you had Dot erase my memories? Why?"

He shrugged. "I liked your mother more than I usually like my partners, but more than that, you became such a great challenge because of that barrier. If Franc and Kali hadn't kept you behind that wall for so long, I might have lost interest." He sniffed the air. "But more than that, I can smell the darkfire inside you. It's strong, almost as strong as Ivy's, and she's a full-blooded demon."

My mind spun with so many thoughts.

So until two weeks ago, I hadn't been here. I had not lived with them; I knew nothing about them. They had faked my death and stolen me from Shane, and told me only lies.

By the moon, Shane.

Now that I knew, now that Dot's spell was wearing off, I could feel it—the mating bond stronger, drawing me to him.

"Did Dot mess with my mind, or did she do something with the mating bond?"

"I asked her to mute the bond as much as she could, so it wouldn't trigger any of your memories," my father said. "She said that was harder than erasing the memories."

A new memory flashed behind my eyes: Me, walking with Roman toward the school. Roman asking me to dinner at his house, and Shane standing in front of the town hall, listening and probably dying on the inside. If it had been Lucille asking him, I would have died too.

I suppressed a gasp. Lucille. I remembered Lucille.

"What about Roman? How did you get him onboard?"

"Actually, Roman was the one who approached Nortrix," my father said. "He wanted to take down Shane so he would have a chance with you. Nortrix realized how he would do anything for you and brought him in on our plans."

Our plans ...

That sparked another memory. Nortrix standing in the main square, placing the crystals in the ground and opening a portal for Paimon. And then ... Paimon revealed he was my father.

Moreover, I remembered how horrified I had been.

Paimon wasn't trying to help the other demons. No, he was trying to gain power and become the next king of the underworld because he was selfish, arrogant, and power hungry.

He didn't care about me or anyone else.

We were only pawns on his game board and he would dispose of us the moment we didn't serve our purpose anymore.

"What will you do with Roman?" I was pissed at him, but that didn't mean I wanted him dead.

He scoffed. "The boy is too eager, and a wolf shifter, but as long as he does what I tell him, he's all right."

"How did you fake my death?" I asked.

Shane had told me he had held my body and cremated me.

"That was Dot again," Paimon said. "She cast a spell over the body of a fallen Whitecrest female wolf to make it look like yours."

My stomach tightened. Poor Shane. He had held and cried for a stranger. I was sickened for this wolf's family. If they didn't find her body, they would never have closure.

I jerked my arms. "So what's your plan now? Now that Dot's spell is wearing off, are you going to kill me?"

"Why would I kill my favorite daughter?" Beside him, Ivy winced. All this time, she had been quiet and avoided looking at me. "No, we'll replicate the spell. Dot is out now, but she'll be back in a couple of hours."

Couple of hours. Speaking of which, how long had it been since we had left the mountain? I looked out the window, but from here, I couldn't see much besides the brightness of the sunlight. Which meant it was probably later in the day.

"So I'm supposed to just wait?" I tried but couldn't erase the bark in my words.

Paimon sighed. "I know you're mad at me right now, but don't worry. Dot will work her magic and you won't remember a thing. We'll be a happy family again." He glanced at his phone. "I have a meeting I need to attend, but Roman should be back soon with your lunch." He smiled at me. "I'll see you later." He squeezed Ivy's shoulders and walked out of the sitting room.

I stared at Ivy, not sure how to feel, but not being able to stop the anger and outrage brewing inside me.

"So telling me I was your best friend was a big fat lie."

She finally lifted her blue eyes to meet mine. "I'm sorry," she whispered. "I'm so sorry. About everything." She stood. "Sometimes I wish he had erased my mind too. It would have been much easier."

I gaped at her as she walked away.

What the hell did she mean?

ALONE IN THAT SITTING ROOM, I forced the panic rising inside of me to surface. I couldn't break down now. I had to do something. If I stayed here, Dot would erase my mind. Again.

I looked around, trying to recognize the place. But Ivy had said we weren't at the mansion, and I hadn't been here before, unless they had erased that from my mind too.

The sitting room was dark and gloomy with old velvet couches, rugs, and dark wood-paneled walls. A door was nested in the wall near the back, probably from where Paimon had come through when I was talking to Ivy. The three long windows in the room only showed the green of some trees and nothing more.

But there had to be a way out of here.

I looked down at my hands and forced my wrists apart. The rope bit down on my skin, but didn't budge. I tried again, this time calling my darkfire to aid me, but only a flicker answered. Were these ropes magic repellent? That was the only explanation I saw.

Still, I tried again.

And nothing.

I could hop to the window and see what was out there. I would probably fall on my face and worm my way there, but it was better than waiting for my doom.

I stood, and promptly sat down as the door across the room opened and Roman walked in, a silver tray in his hands. He closed the door with his foot and walked toward me, a small smile on his lips.

Anger seethed in me. This man had helped Nortrix and Paimon. He had sent Shane to his death, and brought me here to play lab rat to Dot and her spells.

He sat beside me and I scooted to the other corner of the couch, glaring at him.

He sighed and put the tray on the table in front of us. "Raika, I know you're mad at me right now, but you won't be. Dot will spell your mind again." He reached for me. "We'll go back to being a cou—"

"We're nothing!" I slapped his hand away. "Don't touch me!"

Another memory came back to me. Roman in my house when the demons attacked. He tried getting my mother and me out, and ended up being thrown across the room. I thought he had died, and I had felt sad.

"I thought you were my friend," I whispered.

The gleam in his eyes changed. Hardened. "I don't want to be your friend. I've been waiting for you to see me for at least five years, but you haven't! I was always a friend to you, and I was fucking tired of it!"

"If you really cared about me, you would have let me go."

"I thought I could, I swear I did, until I saw you and Shane exchanging glances. The more I paid attention, the stupider I felt for not seeing it before. All the stolen glances, the almost touches, the way he spoke to you, the way he included you in everything. Now I know why he wanted to promote your rank in the pack." He shook his head. "The guy who had always been such a jerk to you was your fucking mate? I couldn't stand it."

"So, now you're the jerk? You're the one playing with me? Don't you see how wrong this is?"

He clenched his teeth and reached for the tray. "It won't be. Soon, Dot will fix this."

I stared at him, my face slack.

Bits and pieces of images rushed in my mind now, of

Roman being by my side since forever. He had always been there for me. He had tried making my life less miserable. And now, he was ruining everything.

Roman grabbed the tray and placed it on his lap. "You should eat something." He grabbed the utensils and cut the chicken pot pie.

How could he sit here and pretend everything was fine?

I lunged at him, grabbed the knife from the tray before flipping it on top of him. I reached down and half-cut, half-tugged the ropes free from my ankles. I smiled when they snapped, and I could move my feet.

Before I could use the knife on the ropes around my wrists, Roman put the tray aside and glared at me. "You want to play dirty? Then I'll play dirty too." I shot up and ran to the other side of the room. "I'll tie you to a chair and gag you until Dot comes back and spells you!"

He came after me.

I dashed out of the room, and into a large basement with cement floors. A long, foldable table and several chairs stood to the left, a rickety desk with two monitors and electronics to the right, and several hanging naked lights. What was this place? I didn't care, as long as I got out of here.

A set of stairs leading up were along the farthest wall. I ran to it.

A door to the side opened, and Ivy and Rotgar stepped out.

"Raika? Wait!" Ivy yelled.

I didn't stop. A second later, I ran into a darkfire wall and fell back, hitting my hips and shoulder hard on the rough floor.

I groaned, pushing to my knees.

Roman, Ivy, and Rotgar stood in front of me—Roman

with his hand turned into claws, and Ivy with darkfire in her open palms, and Rotgar with an amused expression on his face, as if he was enjoying this.

"Don't make me use this," she said.

I almost laughed at that. "Why? Don't demons relish hurting others?"

Her eyes softened. "No, we don't."

I faltered, but only for a second. I shot to my feet and ran.

Only to stop once more, frozen in place. "What ...?" I could barely move my lips.

Laughter filled the room as Dot made her way down the stairs. "I heard you've been a naughty girl, but I didn't think you were this naughty." She walked up to me and winked. "I like it."

"When can you do the spell?" Paimon asked from somewhere behind me.

She looked at him. "Give me about an hour to get everything ready."

"You should put her inside a witch's circle before she causes more trouble," Rotgar said.

Dot wiggled her fingers.

I floated in the air until I was right in the center of the room. Dark light shone from the floor as she etched a witch's circle with her magic. She closed her hand and the magic left me. I fell to my knees with a *humph*, pain shooting up my legs, and barely braced myself before I toppled on my face.

"That should contain her," she said, walking away.

A phone beeped and Ivy picked hers up. She glanced at the screen. "He's here."

"I'll go get him." Rotgar ran up the stairs.

He? He who?

Dot disappeared through the door in the back of the

room. Paimon walked to a cabinet behind the couch where I had been seated, and picked up a bottle of whiskey and glasses. Roman followed him, probably in need of a drink. I could use one too.

Ivy paced the room, not far from me.

I pushed to my feet. "Since I'll forget everything anyway, tell me what's going on?"

Ivy stopped pacing. She looked at me, then at Paimon, but he seemed distracted with his drink. Her eyes met mine again. I didn't think she would tell me anything, to be honest, but she surprised me when she took two steps closer and said in a low voice, "Your mate found out where we lived. He was there, faced Paimon, Dot, and Rotgar, and then sent a bunch of demon hunters to get them. Paimon, Dot, Rotgar, and the other demons fled here."

I suppressed a gasp. Shane had done all that. I schooled my features to remain nonchalant. "Where is here?"

Ivy shook her head. "I'm already telling you too much."

"But I will forget everything."

"Exactly, so why bother?" Her voice was soft and sad.

I didn't have an answer for that.

Footsteps echoed from the stairs. Rotgar walked down first, followed by Kaz. The bounty hunter had come back too. What had happened to the dragon, then? And to Shane?

Kaz halted beside Ivy, but Rotgar went to the bar cabinet.

Paimon downed the amber liquid from his glass and marched to the bounty hunter, not too pleased. "I thought I paid you to capture the dragon for me, not to come back empty-handed."

"I didn't come empty-handed." Kaz picked up a shiny, dark dragon scale from his bag and offered it to Paimon. "I've lost the dragon. It seems she moved on to Ontario. I was on my way there when I talked to Ivy."

"He told me where he was going, and I remembered there had been several scales on the mountain," Ivy said. "Since we're on the path to the dragon, I thought it would be a good idea if he brought a scale or two for you, Father, so you can recharge."

Ontario? Where the hell were we?

Paimon turned the scale in his hand. "You brought only one?"

Kaz shook his head. "I brought a bag full. It's upstairs."

Paimon nodded. "Good. However, our timetable seems to have tightened. I'll pay you double what we first agreed if you can capture the dragon in the next twenty-four hours."

Kaz's brows knotted. "I'll do my best. Just ... I'm parched. Do you have water?"

Ivy looked at Paimon. He shrugged. Ivy gestured to where Roman was with a drink in his hand. "Here." She walked past me with Kaz, toward Rotgar and Roman.

As he crossed the witch's circle, Kaz looked at me for a brief moment, his expression hard.

Ivy grabbed a bottle of water from the cabinet and handed it to Kaz. "Thanks."

My eyes shifted to Paimon, who still stood where the others had been, holding the dragon scale in his hands. He smiled, closed his eyes, and inhaled deeply. The dark scale shone for a moment, and then its magic was gone. Paimon exhaled. "This feels—" He dropped the scale. His hands shook, his brows curled down. His eyes met mine, full of anguish.

I took a full step back.

"Father!" Ivy shouted. She ran to him. Paimon fell to his knees. She looked at Kaz. "What have you done to him?"

Kaz didn't answer. Instead, he threw his bag and his crossbow to the side, took off his vest, exposing his chiseled chest, and flexed his arms.

And then he shifted.

He gained at least another foot and his shoulders widened. Tiny dark scales covered his torso and arms, and large, dark webbed wings sprouted from his back.

My mouth fell open.

Kaz was a dragon shifter!

He pushed from the floor, his wings taking him up. He turned his head up, opened his mouth, and a thin jet of fire raced to the ceiling. It exploded with a boom, the wood and concrete pieces falling to the floor.

Then four people jumped in.

20

SHANE

EVELYN, ASH, ARIELLA, AND I JUMPED THROUGH THE HOLE. WE landed on the floor in the basement and I found Raika in the witch's circle. Her eyes met mine and the recognition in them brought relief to my muscles. They hadn't recast the spell yet. She hadn't forgotten what had happened in the tunnels and in the goblin village.

She might not remember everything yet, but I knew she was remembering more and more.

"Watch out!" she shouted.

I glanced to the side as Dot ran from a side room, her hands up and dark magic at her fingertips. Evelyn threw her magic at Dot, a huge bolt that hit her in the face, knocking the witch to the side. Dot wasn't down, but she would be dazed for a few seconds.

Ariella sent bolts of light at Ivy, Rotgar, and Paimon, but Ivy raised a wall of darkfire in front of them both. Ariella increased her attack.

Kaz turned to Roman, who had shifted and lunged at the dragon shifter. Kaz dodged Roman's attack, taunting him.

When Ariella told us her plan—to have Kaz call Ivy and say the dragon had moved to another state and he had a gift for Paimon, a gift with magic that would counteract his dark one and weaken him—we all agreed to it. Kaz called Ivy and she didn't hesitate to tell him where they were hiding, and to my surprise it wasn't even that far away: an abandoned office building on the outskirts of Montreal.

When hashing out the plan, Kaz revealed what he was. We were all in shock. We had all thought dragons and dragon shifters were extinct, and now we were seeing both.

"We aren't extinct," Kaz said, "but we were close to it."

I gawked at him. He was impressive. His frame had enlarged, his skin had become tiny scales, and his wings ... by the moon, they were huge and dark.

Kaz threw Roman to the side. The wolf shifter flew through the air and slammed into the wall. He fell to the floor with a whimper and didn't get up.

I watched for a second, trying to feel a little remorse since he had been one of my wolves, but I couldn't. Roman had betrayed not only Raika and me, but the entire pack. He had turned to our enemy and aided him.

That was unforgivable.

"Evelyn, now," I said through gritted teeth.

The witch grabbed vials from her bag and threw them at the witch's circle. The glow from the circle faded. Raika reached forward; she gasped when she stepped through it.

I couldn't contain myself. I ran to her. To my surprise, she met me halfway. She wrapped her arms around my neck, and I held her tight against me. By the moon, how good it felt to have her back with me.

I held on to her while the others fought the battle.

Dot was up again, and Evelyn and Ash battled her. Before

coming here, I had told them I wanted Dot alive, if possible. She was the only one who could break my damn curse, and I needed her. I saw as Evelyn struggled to rein in her anger and not fire any killing blow, while Dot didn't hold back.

Evelyn flung a vial at Dot. It fell at her feet, breaking the glass, and a dark cloud of smoke enveloped Dot. When the smoke was gone, Dot had fainted to the floor. Evelyn and Ash secured her arms and legs with magical ropes, so she wouldn't be able to escape.

On the other side of the room, Ariella's magic and Kaz's fire broke through Ivy's shield, but Rotgar brought another one up. Ivy and Rotgar grabbed Paimon's arm and helped him up. The three of them ran to a side door and disappeared through it. The shield fell and Ariella dashed to the door.

"It's locked," she yelled. She brought her hands up to blast it.

"No," Raika said, her voice faint. But Ariella heard and stopped. "I ... Please, don't. Not yet. I ... I have to work through my feelings, but there's one thing I know: Ivy isn't as bad as she seems. I don't want to hurt her."

Ariella looked at me. Ivy and Rotgar had taken Paimon to the rest of his demon gang who had been hiding in this abandoned building. If we went after him, we would have to face them all, and right now, all I cared about was taking Raika from here. And Dot too. We couldn't lose Dot.

I nodded.

Evelyn ran up the stairs. "I can hear the demons coming this way. We need to go. Now." She and Ash were the first to leave.

Kaz picked up a limp Dot in his arms and went up next. Ariella followed.

I offered my hand to Raika. When she took it, my heart squeezed. We glanced at where Roman was on the floor.

"I can hear his heartbeat," I said, a little annoyed he was still alive.

"Leave him," she said. "He lost his bargaining chip with Paimon, and now he's packless. Being a lone wolf will be punishment enough."

She was right, of course.

Holding hands, we left this damn place.

ASH SPED AWAY from the building and drove at top speed for at least two hours. As soon as we left, I called Doreen and let her know where we had seen Paimon and that he was weak, thanks to Evelyn's weakening spell. Though, it wouldn't last long.

When the sun was setting, he stopped the car a spot away from their car, in the parking lot of a busy mall in north Vermont.

We all stood between both cars.

I extended my hand to Kaz. "Thank you for helping us."

Kaz shook my hand with a firm grip. "My pleasure."

"Good luck with the dragon," Ariella said.

We also hugged and thanked Evelyn and Ash, who wanted to help Kaz with the dragon.

The three of them hopped into the other car and drove away. I knew this wouldn't be the last time we saw them. It never was. The supernatural world had a way of pushing everyone together at one point or another.

"Ready to go home?" I asked Raika.

"Ready to recover all my memories," she said, her tone a little quiet.

We returned to the car—me behind the wheel, Raika in the passenger seat, Ariella in the backseat, and Dot in the trunk.

As I peeled away from the parking lot, Dot stirred and screamed through the gag over her mouth.

"On it." Ariella twisted in her seat and let a few drops of the potion Evelyn had given us fall over the dark witch. Instantly, Dot fainted and quieted down. "So much better."

I drove the rest of the way mostly in silence, though I kept stealing glances at Raika. I still couldn't believe she was right here with me, in the flesh. I felt as if I would blink, or stare for too long at the road, and then she would disappear. Poof. Gone, like a dream.

At some point, Ariella closed her eyes, and I knew she wasn't really sleeping, but I took that as the opening I was waiting for.

I glanced at Raika and asked, "What have you remembered so far?"

21

RAIKA

I looked at Shane from across the seats. "Not much."

Another memory came rushing to me. When we were driving back from somewhere, I didn't know where. We had argued, and he was mad at me, or I was mad at him, but we weren't talking. And then wolves with white marks flipped the truck and attacked us. Shane turned into the Shadow Wolf and killed them all. After that, we embraced and whatever problem we had had was gone.

By the moon, how I wanted to remember it all right now. It hurt to look at this beautiful man, feel so many things stirring inside me, feel the tug of the mating bond, but not being able to remember everything we had lived through together.

I knew not everything would be good, but I knew that with him by my side, I could endure it all.

I reached across the seat and slipped my hand in his. One corner of his lips tugged up. He intertwined his fingers with mine and brought my hand up. He placed a soft kiss on the top of my hand, then rested our hands on his leg.

I liked this.

I liked him.

A little while later, Shane let go of my hand and called someone using the truck's Bluetooth system.

"Hey, Killian, it's me."

"You fucking bastard!" Killian shouted. "I've been texting, calling, and you decided to ghost me? If it weren't for Rue and Dom, I would have sent the entire DuMoir army after you!"

"Glad to know you care."

Killian let out a string of curses. "Next time I see you, I'll kill you."

"I'll let you punch me. We'll arrive in a little over thirty minutes."

"We?"

"Yeah, Ariella, me, Raika, a—"

"Wait. Did you say Raika?"

Shane looked at me. "Yes, my Raika."

"How—?"

"I'll explain everything when we arrive, but I wanted to tell you, I'm bringing Dot too."

The line went silent. "I'll get a cell ready for her."

"Thanks." Shane let out a long breath. "Killian, don't tell my pack or my family we're back. We need to do a few things before they know."

"All right, I won't tell anyone. I'll be waiting for you at the castle's main entrance."

"See you soon." He hung up and glanced at me. "Ready to have your memories back?"

My stomach tightened. "I can't freaking wait."

THE CASTLE WAS MAGNIFICENT, made of stones and with turrets and balconies. Wide stone stairs led to dark wooden doors that had to be at least sixteen feet tall.

Killian waited for us right before the giant doors, along with a few others. Shane killed the engine and Ariella opened the car's door. "I'll go ... talk to them."

Shane nodded. Ariella left, closed the door, and walked to the others.

Shane asked me, "Do you remember anyone here?"

I looked at them again, all lined up to welcome us. I shook my head. "No one."

"You'll remember everyone, but still ..." He pointed to the line of people standing outside, their eyes all on me even though they attentively listened to Ariella, the shock apparent in their faces. "In the center are Killian and Lavinia, our good friends. Then there's Thea and Drake to their right, and Almae to their left."

A new memory popped in my head. Of me naked after fighting a demon and the three witches—Lavinia, Thea, and Almae approaching me. Almae put a jacket on my shoulders, then left with Thea to free the pack, while Lavinia and I went back to Shane.

"I saw the witches in a memory," I told him.

He smiled at me. "You're remembering more and more, but we'll fast track that."

The car shook and a muffled scream came from the back. Dot had woken up. Ariella opened the trunk and pulled her out. Drake snapped his fingers and a group of vampires surged from the corners of the building—holy moon, they had been there the entire time?—grabbed the witch by the arms, and carried her inside the castle.

"Ready?" Shane asked.

I wasn't, but that was beside the point. I nodded. Together, we exited the car and I felt like I had stepped onto a stage to sing and had lost my voice. Everyone was looking at me, especially Lavinia, Killian, and Almae, as if they were seeing a ghost.

Thea came forward. "Welcome to DuMoir Castle, Raika. Ariella told us you don't remember much. That must be confusing and a little terrifying, but don't worry. We'll fix it right away." She gestured to the large double doors of the castle. "Come with me."

Wishing I could shrink into myself, I followed her through the immense castle's foyer and large hallways, until we arrived at what looked like a sunroom.

"This is where Thea and the others make their potions," Shane said from behind me. I was glad he hadn't left me alone. Right now, he was the one I knew the most.

Thea pulled out a stool from under one of the long tables and patted the top. "Sit here, please."

I hesitated, but sat down. Almae and Lavinia grabbed chalk from the table and started drawing a circle around me. I tensed.

For a quick second, I panicked. What if this was the spell? What if these supernaturals had messed with my memory, and made me believe things that weren't true? Who should I trust? Who was telling me the truth?

I looked at Shane. He held my stare, his chocolate eyes so sure and proud ... the feeling in my chest tugged hard.

Him.

I could trust him. Now and forever, he would never lie to me, not on purpose. I knew that surely as I knew I could read and write even though I didn't remember being taught how.

I relaxed a tiny bit.

"Don't worry," Almae said. "We're here to help you."

With the circle closed, the witches stepped outside the white line and joined hands.

"Ready?" Thea asked.

Not trusting myself to speak, I nodded. Then I lifted a hand. "There's one more thing. Paimon told me Dot numbed the bond's magic too." I looked at Shane and he was fuming. "They thought I would break free if I could feel the bond."

"We'll break that one too," Almae said.

The witches chanted something I couldn't understand, their voices low, but strong. Magic sparked from the white line and rose into the air like small white fireflies.

The hair on my arms rose and the magic enveloped me. I gasped as it reached inside me. It started as an odd sensation, but as it reached my head, it expanded, and it hurt.

I closed my eyes and groaned.

"What's going on?" I heard Shane asking.

"Stay back," Killian warned him. "Trust them."

The magic rummaged through my mind, like a bird flying through a thick forest, fast and sharp and true. It poked and prodded, making me dizzy. A sudden pang cut through my skull—they found it. The spell. Broken and faint, but still there. Both magics warred for space, for control, for my sanity.

I fell to my knees and gasped for air as the pain increased.

"Raika!"

"It's almost done," someone said, their voice strained.

Another thread of magic wrapped around my heart and prodded at the strings that pulled me to Shane. They swirled around them, cleaning them up.

A second later, the spell exploded, sending pain irradiating everywhere. I think I blacked out for a moment, because when I blinked, I was on the floor, and everyone was over me.

Shane put his arms under my back and helped me sit up. "Are you okay?"

I closed my eyes and let it all quiet down for a moment. There was no pain; there were no magical war in my mind. "I think—" I gasped as the memories flooded my mind and I suddenly remembered everything.

"What is it?" Shane asked, his voice pained.

"I ..." I stared at him, tears in my eyes. "I remember."

He let out a long sigh of relief.

Thea smiled at me. "I'm glad it worked." She ushered everyone out of the room. "Let's give them a moment. They will find us later when they are ready."

"That will be tomorrow," Killian muttered.

"Or next week," Lavinia added.

As they walked out and left us alone, I smiled at Shane. But I couldn't stop all the emotions and memories swimming in my mind. It was like I was seeing a replay of all the big moments of my life, feeling it all again in fast succession, and I couldn't stop it.

Minsi's tenth birthday, her kidnapping, being with Shane in that fissure, the bond snapping, the demons attacking, my mother dying, the pack burning, Shane leaving ...

And more recently, when Nortrix brought Paimon to the pack lands, the dragon woke up and attacked us, and Roman taking my hand and pulling me to the side with the pretense of saving our lives. But he had hand delivered me to Paimon.

"My dear daughter," he had said. "Everything will be all right."

And then I blacked out and woke up in his house—no,

Ivy's house—and they told me lies on top of lies, and I believed them all.

I pressed my hands to my face, wishing I could erase the last two weeks from my mind forever.

"Hey." Shane wrapped his hands around my wrists and pulled my arms down. "Don't hide from me."

"I can't believe I forgot you." My voice broke.

"But you didn't. Not really. When I was there with you, you knew who I was." A tear escaped and Shane wiped it away with his thumb. "Even if you didn't remember me, you knew who I was in here." He pressed his finger on my chest, right where my heart was.

A sob rose in my throat. "And you thought I was dead." Dear moon, if it had been the opposite. If I had thought he was dead ... I didn't know what I would have done. I would have died with him.

"That was actually the second time." His lips turned upside down. "I don't recommend it." I punched him in the shoulder. "Ouch. I'm serious! Please, don't scare me again. I can't take it."

I knew what he meant.

And I wanted him to know that.

22

SHANE

Raika crawled on my lap, pushing her ass right into my thighs, and wrapped her legs around my waist. She cupped my face and leaned into me. A growl escaped my lips as I wound my arms around her back and met her halfway.

Dear moon, I still couldn't believe she was here. She was alive and with me, with her memories back, and her love for me too.

Holding on to her, I moved and took her down. She lay on the hard floor and for a moment, I looked at her. Her long, wavy black hair formed a halo around her, and her bright blue eyes shone like the stars. She bit down on her lower lip, reaching for me. Damn, she was gorgeous. I pressed my body to hers. I didn't even care where we were, who might see us. I just needed her, and I needed her now.

I kissed her again and moved my hips. Raika gasped. She wound her legs around my waist, tugging her feet on my ass. I smiled against her lips, glad to see she wanted this as much as I did.

I broke the kiss and reached for my chest. These clothes needed to come off right now.

The castle shook and Raika stiffened. "What was that?"

I pushed up on my arms and looked down at her. "It's probably Aurora."

"Who?"

"Drake and Thea's seven-year-old daughter. She's a half-vampire, half-witch, and powerful. She has been having night terrors, and each time she does, she sends ripples of magic through the castle."

She frowned. "Poor thing."

"Yeah, but—" I snapped my head to the side. Rapid footsteps crossed a nearby hallway. "Something is wrong." I shot up, took Raika's hand in mine, and helped her up. She landed in my arms. I leaned into her and brushed my lips on her. "We'll continue this later."

Pink spread over her cheeks. "I'm counting on that."

I growled and kissed her one more time. Dear moon, I loved when she said that. Still holding her hand, I guided us through the castle's hallways. Raika looked around as much as she could, taking the splendor of the place in. We arrived at a side corridor, where a handful of vampires gathered around.

Prince Cain and Lyra saw us coming and turned to us.

"Shane," Cain said.

"What is going on?"

"It's Dot," he said. "She got loose when we were taking her down to the dungeons, and she spelled some of our own to attack each other."

"What? Where's she now?" I asked, my voice tight.

"Queen Thea and Almae sedated her," Lyra said. "She's in

her cell, inside a witch's circle. Even so, Thea plans on keeping her sedated."

I frowned. "But if she's sedated, she can't break my curse."

"It won't be much." Thea walked out of a door to our left. "It's enough so she can't use her magic against us."

"She'll need her magic to break my curse."

Thea nodded. "Yes, and when that happens, we'll prepare a safe space and take all the necessary precautions."

My grip on Raika's hand tightened. This didn't sit well with me. "Is it safe to go down there now?"

Thea nodded. "I had to knock her out for her to stop and to properly secure her, but she just woke up. Still dazed, but you should be able to talk to her."

She stepped aside and let us pass.

We crossed through the doorway and into another long corridor. Two vampires stood at the end of the corridor where a set of stone stairs led down. They nodded as we walked past them and down the stairs. At the end of the stairs, two other vampires stood guard. A thick wooden door greeted us a few feet from the stairs. One of the two vampires guarding the door opened it for us, then promptly closed it behind us. Another long corridor stretched in front of us, though this one was lined with wooden doors with small openings on the top. Toward the back, the doors changed into ones made of bars, and Dot was in one of them.

She was seated crisscross in the center of the medium-sized cell, a white witch's circle around her, and bright blue cuffs around her wrists.

She lifted her head, her long dark hair spilled from her face, and smiled at us. "Shane! Raika! You've come to see me!" Her words were slurred, and her head and shoulders swayed to the side. "To what do I owe this pleasure?"

"Cut the crap, Dot," I barked. "You'll undo my curse."

"Oh, the curse." She nodded. "Riiight. Hm, but that's such a fun curse. I haven't seen it in action in months. Tell me, how many people have you killed in your Shadow Wolf form?"

I clenched my hands into fists. "You—"

Raika placed a hand on my chest. "Just do what he says, Dot."

Dot turned her heinous grin to Raika. "Little wolf, I—"

Rage surged in me. "Do not talk to her!"

Dot's eyes shone with amusement. "Is that anger I hear in your voice? Hm, I actually can see it. That's fabulous. I would love to see the Shadow Wolf right now."

I took a deep breath, trying to calm down. I wouldn't give her the satisfaction of seeing me losing my shit. "Here's the deal. You will break my curse one way or another. Option one, you can break my curse nicely, or option two, I'll torture you, like you tortured me, until you agree. I'll make you wish you had agreed sooner."

She stared at me blankly. "You don't scare me."

A growl rose from my throat. I leaned the bars and barked, "You should be scared."

Her smile widened and I suppressed a shudder. She was insane, like all the other Nightmist witches I had met.

Without any more to say to her, I held Raika's hand and marched out of the prison.

Once we were outside the castle, Raika tugged at my arm. "Are you okay?"

"I'm great," I said, my voice high. I let out a long sigh. "I really am great, though. You're here with me, unharmed and whole, and we have Dot. Soon, she'll break my curse, and everything will be fine." Or almost everything. There was still

Paimon for us to deal with. I frowned. "How about you? Are you okay after confronting her?"

Raika's shoulders drooped. "I'm ... I don't know. While I was with them, Dot was like a cool, crazy aunt. If only I had known she was spelling my mind so I couldn't remember anything, and muting the bond." Raika shook her head. "I was so naive."

"Hey." I cupped her face. "You're not naive. You didn't know anything and you did the best you could."

She rested her head on my hand. "I'm just glad I'm back beside you."

"I second that." I leaned into her, pressing a soft kiss on her forehead. "Now let's get you home."

23

RAIKA

It was so late, but Shane said certain things couldn't wait. So, as we walked from the castle to the village, he called Dom and let him know we were coming.

"We?" Dom asked, confused. His voice was faint to my ears, but I still could hear it.

"Yeah," Shane said. "Just get Minsi and Tyren up, if they are sleeping. And call Lucille. She'll be mad at us if she misses this."

"Man, you're scaring me."

Shane's lips curled up and his eyes met mine. "It's a good thing, Dom. A wonderful thing. Just get everyone together at my house. We'll be there soon."

He turned the call off and pulled me closer to him, with his heavy arm around my shoulders. I liked this.

As we approached the village, my heart beat faster and my hands dampened. I hadn't seen them in a little over two weeks, but during that time, they had all been erased from my mind. I had forgotten all we had lived through together and how much they meant to me.

I never wanted to forget any of them again.

Shane kissed the top of my head. "You're tense."

"I'm nervous."

"Why? You're going to see your family. They love you."

"Not because of that, but ..." I let out a long sigh.

Shane halted, making me stop with him, and faced me, his hands on my shoulders. "Raika, what is it?"

I looked at his beautiful face, at the sharp angles of his chin and jaw, his deep chocolate eyes, looking at me with so much worry. If I could etch them into my mind forever and nothing, no one could ever erase them.

I was so afraid of losing him in any way, but it was a special kind of horror to be alive and not remember him at all.

"I don't want to forget anything again," I said in a whisper. My throat closed. "I don't want to forget you."

Shane wrapped his arm around my waist and pulled me flush to him. He buried his head in my hair and held me tight as I let one stubborn tear escape my eyes. I splayed my hands on his shoulder blades, as if I could keep him like that forever.

"I'm so sorry you had to go through this, my love," he whispered, his lips brushing my neck, sending a shiver down my back. "As your mate, it's my responsibility to protect you, to not let anything happen to you, and I failed. That knowledge kills me."

I pulled back and stared into his eyes. "Shane, it wasn't your fault. We had too many enemies, too many things going against us, it was impossible to fight it all."

He nodded. "That might be true, but I still failed." He cupped my face. "It killed me. To lose you again. I only hung on because of my siblings, because of the pack."

I clutched his shoulders. "I'm glad you didn't do anything stupid, or you wouldn't have found me."

He let out a hollow chuckle. "I did something stupid. I abandoned the pack to go after Paimon."

"And yet, you found me."

A corner of his lips curled up. "That was fate guiding me to you because we're meant to be together. We are made for each other."

I rose on my tiptoes and pressed my lips to his. He pulled back. "Hey!"

He chuckled. "I want to say something else." He ran his thumb over my cheek. "I love you, Raika. You're the most important thing in my life, and I'm so sorry I let you down. I promise you, I'll do my best so it never happens again."

My eyes brimmed with tears. "One, you didn't let me down. Two, you saved me. And three, I love you too." This time, when I went for him, he moved for me too.

His lips captured mine and I surrendered to him. I was his, now and forever. I wrapped my arms around his neck and melted into him as he deepened the kiss. His big, warm hands snaked around my waist and a low rumble started in his chest.

Something vibrated between us. Shane broke the kiss and grabbed his phone from his pocket.

"A text from Dom asking what is taking so long." He lifted an eyebrow.

I smiled. "You shouldn't have told them to get together now. We should have gone into your room, where I could enjoy your hot body." I skimmed my hands down his chest and stomach. Shane groaned. "And then tomorrow, we could have called them all for breakfast."

He waved his phone at me. "I can arrange for that right now."

I slapped his side, and he made a pretend-hurt face. "They probably woke up Minsi and Tyren for this. You won't send them back to bed now."

"Damn, I know." Still, he leaned into me and kissed me again. He moved his lips against mine, slow and deep, savoring every little bit of this slice of heaven. He groaned and broke the kiss. "I better stop now before I push you to those trees—" He jerked his chin to the tree line marking the forest entrance. "—and take you right now."

"I wouldn't be opposed to that."

He groaned again. "You're not making it easy."

"What can I do? I like seeing how much you want me."

"You have no fucking idea." He entwined his fingers with mine, brought my hand to his lips, and kissed the top. The strings around my heart tugged hard. "Now let's go before I lose control."

Hand in hand, we walked the rest of the way. The village came into view and I took it all in—several old-style houses lining a square grid with cobblestone streets. Streetlamps and lights from house porches illuminated the village at this time of night. A lake made a thick C around the village. Beyond the lake was a winery, but half of it had been destroyed years ago.

I glanced up at the moon, half-hidden behind fast moving clouds. It was almost full, and if Dot didn't agree to break Shane's curse, we would soon have to lock him in a cell.

I didn't want that for him.

Shane steered us into the manicured front yard of one of the bigger houses I had seen in the village so far. We could see lights on through the window. As we approached the front door, my heart squeezed.

The door flew open and Dom stared at me, his eyes huge. "What the ...?"

Before I could step into the house, Minsi and Tyren appeared beside Dom. Behind them were Rue and Lucille.

"Oh my heart," Rue whispered.

But my attention was on Minsi and Tyren. The teenager's face paled and he went completely still, while the younger girl started trembling from head to toe. She scooted back, her breathing coming in shallow gasps, her hands coming to her face.

The first signs of a panic attack.

I let go of Shane's hand and rushed inside the house. "It's okay, pretty girl." I wrapped my arms around her and pulled her to me. "It's really me. I'm here, and I'll take care of you." I pulled back and bent down at the waist so I could look at her at head-level. "Take a deep breath." She didn't do it right away. "Come on, follow me. Like this." I demonstrate it. She inhaled deeply, her breathing interrupted by gasps. As she exhaled, her gaze locked on mine, tears brimmed in her eyes. "Oh, sweetheart." I wiped the tears away and embraced her again. "I'm so sorry for scaring you."

Her face pressed on my chest and she clutched at my clothes, as if afraid I would disappear again. I held on to her and looked around the room. Rue, Lucille, and Dom looked at me as if I were a ghost, but wonder filled their eyes.

"Hi," I mouthed.

Tyren though stared at me as if I was a nightmare. "How is this possible?"

"It was one of Paimon's many tricks," Shane said. He told

them a quick version of how Paimon faked my death, erased my memories, and played with us all.

"I thought you would be happy to see me," I said to Tyren.

"I am, but ..." He gulped.

"Just come here." I hooked one hand around his neck and pulled him to me. He didn't resist. He melted into me, one hand around me, the other around Minsi. A whimper came from his throat, letting me know what he couldn't say with words.

I looked at Shane and he had such a bright, satisfied gleam in his eyes, it warmed my heart.

Lucille clapped her hands. "This calls for a celebration!" She ran into the kitchen.

Rue gasped. "We need food!" And she ran after Lucille.

Dom gestured toward them. "I'll just ... yeah." He went to the kitchen with Rue and Lucille.

Shane stepped into our embrace. The four of us, together. Forever.

"I love you all," I said, my voice breaking.

"Damn, you beat me to it," Shane said with a chuckle. "I was about to say it."

"I love us too," Minsi said.

I stilled. Shane looked at me with wide eyes. She never said anything! This was amazing! I laughed.

"Ditto," Tyren mumbled.

I tightened my hold on all of them, wishing that fate would be kinder to us and would never take them away from me again.

WHEN WE REALIZED the get together was quickly turning into a party, Shane texted Killian, who showed up with Lavinia. Now that I remembered them, we hugged, and Lavinia told me with tears in her eyes that she was glad I was back.

"Oh, I have something for you," Shane said. He grabbed one of the pretty flowers from the mountain and handed it to Lavinia. "I had almost forgotten it, but thought you might like to do some experiments with it, see if you can use it in a potion."

"It's so beautiful." Lavinia held the flower like a precious jewel. "It'll be a shame to destroy it." A wide smile spread over her lips. "But I also can't wait to start!"

Ariella joined the party. I hadn't officially met her until now, but she was a good friend of Shane's, and if he trusted her, then so did I.

Rue cooked and Lucille distributed the booze. There was beer and wine for the adults, and soda for the kids. I asked Rue if she wanted any help, but after hugging me tight, she shooed me from the kitchen every time I checked on her, telling me I should sit down and relax.

I did relax, and I felt loved and happy. I was surrounded by family and friends, and it felt like heaven.

I knew this feeling wouldn't last, so I hung on to it with both hands.

Rue made spaghetti and meatballs, and when she brought it to the table, she apologized for cooking something so simple. She didn't have time to make something more elaborate.

"I love your spaghetti and meatballs," I told her, and it was the damn truth. Everything Rue cooked was perfect.

We all sat around the small table, our arms and legs touching, but as I looked around the table, my heart so full, I wouldn't have traded it for anything. These little moments made life worth living.

I raised my glass high. "To family and friends."

"To family and friends," they all repeated, raising their glasses.

"To having my mate back," Shane said, his eyes on mine. "To being able to face anything with her by my side."

Awws echoed around the table, but I had eyes for Shane right now. He leaned into me, pressed his lips to mine in a soft, barely there peck. My toes curled anyway.

We kept the conversation light and fun during dinner and dessert—ice cream and homemade chocolate syrup. There was no destruction, no dragon, no crazy demon wanting the take the underworld back. There was just us and happiness.

Lucille had one glass too many and started playing "I spy" with Minsi, and even Tyren joined in, forgetting about his video games for once. Shane leaned back in the chair, his arm behind mine, his finger playing with my shoulder, as we watched the game and laughed when Lucille's slurred words sounded something else entirely.

Time stretched and the busy day finally caught up with me. I yawned and after that, everyone formed a line to leave.

"I'm glad you're not dead," Dom said.

"Me too!" Lucille grabbed my arms. "Did you know Shane was very grumpy and lost while you were away? Don't ever do that again!"

I smiled at that. At least she didn't sound jealous or mad that I was his mate, and not her.

Dom put an arm around Lucille's shoulders and took her away.

Next was Rue. "Do you want me to watch the kids tonight?" she asked, one of her eyebrows up in her hairline.

My cheeks flamed. "Hm, I don't think that will be necessary."

"If you say so." She hugged me again. "Get used to this. I'll embrace you many, many times."

"I'm not complaining."

She kissed my cheek then left.

Ariella halted in front of me. "It was nice meeting you, Raika."

"You too," I said. "And thank you for helping Shane."

She shrugged. "Anytime."

Next were Killian and Lavinia.

"Rest up," Killian said. "Or not."

Lavinia elbowed him in the ribs, then she flashed a wide smile at us. "I have a gift for you." She picked up a small flask from her purse and offered it to us.

I grabbed the vial. "What is this?"

"Spill some of it behind your door, on the floor," she said, her voice low. "It'll make your bedroom soundproof." She winked and waved at us. "Bye!"

She and Killian zoomed out of the house with their super speed. They didn't even stay long enough to see as the blood pinked up my cheeks.

Holding the vial, I turned to Shane. "What's with everyone?"

A lopsided grin adorned his lips. "They know we have been apart, and we missed each other."

My blush grew redder, I was sure.

We closed the door and went to the couch, where Tyren was seated, his eyes glued to his phone, as if he wasn't really seeing anything anymore, and Minsi was lying down, her head on Tyren's shoulder.

Shane scooped Minsi up and I helped Tyren up. At

Tyren's bedroom door, I kissed the top of his head. "Good night."

"Night," he mumbled with a yawn. He closed the door, and I heard the bed creak as he fell over it.

I turned and stopped at Minsi's door while Shane deposited her in bed. He tucked her in, kissed her forehead, and silently backed away from the room. He pulled the door until only a small crack was open, then he turned to me.

His gaze darkened and a thrill coursed through me.

Our eyes locked, he stalked to me, one step at a time, and I backed away, matching his slow, sensual rhythm. I entered a room, his, and didn't even bother turning on the lights. Shane came in after me and closed the door. I scooted back until I was beside the window. I drew the curtains, so a little of the moonlight spilled in through the blinds and I could look at him, at the perfection that was this man.

My mate.

He marched to me, but before he could touch me, I brought my hand up, the vial resting in my upturned palm. He got the vial from me, uncorked it, and spilled some of the liquid behind the closed door. A faint humming echoed through the room as a blue light traveled from the door to the walls, and then disappeared.

"Now you can scream for me," he said, his voice rough.

Dear moon ...

He rushed to me, but stopped short. He kept one foot between us, while he stared at me with hooded eyes.

A need hit me—a need to touch *him*, to kiss and be kissed, to be taken this badly—but it consumed me in the moment.

"Kiss me," I whispered, my head in a daze.

Shane didn't waste a second. He stepped into me, and

pressing me against the wall with his palms flat on either side of my head, caging me in, he kissed me. His lips were warm and soft and made of pure honey. I melted into his kiss, parting my lips for him. His tongue sneaked in, teasing mine and ripping a moan from my throat.

He groaned, taking my lower lip between his teeth. "Delicious," he whispered, before taking my mouth again. His hands slid down my waist, down to my thighs, leaving a trail of fire across my body, and all I could do was moan in his mouth.

He hooked his fingers under the hem of my shirt, teasing my skin. I gasped, sinking my nails into his shoulders. He groaned again before splaying his big hands on the back of my thighs and tugging on them. My mind on a cloud of pure delight, I let him pull my legs up, and I was half conscious as I wrapped them around his waist. He thrust his hips against mine, rubbing his erection on me. I moaned again.

His lips trailed down my jaw, pausing at my neck. His labored breathing was all I could hear as he thrust his hips into mine again. Helpless, I moaned once more.

"Fuck, these little sounds ..." He bit the tip of my ear, then slid his hands to my ass and pulled me up against him.

I yelped as he crossed the room and deposited me on his bed. Sliding his hot hands over my skin, he pulled my pants off, revealing my lace panties.

I didn't have time to be embarrassed as Shane pressed his hard-on against my center, and I wished my panties would melt away. But then, he let out a hiss and hooked his fingers on the shoulder straps of my shirt. He tugged them down, enough to give him access to my bra. With agile hands, he unclasped my bra and pulled it out—without taking my shirt off.

Shane dipped his head and ran his tongue over the top arch of my breast. My lips parted. I wrapped my arms around his neck and arched my back. Right now, I would do anything he wanted.

He kept playing with his tongue, running it around my breast, until finally, he flicked my nipples. I bucked, wishing he was inside me. He closed his mouth around my breast, and I melted some more. Holy crap, how could it feel this good?

One of his hands snaked up, wrapping around my free breast. He pinched my hardened nipples and I bucked. Pure heat and pleasure swam through me and I wanted more, more, more.

Feeling bold and sexy, I slid my hands over his chest and found the hem of his shirt. While savoring each lap of his tongue and suck of his mouth, I explored his stomach and chest, always in awe of the muscles I found under his warm skin.

He pushed his hips against me again—I shivered.

Biting my lower lip, I undid the button and zipper of his pants, and slipped my hand inside his boxers. He hissed, his teeth closing around my nipples as I ran my hand over his massive hard-on.

Loving the way he reacted to my touch, I moved my hand up and down, up and down, pushing hard against his shaft. Shane shivered, then he grabbed my wrists, and pulled my hands away.

Straightening, he looked at me. "Keep that up and I won't last. It has been a while, remember?"

Two weeks, but who was counting?

He leaned into me and captured my mouth again. I surrendered to the kiss, melting into his arms, sucked from reality and loving every second of it. I tightened my legs around him, and with my feet, tugged him to me. He let out a small chuckle against my lips as he obliged and thrust his hips against mine, rubbing his hard-on over my center. I threw my head back, breaking the kiss. Shane's lips found my neck and he switched between kissing and nipping at my delicate skin.

He grabbed hold of my shoulders and pushed me down, until my back was flat on the bed. Then he knelt in front of me.

I sucked in a sharp breath. Oh …

Shane slipped off my panties with ease, then trailed small pecks from my ankle, up my knees, to the inside of my thigh. I tensed in anticipation, and my hands flew to his silky hair.

He licked my center, and with a loud gasp, my hips bucked and my back arched off the bed.

"You taste so good," he whispered, before flicking his tongue over my clit again.

His finger slid inside me. Then a second one. I slapped my hands on the bed and curled my fingers around the comforter, trying to hold on before I lost it. Before I melted away. Before the pleasure took over and I became a useless pile of pure bliss.

He pumped his fingers inside me, fucking me with his hand hard and deep. Holy crap, this was so good, so hot, so unbelievable …

"Shane." It was a half-cry, a half-moan. "Please."

He sucked on my clit, hard, and I was done for. Pleasure exploded inside me, sending me in a spiral of heat and bliss. With a low chuckle, Shane licked my center one more time, then stood straight. My mind was a beautiful haze, but I couldn't stop looking at him, gawking at the handsome man before me.

Grabbing my hips, Shane pushed inside me in one quick, fast thrust. I cried as his cock filled me. God, he was big.

In a slow rhythm, Shane worked me up. The pressure built up again, but it was different this time. Deeper, more powerful.

"Fuck," Shane hissed. "This is so good."

Shane pulled off his shirt, wrapped an arm under my back, and pulled me up so I was seated on the bed, my breasts pressed tight against his bare chest. He leaned into me and captured my mouth, as his movements sped and he pushed inside me fast, deep, and hard.

I gasped against his mouth and that only seemed to entice him more. Holding on to me, Shane pumped into my core, drawing out the hidden fire I never knew I had.

"I've missed you," I whispered against his lips.

"Dear moon." He groaned. "I've missed you more."

A wave of pure heat rolled through me and I sank my nails into Shane's back, stilling for a moment before the fire exploded, and I melted away in little quivers.

Shane groaned against my mouth. He pushed into me hard once, twice, three times, then broke out in little trembles.

"Holy fuck," he whispered, leaning his heavy body over mine.

I know, I wanted to tell him, but my mouth couldn't catch up with my dazed brain and numb body.

He propped himself up on his elbows and looked at me. "I love you."

I smiled at him. "I love you too."

24

SHANE

IF IT DEPENDED ON ME, RAIKA AND I WOULD LIVE IN TOTAL oblivion to the rest of the world. But as alpha, I couldn't pretend for long.

After waking up and making love to Raika once more, I forced myself to get up, take a shower—where I dragged Raika with me and took her one more time against the shower wall—and face the day.

With a smile on her pretty face, Raika made us breakfast and when it was time to leave for school and training, Minsi and Tyren both complained about having to go when they wanted to be with us.

"We'll spend the morning at the castle, in boring meetings," I told them. That seemed to do it.

Raika kissed Minsi and Tyren when Rue and Dom came for them.

With a hand over her heart, Raika watched as they walked away.

And I watched her, totally taken aback by her, her kind heart, and her love for my siblings. And for me.

I was totally, irrevocably in love with her.

After organizing the kitchen, I remembered Raika's cell phone. I had kept it, though turned off, so I handed it to her. She chucked the one other she had been given in the trash.

Then, Raika and I made our way to the castle.

I glanced at her, so proud and happy she was by my side. But there were pressing matters we couldn't forget. I squeezed her hand on mine and asked, "Want to talk about Paimon? Or Ivy?"

Raika's brows knotted. "I ... I don't know. I mean, I don't know what to think. I know Paimon was playing with me, but Ivy ..." She shook her head. "She was different. I felt she was really my friend, my sister, while I was there."

I could only imagine. Raika had been an only child, practically isolated from the rest of the pack while growing up because she was the omega and no one wanted her near them. But suddenly, she woke up in a world where she had never been alone. Where she had a sister and a best friend.

And that had been a lie.

"I'm sorry."

"Me too."

"The demon hunters are preparing for a war against Paimon. At some point, we'll have to decide whether we want to help them, or if we want to ignore what is going on." I still wanted to be the one to kill Paimon, but if Raika chose to stay out of it all, I wouldn't force it on her. I would stay by her side, no matter what.

"I know." She sighed. "Right now, thinking about confronting him and Ivy makes me anxious and I honestly don't know how I'll react. But I want to believe that if I prepare myself, I'll be able to act and do the right thing."

"So you want to join the fight?"

She nodded. "I think we should consider it. They'll need all the help they can get, and if they lose, it'll affect all of us."

I tugged her to me and pressed a soft kiss on her head. "My mate is wise."

She elbowed me on my side, but not hard. I still groaned as if she had broken a rib. She laughed and that sound was music to my ears.

Unfortunately, we couldn't live in our own bubble. At the castle, Raika and I went directly to Dot's cell in the dungeon. The guards opened the doors for us without any questions.

The witch was in the same position as last evening, a tray of untouched food by her side.

"Have you changed your mind?" I asked, knowing this wouldn't go well.

She didn't say anything, but I could hear her heartbeat and her breathing—slow and steady. She could be sleeping, but I knew she wasn't.

"I'll give you one more day to do this the easy way," I told her.

Her chest moved, and at first, I thought she was having a seizure, but then a raspy sound came from her throat, and as it grew louder, I realized it was laughter.

Dot threw her head back and cackled. She stopped and stared at me, a sick grin on her dark lips.

I held her gaze, unflinching.

I didn't mind forcing her to help me, but the only way for that was torture, and I wasn't looking forward to that. I was sure as I tortured her, I would relive my past trauma. It wouldn't be pretty. Just thinking about it brought a wave of rage forth, and my Shadow Wolf stirred. I inhaled deeply, trying to remain in control.

After a long while, Dot lowered her head and returned to

her previous pose. Like a motionless, creepy doll.

Holding Raika's hand, I took us out of the dungeon.

Once out in the castle's hallway, Raika asked, "Are you okay?"

"Of course," I scoffed. "Dot is nothing. One way or another, she'll break my curse."

"But the full moon is almost here."

"I know." I could feel it, actually, the pull getting stronger and stronger. From now until the full moon, or until Dot did the spell, the Shadow Wolf would make himself known each time I got mad or frustrated. Which was almost every day.

I guided Raika through the castle's hallway, telling her about some of the rooms we walked past, and what was beyond this corridor and that, until we entered a meeting room across Drake's office.

Killian, Lavinia, and Ariella were already here, along with Dom and most of the DuMoir princes. I introduced Raika to them—Prince Cain, Prince Aston, and Prince Dorian. I told her Prince Gray had left to help the demon hunters in their war against Paimon.

A couple of minutes later, Almae arrived with Elisa and Zadkiel—Elisa was Thea's right hand, and Zad was an angel and Elisa's mate. I introduced them both to Raika.

"How are you feeling, dear?" Almae asked Raika.

"Like myself again," Raika answered with a smile.

Another minute passed before Lord Drake and Queen Thea arrived.

"Please, sit," Drake commanded. Vampires didn't have the same power as wolf shifters when it came to that, but Drake's tone didn't leave any room for arguments.

We all sat down around the long, dark table.

"Before I forget," I started. "Lord Drake, I promised something to the goblins we met at the mountain." I explained the promise to send vampires to check out the demon activity in the mountain and why.

Drake nodded. "You did the right thing." He looked at Aston. "After this meeting, send Lyra with a team to check it out."

"Another test for Lyra?" Killian asked. Once he had told me that to become a prince (or princess), a vampire had to pass many tests.

"Something like that," Drake said. "Now, who can tell me about the demon hunters and Paimon?"

"I've talked to Demon Hunter Norah this morning," Prince Cain started his report. "After Shane encountered Paimon at his house in Vancouver, and later at the building in Montreal, they sent teams to find him, but Paimon and his demons were long gone. However, Doreen and Thierry filled them in about the dragon and why Paimon is after her. They sent a team to either capture or kill the dragon."

"Evelyn and Asher are on it," I spoke up. "They are being helped by a dragon shifter, Kaz. He said there's a place where he can take the dragon, where she'll be safe and Paimon won't find her."

"Where is this place?" Drake asked.

I shook my head. "Kaz didn't tell us. He said he won't."

"It's a sacred place," Ariella added. "Like a refuge for dragons and dragon shifters. I think Kaz might not be able to tell us. Like an oath, or something."

Drake nodded. "Prince Cain, contact the demon hunters and tell them what we know about the dragon. Please, let them know to not harm her."

"Yes, my lord," Cain said.

"When we fought Paimon yesterday, I tricked him with

my light magic," Ariella said. "It weakened him, but that won't last long. If we can find him today or tomorrow and fight him, we'll have a better chance of defeating him."

"The best demon hunters are out there tracking him," Drake said. "Soon, we'll hear news about his capture."

I felt Raika stiffen in the chair beside me. I frowned.

"Shouldn't we send another team to aid them?" Killian asked.

Drake seemed to consider that. "Prince Gray is already on site with the demon hunters. He'll let us know if more help is needed. For now, everyone stay put and go on with your normal routine."

With that, the meeting was over. Everyone got up. Some left the room right away, others mingled and talked.

Killian, Lavinia, and Ariella joined Raika and me.

"I'm leaving," Ariella announced.

"Where are you going?" Lavinia asked.

"To join the demon hunters and go after Paimon." She shrugged. "It's not like I have anything else to do."

A part of me wanted to join her. I still wanted to hurt Paimon for what he did to Raika and me, but with the full moon approaching, it would be easy for me to lose control. Besides, I had to take care of my pack. Now that Raika was here and Paimon would be dealt with soon, I had to think of what was next for my pack.

"Good luck," I told her.

We accompanied her to the underground garage, where she borrowed a car, and we said goodbye to her.

"Sometimes I pity her," Lavinia said. We stood at the garage's entrance, watching as Ariella's car turned into a small dot on the long road.

"Why?" Raika asked. "What happened to her?"

"From what I heard, she came from heaven on a mission with a small group of angels. They were ambushed by demons, most of the angels were killed, and Ariella lost her wings. She became a fallen angel, and she can't go back to heaven until she recovers them."

"Can she recover them?" Raika asked.

"I think so, if they weren't destroyed," Lavinia said. "She has been after the demons who attacked her for years now, but they either are good at hiding, or they are all dead. Either way, it seems it'll be impossible for her to get her wings back."

"What happens then?"

"She remains on earth as a fallen angel without her wings."

"Which is why she helps everyone who needs a hand," Killian said. "So she has something to do."

"Lord Drake offered me a place here," I said. "Maybe he can offer her one too? At least it's something for her to do. To occupy her time and mind so she's not obsessing about her wings."

"I heard he already offered," Killian told us. "She's good friends with Farrah and Wyatt, and they offered her titles and positions within the fae court and more, but she has refused it all."

"It seems she likes being a free spirit," Raika said. "Owner of her own destiny."

Lavinia nodded. "It sounds rather mysterious and powerful, doesn't it?"

The car disappeared beyond the bend in the road.

"We should go back." I squeezed Raika's hand. "Will you come back later?" I asked Killian. "I want the council to meet. We should discuss the pack's current situation and what to do next."

Killian frowned. "You're not thinking of leaving, are you? You know that village has been deserted for years. It's all yours if you want to stay."

"I know and I'll bring it up again. I might be the alpha, but my pack's opinion matters to me." I wouldn't repeat my father's mistakes.

"Are you becoming old and wise all of a sudden?" Lavinia teased.

Raika laughed and I glared at both of them.

We agreed to meet and have dinner together later.

On the way back to the village, I texted Dom and told him about the meeting in an hour. Rue asked Lucille to help Vianna with the kids in her place, and Hamill had been notified and ready.

We still had time, so Raika and I stopped at our house.

Our house.

I liked the sound of that.

"Are you hungry?" Raika asked me once we entered the house. She let go of my hand and walked to the kitchen in the back.

"I am, but it's not for food."

She halted and turned to me, her blue eyes shining with mischief. "What do you mean?"

I advanced toward her.

Then froze.

"Raika—"

Someone jumped behind her and wrapped a hand around her throat.

Roman.

Rage surged from within my veins and the Shadow Wolf screamed at me.

"Stay back!" he yelled. His hand shifted into a claw, his

nails pressed along Raika's throat. He wrapped his other arm around her waist and pulled her flush against him.

My vision became a sea of red. "Let her go," I snarled.

"Never!" he shouted. "She goes with me, or she dies right here!"

"Roman, stop this," Raika said, her voice strained. She stretched her neck, trying to avoid his grip, in vain. She jerked against him, but he only tightened his hold. A drop of blood slid down her throat.

"I'm going to kill you." The Shadow Wolf was at my fingertips, and I was having trouble finding a reason not to let it out.

His other arm shifted and his claws pressed against Raika's midriff. "Advance one step and I'll rip her to pieces before you can shift."

"This is insane," Raika muttered. "Roman, you don't want to do this."

"No, I don't, but what other choice do I have?" He took a step back, into the kitchen, putting more distance between us. My body thrummed with the need to shift and pounce at him. "You're mated to him. I lost."

"Just ... let me go and we can talk," Raika rasped. "We can—"

"Shut up!" he yelled.

I looked at Raika. My mate was in the arms of the wolf who betrayed his pack, who helped a higher demon take her away from us, who was aiding this demon and his ridiculous plans of taking back the underworld—all because he wanted to be with a woman who was mated to another.

Fury became a white-hot sea and I couldn't control it anymore.

The Shadow Wolf surged forward.

25

RAIKA

I COULD FEEL IT. THREE SECONDS BEFORE IT HAPPENED, I felt it.

Shane lost control over the Shadow Wolf. He shifted in half a heartbeat and advanced on us.

Roman took several steps back and bumped into kitchen counter. I reached for the first thing I could grab—a frying pan from the cooktop—and swung it at Roman's head.

He let go of me and I dashed to the side as Shane pounced on him. Roman shifted, but it was too late. Shane closed his massive claws around Roman's neck and squeezed. The crunching of bones echoed through the kitchen and my stomach turned.

By the moon ...

He let go of a dead Roman and turned to me. His powerful body in a ready stance, his red eyes shining, his sharp teeth bared and drool gathering at the corners of his huge mouth.

"Shane," I whispered, my voice trembling as much as my hands were.

I had seen him like this several times, and I had felt nervous only the first time, because I didn't know what to expect. He had recognized me then and every time since. But this time, it was different. It felt different. We were two days away from the full moon, and the witches had warned him the Shadow Wolf would start taking over more often until he never came back from it.

He snarled.

"Shane, it's me." With minimal movements, I retreated a step. "It's Raika. Your mate." I lowered my arm and grabbed my phone from my pants' back pocket. Knowing I wouldn't be able to text anyone, or even talk on the phone, I simply pressed the call button and put it on speaker mode. Shane took a step closer and snarled again. "It's okay, Shane."

I put the phone on the counter.

"Hello? Raika?" Killian's voice came from the phone.

Shane let out a growl and rushed toward me. "Help!" I screamed before running out of the kitchen.

Shane skidded on the hard floors, but didn't slow down. I raced through the short hallway to the living room and Shane came after me, bumping into the walls, bending the doorways, and ripping the lights on his way.

I ran to the door then paused. No, I couldn't take him out of here. If I did, then I would put the entire pack in danger. I had to keep him occupied until the others arrived and we could subdue him.

Shit.

I dashed across the room and into the small dining table, putting that in between us. Not that I thought the table would save me from Shane.

I clutched the back of a chair. "Shane, stop it! You know me. Please, remember me."

He growled and jumped over the table.

I gasped and ran, but before I took two steps, he slammed into me. He pushed me against the wall, a big hand on my neck, and lowered his head to mine. He snarled, his hot breath washing over my face.

I whimpered. "Shane, please. It's me. Raika. Your mate." He snapped his teeth an inch from my nose and I swallowed a scream. "I'm so sorry for this."

I pushed my hand into his chest and sent my darkfire into him. Just a small jolt, but enough to make him stagger back and let me go.

He straightened and let out a hair-raising howl.

Shit, I only made him madder.

He rushed me again.

I brought my hands up and threw two darkfire bolts at him, one right after the other. These were a little more powerful than the first one, and Shane skidded back, falling to his knees.

But it didn't keep him down for long.

He pushed to his feet again and let out another piercing growl. He charged—

The door flew open and a blue magical shield appeared between us. Shane slammed into it, but that didn't faze him. He turned to the newcomers, Lavinia and Killian.

Snarling, Shane ran at them.

Lavinia lifted her hands and a blue round wall rose from the floor, trapping Shane within. "Quick," she said, her voice strained. Enraged, Shane clawed at the shield. "I won't be able to hold it for long."

Killian held up a gun and pointed at Shane.

"No!" I screamed.

He squeezed the trigger four times. Shane stumbled. He

growled, but it was a weak thing. Then he folded to the floor. The wall disappeared and I ran to him. Four darts pierced his chest.

"Sedative?" I asked.

Killian nodded. "It was the only thing I could think of to stop him without hurting him."

It was a good idea.

I reached for him. The fur retreated and he shifted back to his human form. Lavinia picked up a throw blanket from the couch and handed it to me. I covered Shane's lower body, then cradled his head and moved so my legs served as his pillow.

I ran my hand over his beautiful face.

Lavinia crouched beside me. "It isn't the full moon yet. What triggered it?"

Killian sniffed the air. "I smell blood."

"In the kitchen," I told them.

Killian and Lavinia went to the kitchen. I heard Killian's loud curse. They came back to the front of the house. "I'll clean this up."

"Wait," Shane said, his voice faint.

I gasped. "You're awake."

He groaned, his eyes still closed. "Lock me up. I can't control it anymore."

His head lolled back, and he fell into a deep sleep.

Killian looked at me.

My eyes filled with tears. "You heard him. Let's clean this mess up and lock him up."

I SAT on the floor in front of the bars dividing the room in half. Shane slept in the bed on the other side, still out because of the sedative. Killian admitted giving him a strong dose because he didn't know how much the Shadow Wolf would require to go down. Now that Shane was back in human form, he would be out cold for hours.

This was the room Killian and Lavinia had made for Shane when they first moved here. Shane had confided in them about his curse, and Killian had gotten Drake's permission to modify the room, without explaining why. Drake trusted Killian, but everyone in the castle knew what went on during full moon. It was hard not to, when he became a massive wolf who wanted to murder everyone on sight.

Including me.

The bars were reinforced with magic, and the windows had the same bars and magic on them. The only door on his side of the room led to the bathroom, which had been stripped to the bare minimum, in case he needed to be locked here while in his human form.

Like now.

After bringing Shane here, Killian and Lavinia went back to the village to clean up the house. We decided not to tell anyone about Roman. The wolves in our pack had already participated in a ceremony to honor his death. If they found out he had betrayed us all, kidnapped me, and then tried to kill Shane and me, he would be cursed for eternity. Better to let them believe he had died weeks ago.

My heart hurt, though. Roman had been a good friend, and I was saddened about how things ended with him.

I couldn't believe all of this was happening. Couldn't Shane and I be two wolf shifters in love and raise our family in peace? Why was there a damn curse, a demon who wanted to destroy the world (or take over the underworld), and more terrible things?

People came in and out of the room to check on Shane and me. Lavinia brought me food and sat down with me for a long time. But I didn't blame anyone for not sticking around. For them, it was boring to watch Shane sleep. For me, it was the only thing that I had to cling to sanity.

I called Rue several times, though, to check on Minsi and Tyren. I facetimed with Minsi twice, but she never spoke. She wanted to hear me talk. I made a mental note to have dinner with them, even if Shane was still sleeping. I couldn't abandon them.

Finally, late in the afternoon, Shane woke up. I heard as his breathing and heartbeat changed right before he turned to his side and opened his eyes.

He sat up with a jerk and looked around, confused. I stood and he looked at me. "What ..." He inhaled sharply. "Roman had you. Then—" He pressed his mouth into a thin line. "I killed him, didn't I?"

I nodded. "For the first time, you didn't recognize me."

His eyes bugged. "I attacked you?"

"I'm sorry I used darkfire on you. It was the only thing I could think of to stop you."

He took slow steps closer to the bars. "Did I hurt you?"

I shook my head. "No, you didn't. I'm fine."

He ran a hand through his hair. "But I attacked you anyway." He clenched his hands.

"Shane, calm down. It's fine, I'm okay. Don't get angry. You'll lose it again."

He seethed, his eyes turning red. "I ... can't ... control it."

He shifted into his Shadow Wolf and ran at the bars with all he had. I jerked back as he rammed into the bars and the magic jolted him back. He growled, a sick noise that gave me goose bumps, and came at the bars again. Once more, the magic sparked to life, shocking him back.

I clamped my hands over my ears as my heart ached.

Shane didn't stop. Like a mindless beast, he kept coming to the bars, getting shocked, and then trying again. Each time, he seemed more hurt, more tired, but he didn't stop.

Arms closed around my shoulders and someone steered me from the room. Once in the hallway, the door was closed with a definite thud, and Shane's growls and howls became a faint echo.

"I'm sorry." Lavinia embraced me. "I wish you didn't have to see him like this."

A sob rose to my throat. "He told me this would happen. The Shadow Wolf would take over." I pushed away from Lavinia. "I won't let that happen."

Wiping at my eyes, I spun on my heels and ran down the hallway. I only stopped running when I was inside the dungeons and in front of Dot's cell.

"All right, bitch, here's the deal," I said. "You will break Shane's curse, right now, or you'll have to deal with me."

I half-expected Dot to ignore me, like she had done with Shane earlier today. In the exact same position from before, Dot lifted her head, her slick dark curls parting a little, revealing a dark eye behind it.

"You? That's the best Shane can do? Send you in his place?" Her lips curled back in a wicked grin. "You're wasting your time, little wolf."

"You've been inside my head and you still underestimate me?" I pushed my hand forward, carrying as much darkfire as I could. My magic wrapped around Dot's neck and lifted her clean off her feet. "Isn't it nice that this cell of yours can neutralize your magic, but not mine?" I squeezed my hand and the witch gasped for air. Her eyes widened and she reached for the hand that wasn't there. "Now, you'll listen to me: You will break Shane's curse right now, or you'll see this is nothing. I'll break you like a sad little doll."

I closed my hand, giving one last squeeze before letting go. She fell on the floor on all fours, panting, her head and shoulders drooped.

A wheezing sound came from her.

It grew louder and I realized it wasn't a wheezing sound.

It was laughter.

Dot sat back and stared at me as she laughed, her shoulders and chest shaking. Her laughter became louder and louder, until it hurt my ears. I fought the urge to press my hands over my ears.

Suddenly, she stopped, but the wicked grin still stamped her lips. "I thought you were my friend, little wolf."

"You were never my friend." If she pretended to care, it was because of their plan to make me more docile, so I wouldn't see all the shit they were doing to me. "You were just helping Paimon."

"Smart girl." She cocked her head. "But you'll need more than that to convince me to help you."

I crossed my arms. "All right. Then tell me, what do you want in return for breaking the curse?"

"What I know you can't promise, because the others will never agree."

"Freedom."

She nodded. "Even if you could promise me that, I know the moment I break his curse, the others will kill me. After all, the only reason I'm still alive is so I can break the curse."

I frowned, the wheels in my mind spinning. I glanced to

the side, to the door at the end of the hallway. It was closed and the two vamps standing guard were on the other side. I wondered if with their hearing, they could hear us.

I cast a wall of darkfire across the corridor. That should do it.

"I can promise you your freedom if I don't say anything to the others."

Dot's eyes widened for a brief second. She schooled her features. "I'm listening."

"I'll arrange to take you to Shane. I don't know when, I don't know how, but I'll find a way and it'll be soon. Be ready."

"And after that?"

I clenched my teeth. "I'll arrange for you to sneak out of the palace before anyone finds out about it. I'll give you your freedom."

She seemed to consider it, her eyes fixed on mine. If she was trying to find the lie in them, she wouldn't.

"You surprise me, little wolf." Her grin broadened. "I'll be ready."

I nodded at her, then marched away from the prison.

Now I had to come up with a damn plan and execute it.

I HAD DINNER WITH MINSI AND TYREN. THEY KNEW ABOUT THE curse, so there was no reason for me to lie about it.

"Shane is losing control," I told them as I prepared a quick dinner. I wasn't in the mood for cooking, but they needed nourishment. "He's locked up at DuMoir Castle right now. But don't worry. The witch will break his curse, and he'll be back here with us."

Minsi's anxiety spiked, but Tyren acted before I could. He grabbed a glass full of ice and handed two cubes to her, so she could hold them in her hands. The difference in temperature helped shock the system and break the cycle. Tyren also took her mind off it by telling her a story while I cooked—a made-up, sweet version of Red Riding Hood where the wolf didn't eat the grandma and he fell in love with Red. If only life were that simple.

After dinner, they helped me clean the kitchen, and we watched an episode of a tv show the two of them were following, my mind elsewhere. When that was done, I put Minsi in bed. I thought Tyren would disappear into his bedroom, but he followed me back to Shane's bedroom.

He halted at the doorway and crossed his arms. "Now tell me what is going on."

Tyren was a teenager, but he wasn't little anymore. In fact, in the past month, he had grown another inch and bulked up. Soon, he would be as tall and strong as his older brother.

I sighed. "I can't tell you."

"Why?"

"Because I promised the witch I wouldn't tell anyone, and I'm a woman of my word." I walked to him, placing a hand on his arm. "But ... trust me. You know I love your brother. He's my mate and I'll never do anything that might hurt him. Or you and Minsi, for that matter. Just go to sleep. Rue will stay with you both while I'm gone. Hopefully, Shane and I will be here for breakfast."

He stared at me, a knot between his brows. "I ... I trust you."

A soft smile spread over my lips. That meant a lot to me. "Go to your bedroom. I'll be back soon."

He looked at me for a moment more, then nodded and went to his bedroom. I changed into all-black clothes and soft shoes and then waited for Rue at the front porch. She didn't ask any questions, or say any word. She took me in, nodded, and went in the house.

I stared at the closed door for a second.

When would the sneaking out, the planning, the attacking, the missions end? Would they ever? I seriously hoped it would. All I wanted was to settle with Shane, Minsi, Tyren, and the rest of the pack, and live peacefully.

That seemed like a faraway dream now.

Not wasting any more time, I put my plan into action.

Late at night, I walked to DuMoir Castle. Though this was a vampire castle, most supernaturals were sleeping now. Shane told me that once upon a time, the vampires slept through the day and were awake at night, but when Drake met Thea and they took over the vampire and witches, Drake changed the castle's schedule to accommodate the witches. He changed their way of life for love. Thea was one lucky woman.

I was too. Shane loved me, and I loved him, and I didn't wish for anyone else. I didn't want anything else. Tonight, this damn curse would be gone, and despite still having plenty of problems to deal with, it would be one big weight off our shoulders.

The vampire guards at the castle's doors let me pass without any problem despite the hour. Inside, the castle was dim, with only a light on here and there. A few patrols roamed around the castle every few minutes, but I wasn't worried about them.

I went directly to Thea's sunroom. I found a wall full of potions and elixirs. It wasn't hard to find the ones I was looking for. I grabbed a few vials, filled the pockets of my vest, and walked toward the prison.

Again, the two guards at the entrance didn't even look at me. But they should have. I put on the enchanted mask over my mouth and nose, picked one of the vials, and threw it at their feet. The smoke rose fast, enveloping them. They fainted and slid to the floor. I hooked my arms around theirs and dragged them inside the corridor, so no one could see a pair of vampire guards knocked out.

I descended the stairs and did the same with the next set

of guards. These ones, though, I didn't bother carrying anywhere. In here, no one would see them.

I walked past them, leaving the door wide open behind me, and halted in front of Dot's cell. "Ready to get out of here?"

Seated in the same position as before, Dot lifted her head, and brought her palms up, the blue shackle still around her wrists. "How?"

I showed her the vial in my hand. I uncorked it and let a few drops fall on the cell's lock. It melted with a sizzling sound. I pushed the bars open and stepped into the cell. I grabbed another vial. Though Dot had the magical shackles cast by Thea, I knew she was a lot stronger than me, and without the circle or other wards around her, who knew what she could do? So I brought some insurance.

I showed her the vial with red liquid. "See this? If you break out of the cuffs, or try anything funny, I'll throw this at you, and this will melt you similar to how the other elixir melted the lock. You won't be able to reverse that. Understood?"

She nodded.

Another flask, another potion. I let it drip over the circle's line. A one-inch section disappeared, breaking the circle.

With a long sigh, Dot rose to her feet and stretched, as best as she could with her hands bound. But I wasn't done.

I stepped into the circle and pressed my hand to her chest, sending a wave of darkfire into her. She wobbled to the side, dazed. "You didn't think I would take you out of here at your full strength, right?"

I hadn't done this before, but when I came up with this plan earlier this evening, I asked Thea, Almae, and Lavinia random questions about magic, as if I wished to understand my darkfire better. I knew their magic was different, but some principles were the same, weren't they? I hoped they were. Otherwise, my plan wouldn't work at all. One of the questions was about how to make someone dizzy enough for a few minutes, and how to break it right after.

I grabbed Dot's arm, bathed us in an elixir to mask our scent and sounds, and guided her out of the prison. She stumbled, too dizzy to do anything else. I timed it right and avoided all patrols while we crossed the castle.

Two guards stood at Shane's door—in case Shane broke out of his magical prison. Once more, I threw an elixir at the guards' feet before they saw us and they fainted. I pushed Dot into the bedroom, let go of her, and dragged the guards inside. I tied them up against each other with my darkfire in case they woke up before we were done.

The room was dark enough that I had to wait a few seconds for my eyes to adjust to the moonlight coming from the curtain-less windows.

Shane stirred in bed and sat up.

"Sorry we woke you up," I said, walking to the nearest lamp on a side table. I clicked it on. Yellowish light illuminated a portion of the room.

Shane's eyes widened as he took in the scene in front of him. "What's going on?" He jumped from the bed and approached the bars. "Raika, what did you do?"

"What I had to." I turned to Dot, who swayed, grabbed her shoulders, steadied her, and recalled the magic I had placed inside her to make her dizzy. She inhaled and blinked as if waking up from a dream.

She recoiled from my grip. "Aren't you full of tricks, little wolf?"

I shrugged. "I must be learning after watching you

witches for so long." I showed her the vial in my hand and backed off a few steps. "Remember our deal."

Apprehension hit me hard for a brief second, but I pushed it aside. I released the darkfire from around her wrists. A wicked grin spread over Dot's lips as she stretched her arms over her head.

"Are you ready, alpha?" she asked Shane.

Shane's eyes met mine and his jaw clenched. He didn't seem happy with this, but I knew he wouldn't oppose it either. He looked at Dot and nodded.

I couldn't say I was surprised when Dot raised her hands and released a wave of dark magic at me. I threw up a shield of darkfire in front of me. Her magic exploded against mine, shattering my shield.

"Raika!" Shane yelled from behind the bars.

She dashed to the door, but she hit an invisible wall and skidded back a step. "What the—?" She turned to me and sent a bolt of her magic at me. It sizzled out against the invisible wall.

I grinned. "Did you think it would be that easy?"

She shouted and punched the wall. "What is this?"

I tsked. "I thought you would at least pretend to try."

"What?" she asked, confused.

The two sets of doors on this side of the bedroom opened and supernaturals spilled inside. The wall I had created faded away as Killian, Lavinia, Almae, Drake, Thea, Cain, Elisa, and Zad surrounded the witch. Thea waved her hand and the glamoured circle she had prepared earlier disappeared. Now the circle shone a bright blue.

Dot's eyes widened. "Fucking little wolf. You have no honor. You said you wouldn't tell anyone."

"I told you I wouldn't say anything to anyone." I gestured

to Lavinia. She held a piece of paper in her hand. "But I didn't say anything about not writing it down. I kept my word."

Behind the bars, Shane chuckled.

I glanced at him, proud of myself. I had expected Dot to try to run, but I had hoped she wouldn't. Of course, I would still have delivered her to the others if she had done what she promised.

Now, we would have to come up with another way.

"You little bitch wolf," Dot said through gritted teeth.

"Give up, Dot," I said. "There's nowhere for you to go. Just get this over with and undo Shane's curse."

"Never!" she screamed. The windows rattled and I clamped my ears.

"We can torture you all day long," Drake threatened.

She turned mad eyes at him. "I'm not afraid of torture. You can play with me for a year, a decade, I'm not helping you or anyone. Shane will become the Shadow Wolf, and there's nothing you can do." She faced me again, her lips peeling in her signature crazed grin. "Your mate will be lost forever."

Behind the bars, Shane let out a growl. Without control, every little bit of anger was enough to bring the Shadow Wolf to life. He shifted in two seconds and rammed the bars, his sharp teeth snapping as if he could bite Dot's head off.

I winced, my heart breaking a little at the sight.

Lavinia waved her hand and brought a hazy wall over the circle, so we couldn't see or hear Dot inside. And she couldn't hear us.

"I think she's telling the truth," Lavinia said. "We can torture her however we want, she won't undo the curse."

"I'm afraid to say I agree," Almae said. "Dot is determined to take this to the grave."

My shoulders sagged. "Then what am I supposed to do?" I

gestured toward Shane. He continued ramming against the bars and I wondered if the magic in them would just fade at some point. "I can't leave him like this."

Killian snarled. "Let me take a good bite at her and see if she won't agree after that."

Lavinia slapped his stomach. "We just established that—"

"Wait!" An idea popped in my mind. "The curse was done with blood magic, that's why it has to be a Nightmist witch who has to break the curse, right, because it was a Nightmist who did it."

"Right," Thea said.

I looked at Lavinia. "Then ... what if you bite Dot, take as much of her blood as you can, then perform the spell yourself?"

Her eyes rounded. Lavinia was not only a vampire, but also a powerful witch. "That ... could work. Right?" She glanced at Almae and Thea.

"Technically, yes," Thea said.

"I think so," Almae said.

"But I don't know any curse-breaking spells," Lavinia said.

Almae reached for her and touched her arm. "I know an easy one. I can help you with it."

I looked at them expectantly. "So?"

Lavinia shrugged. "We can try, but I think I won't take all of her blood in case it doesn't work. We might need her."

Dot was one of the last Nightmist witches alive. Her coven had terrorized Minsi, made a deal with Conri, attacked my pack, brought the demons who killed my mother into the pack lands. They had also tortured Shane for six months and cursed him.

I was past the point of caring. "She made it clear she won't help either way. If you need to kill her, go ahead."

"Ready?" Thea asked. We nodded. She lowered the wall and Dot growled at us, looking more insane by the seconds. The witch was starting to lose it. "In three, two ... one." Thea broke the circle.

With her vampire speed, Lavinia rushed to Dot. The witch didn't even see it happening. One second, Lavinia was beside Killian. The next, she was holding Dot against her, her mouth closed around Dot's neck. A thin trail of blood slid down the witch's dark skin.

With a gasp, Lavinia let go of Dot. Her body fell on the floor with a heavy thud. I could still hear her heart beating slowly, but still there.

Lavinia closed her eyes and took a deep breath. "I can feel it. Her magic."

Almae stood by her side. "Call on that magic, hold on to it. Now look at Shane." Lavinia followed the instructions. "Think about his curse. To turn into the Shadow Wolf at every full moon, until it's all he knows and becomes it." Almae placed her hands over Lavinia's. "Now, let me guide you."

Almae closed her eyes, and together, the two of them stood still, their hands touching and out toward Shane. He seemed oblivious to all happening on this side of the bedroom, as he continued running and racing toward the bars, trying to break them.

I bit my pinkie nail, waiting, waiting, waiting. A couple of minutes passed and nothing happened. I wanted to ask what was going on, but I was afraid of disrupting their spell.

Finally, Shane stopped.

"Keep going," Almae whispered.

His red eyes faded, his fur started receding, and he let out a howl. Then he twisted into himself, as if it was hurting.

He knelt on the floor as the Shadow Wolf features disappeared.

A sob rose to my throat. It was working. It was working!

Shane's howl turned into a growl, then a gasp.

Sweat beading his skin, he lifted his head and stared at us. "What's going on?"

My heart hammering in my chest, I approached the bars. "Shane, Dot put a curse on me."

"She did WHAT?" he growled, his chest moved fast, but ...

"No Shadow Wolf," I whispered. Tears brimmed in my eyes.

He realized what I did. His eyes rounded. "You lied. You thought I would turn into the Shadow Wolf." He looked down at his arms. "But ... I'm still me. I was fucking pissed a second ago, but I'm still me."

A click sounded from the door in the center of the bars. The magic on it was gone and I opened it. I knew everyone behind me was exiting the room, carrying Dot with them, but I barely paid them any attention.

I stepped past the bars. Shane pushed to his feet and came to me. We collided, his naked body flushed against mine, his arms around my waist, and his head on my hair and neck.

"It's gone," I whispered.

"Yes, I can't feel it anymore," he whispered back. "Thank you."

"You don't need to thank me."

He pulled back and looked in my eyes. "I do. For everything. You're amazing and perfect and I'm just so damn lucky to be your mate." My cheeks heated up and I averted my eyes. I wasn't good at receiving compliments. Shane cupped my face and turned my head up. "Don't you hide from me. You're mine, forever, and I won't ever let go of you."

I rose to tiptoes. "I'm counting on that."

His mouth crashed against mine.

27

SHANE

THE MOMENT MY LIPS TOUCHED HERS, I WAS LOST. SHE MOANED against my mouth and I felt her body shuddering with the same electric jolt that had run through mine. Fuck, I had to have her. I angled my head and claimed her mouth, pushing my tongue through her parted lips. I wanted to kiss her, I needed to taste her.

I wrapped my arm around her waist, and still kissing her, still tasting her, I pushed her back in the direction of the bed. We stopped kissing long enough to pull her shirt over her head and throw it to the side, then, noticing the bed was right behind her, I pushed Raika until she fell on the mattress.

I crawled over her.

She clasped my shoulder and pulled my body to hers so I was spread over her, pressing her down. She moaned and I dove, taking her mouth with mine.

She moaned and I groaned. Fuck, I loved all these little noises coming from her. My erection grew harder hearing her moans. I was ready for her, so ready, but I wanted to make this last. I wanted to devour her, to taste her, to explore every inch of her body.

I slid my mouth from hers and rained a trail of kisses down her jaw, her neck. Her back arched and then she surprised me. I didn't even notice her hands had traveled south until she slipped her fingers around my groin.

"Oh," I groaned as she closed her hand around my hard-on. Pumping up and down, making me dizzy and achy and needy. My body thrummed, and all I could think was that I needed more. More of this. More of her. More. Now.

She tightened her grip, and I bit the soft spot between her neck and shoulder. Her movements became faster and harder and I couldn't take anymore. Groaning and cursing, I pulled away.

Frozen, she stared at me with big eyes.

I leaned down and brushed my lips on hers. "If you keep that up, this will end sooner rather than later. And I want later. Much later."

Raika smiled that beautiful, unhindered smile that only she could offer me. I smiled back at her before crawling out of the bed.

Again, she watched me, lust and desire stamped in her beautiful blue eyes. I grabbed her ankles and yanked her to the edge of the bed. Swiftly, I pulled her pants and panties off, and knelt before her.

"Oh, oh," was all she said.

I placed a small kiss on her knee and made my way up, and all the while she squirmed and gasped. I bit back a smile. She buckled once I met her center, my tongue running over her clit. Then she stilled. I did it again, and again she buckled. I put pressure on her clit and slid my finger inside her—

she stilled again. Fuck, she was wet and tight and ready. I slipped another finger inside her and started pumping fast and hard. Raika buried her hands in my hair and I groaned. Loving her reaction to me, I sucked on her clit. Moaning, Raika arched her back—and froze. Two seconds later, she was shaking uncontrollably.

With a satisfied grin, I crawled over her.

I tugged her to the middle of the mattress and rested my body over hers. She greeted me with a lazy grin, and I chuckled before taking her mouth with mine. She gasped as I plunged my tongue past her lips and claimed her for myself, but she didn't stop me. Oh no, she parted her lips and opened her mouth wide, giving me full access.

I positioned myself between her parted legs. She broke the kiss and sucked in a sharp breath as I slid inside her.

"Oh ..." she whispered as I buried myself deep and stilled, delighted in her tightness, her wetness, and how fucking glorious she felt.

I started moving. Slowly at first, savoring each rub of her on me. It was too much and it still wasn't enough. With a growl, I pounded into her, taking from her as much as I could. Raika arched her back, and I wound an arm around her waist, keeping her close to me. I grazed my tongue across her mouth, her chin, jaw, shoulder, and down to her breasts. I clasped a hand around one while I slid my tongue along the curve of the other. Raika moaned, arching her back more and more. Like she had done before, she buried her hands in my hair and held my face against her. I teased her, flicking my tongue around her breast, then her nipple, all the while thrusting into her, hard and deep. Raika cried out, telling me all I needed to hear. I sucked on her nipple, then opened my mouth and took as much of her breast as I could. She cried out again.

Shit, she felt so good, so tight, so wet ... and the sounds she made. I wasn't sure I could hold on much longer.

Surprising me, Raika pushed on my shoulders and rolled us over. She straddled me, her hands on my chest, her torso straight and her head thrown back, her hair a dark wave on her back. She started moving. Up and down, up and down, up and down. With each stroke, she went deeper and deeper, and seeing her over me like this, looking like a sex goddess, it made me hot and crazy and needy.

I closed my hands around her waist and helped her as she went up and down, up and down, keeping in rhythm with her, taking her even deeper. Then, Raika slid her hands from my chest to her thighs, up her stomach and to her own breasts. She clasped them and pinched her nipples, letting out a raspy moan. Shit. Oh shit, this was the sexiest thing I had ever seen. And she was here, with me. I was inside her.

I felt my climax building. Truth was, it had been building since she first entered this side of the bedroom.

With a growl, I wrapped my hands around Raika's upper arms and pulled her torso down until it was flush against mine.

"I want you right here," I said, as I slid my hands back to her hips and held on tight as I lifted her a little.

Then, I captured her mouth with mine, kissing her hard as I pounded into her. Raika moaned against my mouth and her nails clamped my shoulders, holding on tight.

"Oh, Shane, keep going ..."

I increased my rhythm. "Like this?"

Her eyes closed, she moaned in acknowledgment.

One, two, three thrusts and she cried out, coming around me. And with another one, two, three thrusts, I came too.

Raika's body went limp over me, her face tucked into my neck, her hot breath tickling my skin. I wrapped my arms around her, enjoying how well we fit together.

"I'm happy like this," she whispered.

I held her ever tighter. "I know what you mean."

28

SHANE

Raika and I didn't sleep that night. After making love twice, we snuggled in bed until the sun rose. When we left the room, we learned Dot had died soon after Lavinia had drained her blood, and they had burned her body at once to make sure nothing crazy happened—like a bloody witch coming back from the dead.

Then Raika and I went back to the house to have breakfast with my siblings.

When we entered the house, Minsi and Tyren were still in their beds and Rue was organizing the kitchen.

She hugged me tight. "I'm so glad you're okay."

The gentleness of her voice and her touch took me by surprise and I found myself leaning into her, welcoming her embrace. We were still so young, and none of us had our parents here anymore. Rue was the oldest, most parent-like figure we had around, and now I realized how much she actually fit those shoes.

It didn't take long for Minsi and Tyren to hear us and come running.

"So?" Tyren asked from across the room.

I smiled at them. "The curse is gone."

Relief washed over his features. We called Dom and Lucille to come over for breakfast, and later Killian and Lavinia also showed up. We were having a sort of early breakfast celebration.

The curse was gone.

I couldn't believe it.

One less thing to worry about.

I glanced around the table. Raika sat to my right, her hand secured in mine. Minsi was beside her, then Rue. Tyren was on my left, followed by Dom, and Lucille. On the other table end, Lavinia and Killian squeezed in with chairs from the kitchen table.

Everyone chatted and ate and laughed. My heart squeezed at the sight. I liked this. Now we needed to be able to hold on to this.

I wished we could stop time and be like this forever. Ignore the rest of the world and live on our own. Create another barrier and hide within to keep us all safe.

But we had tried that before, hadn't we? Even then, the barrier hadn't protected us.

We couldn't hide forever.

There was a war brewing not far from here, against a demon who had messed with us, and from whom I still wanted some kind of justice.

I would allow us a couple of days of respite.

"We should celebrate," I said. Everyone stopped talking and turned to me. "We haven't celebrated anything in a long time. I know we've lost too much, we've suffered for too long, but we need to stop and appreciate what we have, who we have, and celebrate even the little things."

"Wise words," Rue said, nodding her head.

"I like that," Lucille said.

Raika squeezed my hand. "What exactly do you want to do?"

"How about a bonfire and some hamburgers and s'mores at the village's center later this evening?" I asked. "Call everyone from the pack, I'll invite some of our friends from DuMoir Castle,"—I looked at Killian and Lavinia—"and we'll have just a good time among family and friends."

"Sounds like a good plan," Lavinia said.

We finished eating in good spirits, Rue helped us clean up, and then everyone left to organize tonight's party.

We all would have a good time.

THE DAY FLEW BY. While Raika and Lucille took care of most of the party details, I met with the council to see how things were going in town. We talked about our residences and Lord Drake's invitation to stay here permanently. Rue liked the idea, while Hamill didn't sound happy about it. The only other person on the council right now was Killian, and he wanted us to stay. I had to choose at least two more council members to balance things out a little more, but I hadn't even had the time to stop and think about it. Perhaps today would be a good day to observe the wolves in the pack and choose a handful of candidates.

Later, Killian brought over beverages from the castle, while Raika, Lucille, Celina, and Jena got together at Lucille's house to prepare the hamburgers, make sure we had all the buns and patties we would need, and also the graham crackers, chocolate, and marshmallows for s'mores.

When that was done, they all got together in the village's center, where a small green area was, and tidied it up. The women hung colorful lantern papers while the men found some old pieces of wood and assembled a few benches and tables for all of us.

Meanwhile, I borrowed a car from DuMoir Castle and went into the nearest town, Crimson Glen. There was something I needed to do there.

I came back in time to finish helping everyone at the village's center. By the time the sun began to set, we were all tired from working so much, but excited about what the night might hold.

Despite not making it official, Raika was living in my house with me and my siblings, and my bedroom was now our bedroom. I loved that, but I hadn't seen her before the party started. I texted her and she said she had to stop by Lucille's house to help her take the stuff to the party location.

I quickly took a shower, put on nice pants and a clean Henley shirt (I almost put on a button-up shirt, but decided it was too much), slipped something in my pocket, and headed over to the party.

As I walked toward the village's center, I saw the colorful lanterns twinkling in the twilight, and the smell of the bonfire rose in the air. On the side, Dom and Hamill handled the two grills we had found in some houses and cleaned up. On another side, Rue and Vianna kept the kids entertained. Those two deserved some kind of award for their patience and kindness. Jay stood quietly near the grills, a little out of place. I needed to include him in the council meetings or something, to make him come out of his shell and feel less awkward in his own pack. Everyone else mingled between the tables, carrying trays of buns and patties, and drinks.

There weren't many wolves left in our pack, but it was ours, and we would make it work.

However, there was one sight that really pulled at my heartstrings.

It was Raika seated beside Minsi on one of the benches, and Tyren directly behind them, his arms crossed, like a bodyguard-in-training. My family. My life. My heart and soul. Everything I did was for them. I hoped they knew how much they meant to me.

By the moon, if they didn't know, I would make sure to let them know now.

Raika saw me walking toward them. She smiled at me and my heart melted. She looked stunning in her usual clothes—ripped shorts, a black tank top, fishnet thighs, and combat boots. While all the other females had done their hair and dressed up in pretty summer dresses, Raika had been true to herself and put on what made her feel the best, what made her look hot as hell.

And she was all mine.

I halted in front of them, pulled Raika and Minsi up, and embraced the three of them. "I love you all."

"We love you too," Raika said. She tilted her head up and looked at me. "Everything okay?"

"Everything is perfect."

Tyren stayed put for two seconds, then he pushed away, gave me a nod, and walked away. I couldn't blame him. At his age, I probably wouldn't have let our parents hug me like that in front of only my friends, let alone the whole pack. He went to where Hugh was, near the grills.

Raika, though, stayed tucked under my arm, the way I liked it, while Minsi sat back down and turned to her tablet, where a movie was playing.

I kissed the top of Raika's head and handed her the red rose I had plucked from the bush in the back garden.

She smiled as she took the rose. "For me?"

Minsi glanced at us.

"We planted It for you behind the house," I told her. "Right, pretty girl?"

Minsi nodded.

"Really?" Raika's eyes widened a little. "I ... haven't been behind the house yet, but I would like to see this rosebush."

"Whenever you want. It's yours." I took the rose from her and tucked it behind her ear.

She lifted her head to me again. "Someone is mushier than normal."

I shrugged. "Life has been a bitch, but right now, I'm happy."

"I'm happy too."

I leaned down and pressed my lips to hers. Every time I saw her, every time I touched her, every time I thought of her, lust was like the sun after a storm—always there. If we weren't in public, I would have backed her to the nearest wall and ravished her until she was screaming my name.

My pants suddenly became tight.

Thankfully by then, Minsi's attention was back to her tablet.

SUVs from the castle drove into town and our guests arrived: Lord Drake, Queen Thea, Aurora, Almae, Prince Cain, Prince Aston, Prince Dorian, Elisa, and Zadkiel. Lyra had been invited too, but she had left earlier with a dozen vampires to help the goblins.

Some wolves from the pack stiffened, wary of the newcomers. Though this was their land, Drake had asked everyone to stay out of the village to give us privacy, and to not spook anyone who might not like other supernaturals.

But as the evening progressed, a duo of wolves played ballads on their guitar and a small set of drums, people danced and drank together, and everyone seemed comfortable.

I sat on the bench close to the bonfire, Raika snuggled under my arm, and a stick with a s'more in one hand. Minsi sat on the ground, her back against Raika's leg, licking her melting s'more. Across the bonfire, Tyren laughed with Hugh, while stealing glances at a clueless Lucille.

Around us, all of our friends and family had a great time.

I looked up, at the night sky and the full moon shining bright, and inhaled deeply. There wasn't one ounce of the Shadow Wolf left in me. I was fine.

I tucked Raika closer.

Right now, I was more than fine.

"Excuse us." I pushed Minsi away from Raika's legs and tugged Raika to stand with me. Holding her hand, I guided her a few feet to the side, then I turned her to me, put my hands on her back, and started swaying side to side.

Her smile was wide and contagious and it brightened her beautiful face. Dear moon, this gorgeous woman was perfect inside and out and she was mine.

I pulled her closer to me, until her chest was glued to mine, and despite the urge to have her rub her body on mine, I had to keep things PG while out here.

So I just settled for a peck on her lips. "I love you."

"I love you too." She cocked her head. "Are you sure you're okay?"

I chuckled. "I'm okay. I'm great. I'm just trying to appreciate the good things I have." I smoothed my hand up and down her back. "I lost you twice before. That will never happen again, but while you're here with me, I want to enjoy every single second."

Her smile turned lopsided. "Continue saying things like that and we might need to leave the party early."

I whispered in her ear, "I wouldn't be opposed to that."

Others joined us on our improvised dance floor—Killian and Lavinia, Drake and Thea, Eliza and Zad. At some point, Tyren asked Lucille and she agreed to dance with him! And Hamill took Rue for a quick spin and later Dom did the same with Vianna.

Slowly, the hours passed.

Vianna and Rue left with the kids. Drake and Thea took Aurora to bed too, and most of his vampires left with him. Raika also took Minsi to our house and tucked her in. Tyren and Hugh went with her. They promised to watch over Minsi until Raika and I were back.

I started organizing things with Dom, Lucille, and Hamill, but when Raika came back, I couldn't help but take her dancing again. Soon, the musicians left, along with the rest of the pack.

It was only Raika and me, the dying bonfire, and the immense night sky.

"I have the feeling you want to spend the night right here, dancing to no music until the sun comes up again?" she teased.

"Not the entire night. I was planning on taking you back home and making love to you at some point." She smiled. My heart squeezed. "You're so beautiful."

Her cheeks reddened. It was so freaking cute how she still blushed when I complimented her. It was endearing.

I cupped the nape of her neck, bent over her, and pressed

my mouth to hers. She parted her lips and I ravished her mouth, taking it slow, but deep. I wanted to imprint her in my mind, heart, and soul. Hell, she already was.

I slipped my hand inside my pocket, picked up the—

My phone rang.

I frowned. Who could it be at this damn hour? As I pulled my phone from my back pocket, I only thought of Minsi and Tyren.

I looked at the phone. "It's Kaz." He didn't seem the type to call for pleasantries. "Hello?"

"Shane," he rasped from the other side. "I need your help."

29

———

RAIKA

THOUGH SHANE WAS ON THE PHONE WITH KAZ, I COULD LISTEN to their conversation thanks to my wolf hearing.

"What happened?" Shane asked, his voice full of concern.

"It's the dragon," Kaz replied. "Paimon found her."

Oh no.

Shane frowned. "Where are you?"

"Northern New York."

"Wait, I heard the demon hunters were following Paimon into central Canada. That the dragon had been spotted there."

"That was a diversion. Somehow, Paimon fooled every-one. Even Evelyn, Ash, and me. At least for a while. Evelyn and I can sense the dragon's magic and we knew something was wrong. We told the demon hunters, but they said they couldn't send an entire team after a hunch. Only Doreen and Thierry joined us while we separated from the group and followed our senses." He paused, took a deep, croaky breath. "But Paimon did something. He made our connection to the dragon hazy, so we decided to separate again. I lost contact with the others over ten hours ago."

I was shocked. I hadn't spent much time with Kaz, but this was the most he had ever spoken in one go. And he didn't sound all right.

"What happened?" Shane asked.

"I found Paimon an hour ago," Kaz continued. "Right when he was closing in on the dragon."

I pressed a hand over my mouth. "Did he get the dragon?"

"Not yet," Kaz said. "I tried stopping him, but I was one against three dozen demons and Paimon. I was sorely outnumbered." He groaned and I could only imagine he was hurt. "I retreated to call for help. You need to get here before Paimon can pin down the dragon and get her powers."

Shane looked at me. I nodded at him. "Give me your coordinates. We'll be there as soon as we can."

We didn't waste time. Once Shane got off the call, we ran to our house, changed into more tactical clothes and packed a bag, while calling everyone we knew.

Rue would come to stay with the kids, Dom and Lucille were still up and getting ready, Evelyn's phone was off or without reception, and Killian hadn't picked up right away.

After, Shane stopped and turned to me. "We're going after Paimon, your father. And Ivy. Are you sure you want to come with us?"

I frowned, my feelings swirling. "I know Paimon needs to pay. Ivy ... I'm still on the fence about her, but if she's helping him, then we need to stop her too." Though I seriously hoped no one hurt her. "I'll be fine."

Shane didn't look like he believed me. "Are you sure?"

I offered him what he probably knew was a forced smile. "I'm sure." I patted his arm. "Now, let's go."

Killian called back when we were inside an SUV and already outside the DuMoir grounds. Behind the steering wheel, Shane told him what was happening.

"I'll talk to Lord Drake," Killian said. "I'm sure he'll send more vampires with me."

"Raika will text you the coordinates." Shane looked at me and I nodded at him, already with my phone in my hands and typing the coordinates Kaz had sent us.

We rode for four hours into northern New York state at well-above-the-limit speed, and into a deeper part of the wilderness. We took the car into wider hiking trails—thankfully, because it was the middle of the night, there was no one here—until we couldn't anymore.

We took off our clothes, tied small fanny packs around our waists, and shifted. We ran as fast as we could to the new coordinates Kaz sent us fifteen minutes ago. The forest was dark and oddly quiet, but we could see and hear fine with our enhanced senses.

I could smell blood before we found him. Kaz was lying inside a small, dark cave, his hand over his stomach, his eyes closed, his breathing ragged, and his crossbow broken beside him. We shifted back, picked up the flashlight and the healing paste I had stashed inside the fanny packs, and knelt beside Kaz. There were several wounds on his face and shoulders.

I peeled his hand from his stomach. A pool of blood greeted me. Shit. I grabbed a shirt discarded by his side, cleaned the blood as best as I could, but more came from the big gash on the side of the stomach.

"How bad is it?" Lucille asked from behind me.

I looked at Shane from across Kaz's fainted form. "I'm not sure." It was a lie. I knew this was bad and he needed more than my healing paste, but it was all I had right now. I cleaned the gash once more and applied half of the paste before more blood came out and washed it away. "He needs a healer."

"No," he croaked. I hadn't even noticed he had woken up. "My healing will kick in in a second." He tried to sit up and groaned. "I need to help you."

Shane pushed his shoulders down. "No, you need to rest."

I offered him two pills and water. "It's for the pain."

Kaz grunted, but took it. "You have to go, then." He swallowed the pills and took a big swallow of water. "By now, Paimon has the dragon."

"Hopefully she got away," I said.

The dragon shifter shook his head. "No, he came prepared. He was going to catch her. You need to stop him before he can kill her." He pointed to his left. "Go this way. That was where I last saw them about ..." He glanced at his phone's screen. "Thirty minutes ago."

I frowned. Of course he hadn't stayed put and rested, even though he had a horrible wound, possibly fatal. No, he was following Paimon and the dragon. But I understood why. He had to make sure they didn't get away.

I left more pain pills and the healing paste with Kaz. "The vampires will be arriving soon. I'll make sure to send someone here to help you."

"Thanks." He stopped fighting it and closed his eyes.

The four of us shifted back into our wolf forms and followed the direction Kaz had told us to go, Shane in the lead.

About fifteen minutes running, Shane slowed down.

I can smell them, he said into our minds.

I could too. A strong scent of Paimon, Ivy, the demons I got to know, and the dragon. Her misty, smoky scent was the strongest of all.

Which meant ...

We climbed over some rocks and looked down at the vast valley below. The dragon was lying on the ground, dark magical ropes around her massive body. Her eyes were closed, and for a second, I panicked, thinking she was dead, but then her eyes snapped open and she yanked at the ropes, but they held. Orange built up inside her throat, but her mouth was also tied. Smoke billowed from her nostrils and she let out what sounded like a cry.

Poor thing.

Paimon and Ivy stood beside the dragon, gesturing wildly at her while arguing. Rotgar was a few feet beyond them, looking bored. And many, many demons filled the valley, some watching the dragon, others looking out at the surroundings.

Paimon wasn't stupid; he knew someone was coming and he had to be quick and prepared.

My chest constricted. For about ten days, I had believed this demon to be a loving father, a man with kindness in his heart, who really wanted to change the world for the better. But now I remembered the before, the truth. He never had my best interest in mind. All he wanted was more power for himself, and his ultimate goal was to become the king of the underworld, so he could rule over all demons and create chaos.

I couldn't allow that. No matter who he was in my family tree.

But there was something else who made me hesitate.

Ivy.

She could have attacked me when we last met. She could have fought Shane and the others and tried keeping me there. She could have done so many other things. But she had let me go. Plain and simple.

If I tried reaching her now, would she hear me? Or would she attack me?

What now? Lucille asked in our minds.

The vampires might be hours away, Shane said. *If we don't attack now, we'll be too late.*

The four of us against thirty something? Forty? Dom asked. *It might already be too late.*

So we just give up? Shane said. *If we can't stop Paimon, then we at least need to buy some time until the vampires get here.* He turned his head and looked at us with his wolf eyes. *Ready?*

The three of us nodded.

As one, we ran from behind the rocks and down the valley.

The first line of demons didn't even see us coming. I jumped at the back of one and clamped my mouth around his throat, with enough force to snap his neck. I flinched with the sound, but didn't dwell on it. I let his body fall and ran to another one.

Shane and I ran toward Paimon and Ivy, dodging demons who turned to us, or taking them down as fast as we could.

I killed the third one and dodged the fourth, when Ivy's voice rang clear through the valley.

"She's mine." My half sister strolled toward me, like a model on a catwalk, and halted four feet from me. The demons obeyed her and took several steps back. "You don't expect me to fight a wolf, do you?"

I looked around. Shane had reached Paimon, but the higher demon taunted him by shielding himself behind demons, sending them toward Shane, and throwing his dark-fire bolts here and there.

On the other side, Dom and Lucille fought Rotgar and other demons as hard as they could, getting their number down, but not fast enough.

I shifted back into my human form. "You want to fight with darkfire because you know you're better than me there."

Ivy scoffed. "First, please, get dressed."

I rolled my eyes. Really? That now? "I didn't think you were a prude."

"I'm not, but I don't need to see my sister naked, do I?"

Other races weren't as used to nakedness like we were, so I grabbed the long t-shirt I had brought in my fanny pack and hastily put it on. "Better?"

She wrinkled her nose. "Not your best look."

I seethed. "Cut the crap, Ivy!"

"If you insist." She lifted her hands and darkfire blasts flew at me.

On instinct, I ducked and raised my arm to deflect her hits. "That's all you can do?" In turn, I sent her bolts of my own.

For a couple of minutes, we threw darkfire and danced around each other, moving along the ring formed by the demons. In that time, something was clear: Ivy wasn't using most of her magic and neither was I. We didn't hurt the other.

I stopped, facing her as a darkfire bolt zipped toward me and hit me square in the chest. I grunted, my shoulders rico-cheting back, but as I expected, it didn't hurt much.

Ivy's eyes widened. "What are you doing?"

"I won't fight you."

"You must!"

"I don't want to hurt you." I paused. "And you don't want to hurt me either."

She blinked, the frustration apparent in her blue eyes. "I can't let you go."

"Then pretend I knocked you out and stay out of the way. That's all I ask." I didn't wait for a response. She could do the opposite: knock me out while she helped Paimon. But for some reason, I trusted her. I knew she wouldn't hurt me.

I turned and ran through the demons toward Shane—even they didn't touch me.

Like before, Paimon hid behind a wall of demons, while Shane made his way through them. But he killed one and another demon took its place. The barrier never eased up. Behind his demons, Paimon faced the dragon, a dragon scale in his hands. He closed his eyes and the dragon scale shone bright.

"Father!" I yelled.

His eyes snapped open.

A few feet to my side, Shane faltered when he saw me there and a demon took a good hit at him. I winced, but focused on Paimon.

A wide grin spread over the higher demon's lips as he turned to me. He pushed his demons aside and took a couple of steps closer. "Raika, my daughter. I've missed you."

I rolled my eyes. "That's such a lie."

"It's true! You and Ivy were always my favorites. I thought you two would be by my side when I finally conquer the underworld and make it ours." He extended one hand at me. "I'll give you one more chance, child. Join me."

Was he serious? I balked. "Never."

He clicked his tongue. "Alas, I'll have to do what I've done with my other children who rejected me."

I swallowed. "So you'll kill me?" I was hoping he would hesitate, and I would rope him in, buying us more time for the vampires to get here. "Just like that?"

"Oh, no." He took another step closer. Shane let out a growl and advanced toward Paimon, but five demons stepped in his way. "I didn't just kill them. You think I would waste such potential?" His grin turned outright menacing. "First, I absorbed their powers, then I killed them."

I gasped.

He was a freaking monster and he had to go down. I packed as much of my power in a big darkfire bolt and threw it at him. Paimon waved his hand and the bolt broke into a cloud of smoke halfway to him.

How was he so damn powerful right now?

"Have you found another one of your children and killed her in the last couple of days?"

"Something like that." He shrugged. "But don't worry. Before I can kill you, I need to kill the dragon." He turned his back to me and the demons attacked.

"Don't hurt her!" Ivy yelled. She surged beside Paimon. "Just ... push her back."

A throng of demons descended upon me, and Shane too, and kept us entertained. They literally grabbed me by the arms and pulled me back, as Ivy had asked.

Meanwhile, Paimon rested his hand on the dragon's side. The dragon jerked at his touch, but the creature seemed to be weakened and couldn't do much other than cry.

No! He was going to do it!

Desperation clawed through my core and I sent out a wave of darkfire. It washed over the demons around me and knocked a few out. Some others fell back, but for a few seconds, I was free.

"Stay back!" I shouted, hoping they would hear me.

They hesitated, and that was all I needed. I crouched down and pressed my hand on the ground. Darkfire rose around me, taking the demons down. Not dead, but out of commission for a minute. Maybe two? I wasn't sure.

I shot up and gasped.

Paimon withdrew his hand from the dragon and a giant bright white ball of magic floated out of the dragon's body. She let out a long sigh, and her body went still.

"No!" I cried. Without thinking, I ran to Paimon. I rammed into him, pushing him away from the white magic ball. He groaned, losing his grip on the magic. The ball split into two and floated forward.

One into Paimon.

The other one into me.

I gasped again as the dragon's magic exploded inside me and searing hot pain coursed through my body. Everything went black and I fell to the ground.

"Raika!"

I blinked and my sight came back, but my head felt fuzzy and slow. Through the blur, I saw Shane's face as he knelt beside me. Behind him, Rotgar and Ivy grabbed a dizzy Paimon by the arm and dragged him back. The demons surged over us.

Shane cupped my face. "Are you okay? Talk to me!" I opened my mouth but no words came out. What was happening? Shane raised his hand. "Here!"

Grunts, shouts, and zaps sounded all around us.

The blur cleared a little more and I took a good look around. Paimon and Ivy were nowhere in sight, but Killian, Lavinia, and the others had finally arrived and were dealing with the demons.

Killian ran to us. "What happened?"

Shane pointed to his back. "Paimon went that way. He's probably dizzy. It shouldn't be hard to catch up to him."

Killian nodded. He yelled for his vampire to follow him and all of them zoomed past us, after Paimon. I wanted to tell them to not hurt Ivy. Again, she had hesitated. She hadn't hurt me. I didn't want her hurt. But no words came out. It was like my brain and my mouth weren't connected.

Shane stared at me again, his eyes rounded with concern. "Raika, talk to me. What happened? How are you feeling?"

I moved my mouth. "I ..." It was hard to speak. I tried lifting my hand to touch it, but it didn't move.

"You can't speak? You can't move?"

I took in a long breath, held it in for three seconds. When I released it, a little more of the blur was gone and I felt less exhausted. "I can speak." My voice was frail, thin. I lifted my hand a few inches and wiggled my fingers, my movements awkward. "I can move."

On his knees, Shane pulled me to him and embraced me tight. "By the moon, you scared me. I thought I had lost you again." He pulled slightly and looked at me. "What happened exactly?"

"I don't know." I looked down at my hand. "I think ... half of the dragon's magic came into me."

His brows curled down.

Movement on my left drew my attention. Aided by Dom, Kaz dragged his feet toward the dragon, one hand over his stomach, the other reaching out to touch the dragon.

"I'm sorry I failed you," he whispered. He placed both hands on the dragon's side and lowered his head.

"Help me up," I asked Shane. He held my hands and pulled me up. I wobbled on my feet. Shane tightened his grip on me and steadied me. "I'm fine." I wasn't fine, but I knew I wasn't dying. I turned to the dragon. "Is there a way to give it back?" I asked Kaz. He turned angry eyes at me. I almost flinched. "I don't want her magic. I never asked for it. I want to give it back."

"You can try, but that won't do anything." He smoothed his hand over the dragon's scales. "She's gone now."

"I'm so sorry, Kaz," I whispered.

A deafening silence fell in the valley. The demons were either dead or gone, most vampires were out trying to catch Paimon, an ancient dragon had been killed, and I had absorbed half of her magic.

And our enemy had the other half.

30

SHANE

I CROSSED MY ARMS, LEANED AGAINST THE DOORJAMB, AND watched as Raika colored with Minsi at the kitchen's table. Tyren grabbed a Gatorade from the kitchen, waved at me, and left through the back door. He was going to meet with Hugh.

Raika, Dom, Lucille, and I had returned from New York last evening, and Raika had slept through most of the drive. When we arrived home, she ate something and went directly to bed. She slept like a rock for almost ten hours.

But now, she looked fine.

I had asked her this morning how she felt, and she said she was back to normal, albeit with some strange power dancing in her veins. I had taken her to DuMoir Castle, where Thea and Almae looked over her.

"There's nothing wrong with you," Thea declared after about an hour of thorough examination. "But there's a lot of dragon power inside of you now. Right now, we believe it's dormant because it's still getting used to you, but it'll manifest itself soon."

"When it does, what do I do?" Raika asked.

"It might be too much power for one person," Almae said. "Come back when you feel it waking up. We'll help you control it."

"Can we take it out?" Raika asked. "I don't want it."

"We might be able to," Thea said. "But from what we've seen, the magic is attaching itself to you. If we try to take it out, we might hurt you, or worse."

"That's not an option," I barked and that was the end of that discussion.

For now, I watched her like a hawk, afraid of what the dragon's magic could do to her. But so far, she was fine. Normal.

While at DuMoir Castle, I had also heard news about yesterday. Before we left, Killian and his vampires came back, saying they had lost Paimon's trail. He either had disappeared into thin air or sprouted wings and flown away. They had found most of the demons who ran away and dealt with those. They promptly informed the demon hunters of all that had happened, especially the fact that now Paimon had half of the dragon's magic, which meant he wasn't weak anymore and could attack at any time.

After we left, Evelyn and Ash arrived. They helped Kaz take care of the dragon's body. I texted Evelyn and she said that when they were done, Kaz would return to his family, and she and Ash would continue with their original mission: finding dragon bones and keeping them from evil people.

"Time to go!" Raika announced, closing the princess book she had been coloring. "Rue's waiting for you." She took Minsi's hand, and after a glance at me, they exited the house.

We walked with Minsi to the house that had become the children's school. It had a beautiful garden and Rue and

Vianna had organized some games for the kids this afternoon. Minsi didn't seem happy about joining them, but both Raika and I believed it was good for her to have at least a little interaction with other kids. And we knew Rue would watch out for her.

Moreover, I wanted some time alone with my mate.

I slipped my hand into Raika's and guided her around the village, toward one of the lake's banks with its warm, white sand. It was a hot day in the last week of July, and I realized I should have planned to bring swimsuits with us.

We halted right at the edge of the water. Raika leaned her head on my shoulder. "It's pretty here."

"I knew you would like it." I let out a long sigh.

We still had an uncertain future ahead of us, and Paimon was out there, stronger than ever, ready to take over the world. I wasn't sure if his plans still included Raika (to have her join him, or to kill her for her powers), but I wasn't taking any chances. I would prepare our small army and join the fight. Paimon had to pay for all he had done to my pack and to Raika.

I still wanted to be the one to take him down.

But for now, I enjoyed the evening beside my mate.

I turned to her. "Raika," I started.

She looked at me, a soft smile over her closed lips. "Yes?"

"I wanted to do this two nights ago, but I was interrupted." A knot formed between Raika's brows. I picked up the ring from my pocket and knelt in front of her. Her eyes rounded. "I love you more than anything and anyone in this universe, and I'll love you even after I die. I can't imagine life without you and I promise I'll take better care of you. You're everything to me and I want a chance to spend the rest of my life proving it to you." I offered her the ring. "Will you marry me?"

Raika's mouth turned into a little O and she waved at her eyes, suddenly all misty. "Yes!"

The best word I had heard in a while. I smiled and slipped the ring on her finger. I rose to my feet as she looked at the ring. "It's beautiful."

"I thought you would like it."

She rested her hand on her chest. "It's perfect."

She was perfect. I swooped her into my arms and kissed her. She clung to me, her body molding to mine, and a growl rose from my throat. I wanted to take her back home so we could take this further ... or maybe we could go deeper into the woods and—

Her body became hot against mine. At first I thought it was the kiss, the lust we always felt for each other, but then she turned too hot. I hissed and stepped back as she was almost at burning point.

"Raika?" She stared at me, her eyes wide. Underneath her cropped top, her skin turned orange. I reached for her. "What is this?" I touched her and instinct made me pull my hands back right away. "You're burning!"

"I ..." She glanced down at herself. "What the—"

Fire surged from within her and enveloped her entire body.

Raika burned alive.

THANK you for reading *The Night Hunting*! If you liked it, don't forget to pre-order book 4, *The Night Rising*!

If you haven't yet and would like to read how everything

changed for Shane and Raika (aka: Minsi's 10th birthday party, how they found out about the mating bond, and Conri's attack), then click here to download this exclusive book!

Haven't you read Killian's and Lavinia's story yet? Then download *The Darkest Vampire* and start their trilogy now! That's where Shane is first introduced in the story ;)

Also, join my Facebook group to get another exclusive book, *The Light Witch*. You just met Evelyn and Ash and now you can read their beginning!

Last but not least, you can check out the recommended reading order for the Rite World here! You can download, print, and check the books you've already read! Enjoy!

THANK YOU

Thank you for reading *The Night Hunting*!

Reviews are very important for authors. If you liked my book, please consider leaving a review on your favorite online retailer and/or on Goodreads and/or Bookbub, please!

Did you like this book? You can check out other books of mine:

The Darkest Vampire (Rite World: Vampire Wars book 1): a witch releases a dark vampire from a curse, and becomes inadvertently bonded to him.

The Midnight Test (Rite World: Lightgrove Witches book 1): a clueless witch is invited to join a powerful coven—but only if she aces a difficult test.

The Demon Kiss (Rite World: Blackthorn Hunters Academy book 1): a fast-paced story about a young woman who finds out she's a demon hunter, and the half-demon intent on protecting her against all evil.

The Vampire Heir (Rite World 1: Rite of the Vampire): a

dark and mysterious paranormal romance about a vampire and a young woman with a secret.

The Warlock Lord (Rite World 4: Rite of the Warlock): a thrilling and kick-ass paranormal romance about a werewolf and warlock.

The Wolf Forsaken (Rite World 7: Rite of the Wolf): a heat-wrenching tale about a lost wolf shifter and a fae princess on the run.

Heart Seeker (The Fire Heart Chronicles book 1): an urban fantasy series about a young woman who finds herself at the center of a mysterious supernatural world.

Destiny Gift (The Everlast Series book 1): a post-apocalyptic urban fantasy series about a young woman with a special power that can save the world.

DON'T FORGET to sign up for my Newsletter to find out about new releases, cover reveals, giveaways, and more!

If you want to see exclusive teasers, help me decide on covers, read excerpts, talk about books, etc, join my reader group on Facebook: Juliana's Club!

ABOUT THE AUTHOR

While USA Today Bestselling Author Juliana Haygert dreams of being Wonder Woman, Buffy, or a blood elf shadow priest, she settles for the less exciting—but equally gratifying—life as a wife, a mother, and an author. She resides in North Carolina and spends her days writing about kick-ass heroines and the heroes who drive them crazy.

Subscribe to her mailing list to receive emails of announcement, events, and other fun stuff related to her writing and her books: www.bit.ly/JuHNL

For more information:
www.julianahaygert.com

facebook.com/julianahaygert

twitter.com/julianahaygert

instagram.com/juliana.haygert

goodreads.com/juliana_haygert

pinterest.com/julianahaygert

bookbub.com/authors/juliana-haygert

youtube.com/julianahaygert

tiktok.com/@julianahaygert

ALSO BY JULIANA HAYGERT

To find links and more info, go to:

www.julianahaygert.com/books/

Shorts

Into the Darkest Fire

Standalones

Daughter of Darkness

Rite World: Night Wolves

The Night Calling (Book 1)

The Night Burning (Book 2)

The Night Hunting (Book 3)

The Night Rising (Book 4)

Rite World: Vampire Wars

The Darkest Vampire (Book 1)

The Darkest Witch (Book 2)

The Darkest Magic (Book 3)

Rite World: Lightgrove Witches

The Midnight Test (Book 1)

The Midnight Spell (Book 2)

The Midnight Flame (Book 3)

Earth Shaker (Book 2.5)

Sorrow Bringer (Book 3)

Soul Wanderer (Book 4)

Fate Summoner (Book 5)

War Maiden (Book 6)

The Everlast Series

Destiny Gift (Book 1)

Soul Oath (Book 2)

Cup of Life (Book 3)

Everlasting Circle (Book 4)

Willow Harbor Series

Hunter's Revenge (Book 3)

Siren's Song (Book 5)

Breaking Series

Breaking Free (Book 1)

Breaking Away (Book 2)

Breaking Through (Book 3)

Breaking Down (Book 4)